The Miseducation of Tabitha Stone

'Your grades have been very poor, Miss Stone!' he snapped. 'What have you got to say for yourself?' His fingers drummed impatiently on his knee.

Tabitha knew the part she had to play. She dropped her head, lacing her fingers behind her back like a naughty schoolgirl. 'I'm sorry.'

'Not good enough!' He thumped his palm down on the leather surface of the desk, and even though Tabitha knew it was a game, she jumped nervously. 'Since you seem incapable of making up your credit academically, we're just going to have to find another way for you to do it. Aren't we?'

'Yes, Professor Sinclair,' she whispered, then realised a moment later what she'd said. Her eyes jerked guiltily up to Jake's but the words seemed to be just what he wanted. There was a charge in the air unlike anything she'd felt in their previous encounters. She knew that it was dangerous, and maybe unhealthy, but she could feel her centre warming with her excitement.

He let the silence rest for nearly a minute, an invisible tension stretching the air between them. 'Take your clothes off,' he said finally. 'And fold them neatly. I hate disorder.'

The Miseducation of Tabitha Stone

Emily Durkheim

Cheek

In real life always practise safe sex.

First published in 2006 by
Cheek
Thames Wharf Studios
Rainville Road
London W6 9HA

Typeset by SetSystems Ltd, Saffron Walden, Essex

Printed and bound by Mackays of Chatham PLC

ISBN 0 352 34071 1
ISBN 9 780352 340719

All characters in this publication are fictitious and any resemblance to real persons, living or dead, is purely coincidental.

This one's for Team Fiction:

PDE, Kerrence, Bodle, Simon, Maz, Claude & Kathleen

With big thanks to Adam Nevill

and to Xanna Eve Chown for some extremely useful pointers

Prologue – Los Angeles

Tabitha should have been home five hours ago, which by definition meant it must be a great party. Brad had hired out the VIP room of the Trash Lounge, had even hired the exclusive venue's regular DJ to play here just for them, funky house pumping out over the state-of-the-art sound system at ear-bleeding volumes. There were a hundred people in the room, and every one of them was Tabitha's friend. Jess and Alton drifted past, arms wrapped round each other even though they'd been bitterly rowing just last night, and smiled the glazed smiles of the chemically happy. Tabitha smiled back, but she knew there was something tentative and not quite sincere in it.

She was 24. She couldn't believe it. That was old, wasn't it? That was the sort of age people started settling for husbands, pumping out babies. She found a sudden wave of sadness washing through her system on a tide of alcohol. Her early twenties were gone.

But the music was loud and good, the cocktails were better, she was at one of the coolest clubs in the whole of LA and there was no reason she couldn't be back here, drinking the same cocktails with the same people, for her next birthday party and the one after that. A crowd of her friends seemed to sense her momentary melancholy and congregated around her in a crush of Maria Cornejo pants and Donna Karan dresses; they pulled her to the centre of the dance floor, and she released the tension in her body and threw her head back in a simulated pleasure which soon became genuine as the skipping treble and deep bass of the music took her to a good place.

An hour or so later she staggered into the restrooms on an urgent make-up repair mission. Her reflection stared back at her, the loose black curls of her hair plastered to her neck, and dark smudges of mascara under her eyes. Not too bad, she decided, in a heroin-chic kind of way, but not really the look she was going for. Carefully – she was buzzing from the alcohol, her movements a little exaggerated with effort – she started reapplying her eye shadow, the shade expertly chosen to bring out the blue in her eyes and de-accentuate the strange brown fleck in the left which one of her exes had called cute but which she had always hated.

Her nose, as it always did, seemed to be mocking her with its perky uptilt and light dusting of freckles that no amount of foundation seemed able to hide for long. Since she was thirteen she'd been begging her father to let her get some work done on it, but he'd always hated the idea of a surgeon cutting into her for any reason other than a medical emergency. Ironic, really. The film and TV actors he'd made his fortune representing as a lawyer had founded theirs on exactly that sort of cosmetic surgery. But he'd been deaf to her protests and as he held the purse strings she had no choice but to accept it. The same ex-boyfriend had told her that the nose was cute, too. No wonder she'd dumped him.

She applied a last brush of rouge to her cheekbones, then made to head back out.

It was seven-thirty by the time she came home. Her father was waiting for her in the living room of their Hollywood Hills mansion, face stormy. He was always up and working by this time of the morning, but on this occasion something about the puffiness of his eyes and the drawn-down look of his mouth told her that he hadn't been to bed at all.

'Morning, Daddy,' Tabitha said, breezing past him into

the big open-plan kitchen that backed on to the swimming pool and ocean view. The alcohol felt like it was starting to calcify in her head, the pleasant dizziness turning into a migraine-like nausea, and she knew that if she didn't begin the rehydration process soon she'd be feeling like death for the rest of the day.

She stopped, though, with the glass of water halfway to her mouth when she saw the large oak and steel kitchen table. It had been carefully set for two, a lavish meal spread over it. The meal was clearly several hours old, cold and congealed, and the champagne which had been poured into two flutes was flat. It was spaghetti bolognaise, the one dish her father had ever learnt how to cook, so Tabitha knew he had prepared it himself. She felt a hard lump in her throat.

'I'm sorry, Daddy,' she said, turning round to face him reluctantly.

He shrugged, his face expressionless. 'Why should *you* be sorry? It's my fault for expecting you to actually do what you said. It's not as if you ever have done before.'

That stung, and Tabitha felt herself growing angry, a knee-jerk response to any criticism from her father. 'I know I said I'd be back early last night, but that was just, you know, a remark in passing. Jessica and Brad booked the Trash Lounge for me, and it *was* my birthday.'

Her father looked at the carefully laid table, the little vase of wilting daisies in the middle, her favourites since she was a little girl, which he must have gone out to pick himself because no flower shop would sell a bouquet as scruffy as that. 'I know,' he said quietly. He sounded washed out, not even really pissed, just very, very tired.

'We can have a meal together tonight, Daddy,' Tabitha told him.

He shook his head, though she couldn't tell if that was a rejection of the offer or just a reflection of his feelings. 'Go to bed, Tabby,' he said. 'I don't really want to talk to you right now.'

* * *

When she woke five hours later feeling not exactly better but at least human, she found him sitting at his desk in the office, files and paperwork spread around him in neat stacks as tidy and squared-off as his mind.

She didn't think her bare feet had made any noise on the mosaic-inlaid marble floor, but she saw his neck stiffen, the bristly grey hairs on it standing out straight as soon as she came in.

'It's my fault,' he said, without turning around.

She took a step back at that, wrong footed. Her father didn't ever admit to a mistake. It was one of the qualities they shared. 'Don't be silly, Daddy. I should have told you I wouldn't be coming back last night.'

He did turn round at that, and she took another step back when she saw the hard, uncompromising expression in his eyes. 'I'm not talking about last night. I'm talking about ... I'm talking about *you*, Tabby, the way you turned out.'

Tabitha's skin prickled. 'What about the way I turned out?'

He waved a hand at her, a vague, useless gesture, as if he didn't know where to begin. 'You're –' he started, then seemed to think better of it. His face softened slightly. 'I knew it was difficult for you when your mother walked out on me ... on us. I tried to make allowances for it.'

Tabitha ventured a small smile. 'You did. You've been great.'

He nodded. 'Yeah, that's exactly the problem. I've been too busy making up for you having a mother who'd walk out on her ten-year-old daughter because she wants to "find herself".' He made inverted commas in the air with his fingers, the pain still pungent in his voice, even after all these years. 'And I've let you turn into exactly the sort of selfish bitch your mother was.'

Tabitha felt tears gather in her eyes, burning with a combination of hurt and anger. 'How can you say that? I'm *twenty-four*, I'm allowed to have fun!'

'And when does the fun stop?' he asked. 'I've been

paying your school fees for six years now, and you've barely pulled together enough credits to pass year two. And most of those were in Media Studies.' The contempt was thick in his voice. 'What is your life going to be, Tabitha? Just one long party?'

'Why not?' she said defiantly. 'You can afford it. Why *should* I work if I don't have to? Maybe if you'd let Mom have a bit more fun instead of always going on at her about spending a few hundred dollars on a new pair of shoes she wouldn't have walked out on us in the first place.'

She saw his jaw muscles working under his skin, but his voice came out hard and controlled. 'Maybe. Maybe I'm making a terrible mistake with you too. But, however this turns out, it's got to be better than the kind of person you're turning into right now.' He looked back down at the papers on his desk, almost as if he was dismissing her.

It took a few moments for what he'd said to sink in. 'Wait a minute – how *what* turns out?'

He looked up at her again. The expression on his face was one she'd only seen him use with clients, never with her. Absolutely resolute. 'You're going back to school, Tabby.'

'I'm already at school.'

His expression didn't shift and she realised that it was time for a tactical withdrawal and regrouping.

'But I'll work harder, I promise.'

He left the kind of silence cops leave when they hope suspects will fill it with a confession and, as it always did, it had pretty much the same effect on her.

'I'll stop cutting classes, too.'

'Yes,' he said finally. 'You will. I'm giving you an ultimatum, Tabby. You're twenty-four now, nearly a quarter of a century old. If you don't have your degree by the time you are twenty-five, I'm cutting you off. Without a cent.'

It sounded so absurdly Victorian that for a moment

Tabitha was tempted to laugh. But she could see that he meant ever word. 'You've got to be kidding!' she exploded. 'There's no way I'll be able to do that – I've barely been to a class in two years, and it's already halfway through September. I've missed two weeks of school already.'

He nodded. 'You're right. There's no way you'll be able to do that here. Not with those "friends" of yours –' he made the quotation-marks gesture again '– not with your layabout entourage to distract you. That's why I'm sending you away to study. Far away.'

'You're *sending* me?' Tabitha's indignation wilted in the face of his steely resolve. The words 'without a cent' were still ringing in her head. More tentatively, she asked, 'You're sending me where?'

He looked back down at the desk again, and she saw that one of the piles consisted of print-outs of online school prospectuses. 'New York.'

She relaxed. A West Coast girl through and through, she was still willing to admit that the Big Apple had its points. And she was sure she could persuade her friends to visit for regular Manhattan shopping sprees. Say what you would about the East Coast, you couldn't beat Fifth Avenue.

'Well,' her father said, studying her face carefully, his own showing a glimmer of what might have been satisfaction. 'I suppose it would be more accurate to say New York *State*.'

He took a prospectus from the top of the pile and pushed it round to face her. The front cover looked blank, but after a moment she realised that it was just a vista of white snow. The name of the school had been written in the snow, white against white. Adirondacks University.

Tabitha shivered suddenly, as if the picture had breathed out a cloud of icy air towards her. She didn't know exactly where the Adirondacks was – geography was a subject she'd flunked at high school and seen no need to put any remedial studying into since – but she was damn sure it was nowhere near the Five Boroughs.

Then she noticed another little pile on her father's desk, a multicoloured little mountain of what she had at first taken for pot pourri. Now, though, she realised that the flakes were composed of plastic. And that the plastic had numbers on it.

'What are those?' she asked quietly. Her voice came out husky, and she became acutely aware that she was still hungover, her mouth filled with the musty after-taste of last night's revels.

'Your credit cards,' her father said calmly.

'You cut up my cards?' Her voice rose to an indignant squawk. 'You sneaked into my room while I was asleep!'

'Maybe if you'd had less to drink you might have woken up and caught me at it.' He seemed entirely unrepentant, which only fuelled her anger.

'So what am I supposed to do for money while I'm slaving away at Deliverance State U?' she demanded. 'Maybe I can play the banjo in the town square. I hear they're partial to that kind of thing out there.'

'You're thinking of the Appalachians,' her father said dryly. 'And you'll have plenty of money. I'm giving you an allowance – I asked the school what they thought was average for a student there, and that's what you're getting. It should be more than enough to pay for your food and books. You won't need to worry about getting yourself an apartment,' he added. 'I've booked you a room in the dorms.'

Tabitha stared at him, speechless. A part of her was still expecting his face to split into the wide, mischievous grin he wore when they were joking with each other and which, she realised, she hadn't seen very much of in the last year. But he remained stern, his features set hard, the sharp cheekbones he shared with her jutting through his cheeks in a way that made him look older than his

52 years, the fine grooves of wrinkles like a cage around his eyes, keeping any softer feelings imprisoned inside and out of sight.

'I'm giving you a chance, Tabitha, a *last* chance, to prove that you're still the great girl you used to be. Don't let me down.'

PART ONE

First Semester

Chapter One

Don't Get Lost in Heaven

Tabitha could accept that her father hadn't flown her to her new school on his private jet. He was making a point and he wanted her to know it. But to make her fly coach. *Coach!* She'd never been so humiliated – or so uncomfortable – in her life. She'd secured a window seat, at least, but all that meant was that she had plenty of time to watch the uninspiring view scroll by beneath the wings of the little puddle-jumper her jet had connected with.

She hadn't known there were that many trees in the world. Apart from the occasional flash of red and orange where the leaves were putting on an early Fall display, the foliage was a uniform dull dark green, as impenetrable as algebra.

Shit. She still couldn't quite believe this was happening. She kept trying to tell herself that it was less than a year, ten months really, but that was still five per cent of her life so far, and that was assuming she actually graduated at the end of it all. What was she going to do if she didn't – would her father really leave her, broke, to look after herself? Tabitha remembered again the angular stubbornness of his face as he'd given her his ultimatum, the deep silences which had widened between them in the few days between it and her departure, and was very much afraid that he would.

The landing was bumpy, but the airport so small that she was out in under ten minutes. Her father had promised to have a car waiting for her at the other end, since she'd been unable to bring her own imported soft-top MG and even he had accepted the argument that he couldn't send her to Hicksville NY and then expect her to get by on public transport. The keys had been sitting in her back pocket for the entire flight, but she walked past the car five times in the airport's small parking lot before she realised that it really was the one her father had bought her.

An *economy* model? It was ten years old and the ugliest beige she'd ever seen, a deliberate choice on her father's part she was sure. She cursed and gave the rustbucket a kick. A gentle one – it looked like it would fall apart if she hit it too hard.

It ran OK, she discovered on the drive out from Lake Placid to the school, though with an ominous low growl somewhere in the back of the engine's throat, which suggested that was likely to be a temporary state of affairs. She just hoped it would last the journey. Adirondacks U was the definition of out of the way – barely a dot on the map she'd bought in a gas station outside the airport – and half the roads that led to it didn't seem to be signposted, let alone paved. She was sure it had been at least five miles since the last house, and the inhabitants of that were probably close relatives of Norman Bates.

The sun was setting too, spreading a red glow over a horizon which suddenly revealed itself far ahead of her when she crested a sharp rise, catching glints of gold in the leaves of the endless trees. She supposed it was kind of pretty, but it was the kind of pretty you wanted to admire from a distance, not up close and personal.

There was another glow ahead of her, she realised, the warmer orange of street lighting. A small town, maybe Crystal Lake – and yes, there at the far left side, she saw the lights terminate in a gentle curve, and the other side of it the oily sheen of deep water at dusk. She was almost there.

She thought she might have to ask directions to the school once she arrived in the town, but it was hard to miss. Aside from Main Street, there didn't seem to be anything in Crystal Lake *but* the university. She counted a grand total of two restaurants, and one of those was a pizza joint. There was a bar, too, but it looked like the kind of place that would be full of people drinking to forget. After a few weeks in this backwater, Tabitha thought she might be joining them.

A security guard, sleepy eyed and sandy haired, stopped her at the gates to the university, and directed her to park in the lot on the left. He told her he'd walk her to the dorms himself – there was only the one for girls, as this was a small place, but hey they always say size doesn't matter. He laughed at a joke he'd clearly made several hundred times before.

Tabitha smiled politely, but the smile slipped as she got her first proper look at the place that would be her home for the next year. A central square of grass, severely mown, was circled by frowning red-brick buildings four and five storeys high. The only light thing she could see was the white clapboard church in the centre.

'The dorm's right in back here,' the guard said, leading her through an ivy-covered arch and into a further smaller courtyard, this one built of a paler, anaemic-looking brick.

'Great,' Tabitha said, scanning the blank windows of the block for some sign of life.

He smiled, either unaware of or indifferent to her lack of enthusiasm. 'The rooms aren't large, but then you weren't expecting a palace, were you?' He nudged her in the ribs, then pressed a small bronze key into her hand before she had a chance to react. 'You're up on the second floor, room 23B. You're roommate's been settled in a couple of weeks, so you'll have to take the smaller bed by the window – like they say, you snooze, you lose.' With that, he strode back across the square towards the front gates, whistling an out-of-tune version of what sounded like a Britney Spears song.

A roommate. In her horror at everything else, it hadn't occurred to Tabitha that the dorm room her father was forcing her into wasn't even sole occupancy. She hoped this unknown girl would at least have the decency to be out when Tabitha arrived, giving her a chance to settle in in peace.

But of course she wasn't. When Tabitha knocked tentatively on door 23B – the last in a long institutional green corridor – there was a gruff shout from inside that might have been 'wait a moment' and a second later the door was yanked open to reveal a wide unpretty face above a body that didn't look like it had ever seen the inside of a gym.

'Yes?' the girl said, eyeing Tabitha suspiciously. Her eyes caught the two suitcases on the floor behind Tabitha, all that the baggage allowance in coach had permitted, bulging with the pitifully few clothes Tabitha had been able to squeeze in.

'Hi!' Tabitha said with bright insincerity. 'I'm Tabitha – your new roomie.'

The other girl had clearly realised this already, and looked no happier at the prospect than Tabitha was. She hesitated a moment longer, as if seriously debating whether to let Tabitha in, then stepped grudgingly to one side. 'I'm Fiona,' she said. 'They told me you'd be coming.'

The room was a little nicer than Tabitha had expected. Hardly a suite at the Four Seasons, but there was a pretty floral print on the walls, and a vase of flowers beside one of the neatly made beds. Fiona was obviously tidy, if nothing else.

'That mine?' Tabith asked, gesturing at the small single bed beneath the window.

'Hope you don't mind, but you have turned up a week after classes started.'

Tabitha was sure she wasn't imagining the edge in Fiona's voice.

'Yeah, I like to be fashionably late – wouldn't want to be a geek and turn up at the start of the party.' Tabitha flipped open her cases to see that all her clothes had been crushed in transit, probably buried under two tonnes of other suitcases in the hold of the plane. Tabitha caught herself thinking that a laundry would soon get them back in shape, then realised that with her father's allowance she could barely afford washing powder, let alone an express service.

The thought was so depressing that she gave up on the idea of unpacking, leaving the case open on her bed with her wrinkled sandy Versace blouse sitting on top like a miniature patch of desert, and headed for the door.

Fiona raised a brown unplucked eyebrow. 'Where are you going?'

'For a walk,' Tabitha told her, hooking her purse over her shoulder.

The other girl looked incredulous. 'A walk where?'

'Oh, I don't know. I mean, with all these acres and acres of trees around, I guess it *is* going to be difficult to find somewhere.'

'You're going for a walk in the *woods*? At night? Are you completely crazy?'

'This is fun,' Tabitha said. 'Are we having a conversation that's entirely in questions?'

'At least take a flashlight!' Fiona shouted as Tabitha shut the door on her.

Tabitha did have an elegant little penlight she kept in her purse in case of emergencies, like inadequate restroom lighting to fix her make-up. But, as she soon discovered, the feeble beam of light barely penetrated the thick darkness between the trees. She didn't know what she'd been expecting – some kind of clearly marked path dotted with tasteful lanternesque street lights, she supposed – but within four paces she was pushing her way through thick undergrowth and within twenty she'd lost sight of the glow of the college buildings behind her, so that she could have been miles from civilisation rather than a few paces.

She knew, of course, that she ought to turn back. Not

only was this not safe, but it wasn't much fun either. But she was damned if she'd crawl back to Fiona with her tail between her legs, so she set her mouth in a grim line and pressed forward, ignoring the trailers which twined and scratched her.

Her determination lasted all of ten minutes, until a particularly determined bramble caught her Armani pants and she felt the soft material snag and then rip. She cursed and dragged it away, worsening the tear. The material had split along a good ten inches of the seam, exposing the tanned skin of her thigh to anyone who might be looking. Probably a grizzly bear, knowing her luck. She sighed, swallowed her pride and decided to turn back.

At which point she realised that she didn't know where 'back' was. Given the slow progress she'd been making, forcing her way through the matted snarling undergrowth, she assumed she'd have left a trail behind her a mile wide. But, when she shone her feeble penlight all around, the woodland looked exactly the same in all directions.

Tabitha could feel the beginnings of panic tightening her stomach, but with an effort of will forced herself not to give in to it. She'd just keep walking in a straight line, didn't matter which direction. She was bound to hit a road sooner or later, even out here – wasn't she?

After what felt like hours of desperate scramble through ever-thickening vegetation but according to her watch was only 45 minutes, she realised that she would have been better just to stay where she was – which couldn't have been very far at all from the college grounds – and wait for daylight. Now she could be a good two or three miles away, and even daylight might not bring rescue. And there were noises, too, noises that might actually have come from bears, maybe even grizzly ones.

At that point, real panic set in. A surge of adrenaline rushed through her body and the only thing she could think to do with the energy was run, blindly, animal instincts taking over from rational thought. Her breathing was the loudest sound in the forest, and after a couple of minutes of the mindless flight she dropped her light, leaving her running in absolute darkness.

Except that she realised that there *was* a light somewhere behind her, and a sound other than her own breathing, the sound of another living thing. Her first reaction was to run faster, further, get away from her pursuer, but her mind was gradually re-establishing dominance over her body and she was able to halt her headlong flight long enough to realise that the thing behind her wasn't just making noise, it was speaking.

She stopped, panting, and the words became clearer.

'Hey – wait up! What in hell do you think you're doing out here?' The voice was deep and male, rough but not unpleasant.

Tabitha drew in a harsh shaking breath, then let it out again. 'I'm – I'm lost,' she said.

'No shit.' The man was suddenly standing in front of her, having somehow found his way through the twenty feet or so of forest between them without making a sound. His flashlight – a big black industrial model, far more powerful than hers – was trained on the ground in front of him, but enough light washed back for her to get a sense of his face, like an artist's impression: hair as dark as her own, but straight and cut ruggedly to shoulder length, which he'd probably done himself. He was young, maybe no older than her, but the weather and hard work had roughened the skin of his face and it was blasted a crimson red from sun, or wind, or both. And he was big, the muscles of his arms bulging out of the shabby denim of his work shirt.

Tabitha found herself unconsciously patting at her hair, trying to get it into some kind of order – though she suspected it was a lost cause. He was looking her up and down, frowning, but his gaze lingered on her breasts on the way back up.

'I think I may have taken a wrong turning somewhere back at the last pine tree,' she told him when his gaze had returned to her eyes. 'Do you think you can point me back in the direction of Crystal Lake?'

He smiled slightly, a cheeky grin that made him look like an overgrown high-school kid. 'Yeah, I think I can do that. The name's Gerald, but you can call me Gerry.'

In the end, though, they decided they'd do better to walk back to Gerry's cabin, which he told her was only a few hundred metres away, and from which he said he'd heard her crashing through the woods like 'a moose on heat', and he'd drive her back in his pick-up from there.

The short walk back, him leading, courteously pausing every few strides to help her over a tree root or hold a branch out of her way, was accompanied by a small lecture on the stupidity of wandering off into the woods alone at night, or at any time. Tabitha didn't mind particularly as she wasn't paying much attention, most of it being taken up with a study of his ass. The jeans he was wearing weren't particularly tight but the muscles in his rear were straining against them nonetheless. Tabitha was damn sure that they had been built up by hard work rather than endless sessions in an air-conditioned gym.

She was surprised to find herself feeling horny. The after-effects of the adrenaline, she guessed – they always said near-death experiences filled you with a powerful urge to reaffirm the fact that you were still alive. And after splitting up with Chris amicably three months ago – a definite fizzle of a relationship end – she'd been pretty solidly celibate. If she was going to be exiled to Hicksville for ten months, she thought she might as well take advantage of whatever was locally on offer. She didn't get the impression Gerry would be too difficult to persuade; stuck away in the woods like this he must be positively starving for female company.

'This is it,' he said, shyly holding open the door of a

rather more spacious cabin than she had expected. There was a log fire burning on the inside, a fur rug tossed casually in front of it that looked like it came from a home-skinned bear. But the first thing that drew her eye, as he shut the door behind her with a suddenly ominous thump, was a row of axes seemingly stuck into the wall, ten of them at least, as if he'd got bored one night and thrown them one after another to relieve the monotony.

She swallowed past a suddenly dry throat. She hadn't really considered that animals weren't the only predators the woods might contain.

He saw the direction of her gaze, sensed the tension in her body and smiled easily. 'Axe-throwing trophies,' he said. 'Take a look.'

After a moment's hesitation she stepped closer and saw that, yes, each axe was indeed mounted on a board with a date and a place name inscribed on to a plaque beneath it. 'Axe throwing?' she said.

He nodded. 'Big sport out in the woods. I've been State Champion twice. Missed out by a whisker this year, though.'

She studied him to see if he was joking, intending to make a sarcastic quip, but he just looked bashfully proud. 'You must have really strong arms,' she said instead.

He shook his head, taking the remark at face value rather than the thinly disguised flirtation she'd intended. 'It's all in the wrist.'

'Yeah, I guess that would come in handy too,' she said, and this time he got it. His eyes narrowed, then widened, and she saw his Adam's apple bob as he swallowed.

He stepped a little closer, close enough for her to smell the fresh sharp scent of his sweat. 'So what exactly is a girl like you doing out in the woods at night?'

She smiled coyly. 'Oh, I was just admiring the local scenery.'

'Round here, the scenery's more dangerous than it looks.' He took another step closer, close enough that she had to crane her neck up to look into his face, to see the faint beard stubble on his cheeks and chin, surprisingly soft looking, as if it was just growing in for the first time.

Tabitha never did this kind of thing normally. She wasn't a girl for one-night stands and was certainly enough of a city girl not to trust a stranger, not to go home with a man till she'd checked out everything about him: salary, bank balance, zip code. But her whole life had just been turned upside down and she wanted something to hold on to, even if it was a stranger.

He reached out a hand, ran it gently through her hair. She leant into the touch, enjoying the contrast between his rough exterior and the gentle gesture.

'Pretty girl like you needs to be careful wandering about round here,' he said seriously. 'People might take advantage.'

'Maybe I like being taken advantage of,' she whispered.

His hand stopped in her hair, fingers tangling in the curls at the nape of her neck. His index finger moved up and down, gently stroking the delicate skin there, and she shivered.

He leant down until his lips were only an inch from hers, his breath washing warm over her face. 'You don't have to do this,' he said. 'I can take you straight back home.'

'Well, you *could*,' she said, and closed the distance between them.

She was used to men whose technique was so polished it was like they'd actually studied it. His kiss was more like the first few she'd ever known back in Junior High, rough and demanding, tongue thrusting in as soon as her mouth opened. In someone less manly it might have been off-putting, but she found herself responding to the demand, to the obvious hunger he felt for her, and opened her mouth wider, then bit down gently on his tongue before pulling back to run her own over his lips.

He let out a low guttural groan. His hands, which had

been gently pressed against her back moved down to her butt, squeezing it almost hard enough to hurt. She enjoyed the sensation for a moment, then took his hands in her own and guided them round to her front. He got the message loud and clear, fumbling with the buttons of her blouse in his haste and tearing the last two when his large fingers couldn't undo the delicate clasps quickly enough.

As soon as her breasts were free, still enclosed in her frivolous scrap of a bra, he dropped to his knees in front of her, his head level with her clavicle, and took the right breast in his mouth. The sensation of the heat and moisture of his mouth through the thin material was intense and she held him to her for a moment before pulling his head roughly back by his thick black hair and reaching up to undo the front clasp of her bra. The feeling of his mouth against her naked flesh was even better, a deep suction against her nipple, and she let out a low groan of her own.

A few minutes more of that and she was more than ready for him, but he didn't seem to want to hurry, intent on savouring her, like a starving man who eats his first meal slowly, enjoying every bite.

When he pulled her down on to the fur rug beside him she reached for the fly of his pants, but one large hand stilled her while the other hurriedly stripped the open blouse from her shoulders, fumbled then released the zipper on her own pants. His eyes, brown and deep, were burning with desire as they swept the prone length of her body, clothed now only in the skimpiest pink panties.

He brought his mouth back to her breasts, sucking harder, then biting, his big jaw encompassing nearly the whole of each pale globe, leaving a ring of red round each before trailing down her stomach, branding her with a trail of nips and sucks as he went.

He released her arms as he moved further down her body, but she left them stretched above her head, enjoying the feeling of being a passive victim to his desire.

Then his mouth found her core, and she didn't think about anything at all except the pulsing build of feeling that started there and spread warm through the rest of her body with each rough thrust of his tongue inside her. His hand went up to her breasts as he worked, pinching and twisting the nipples, more for his pleasure than hers, she thought, but somehow that was even more of a turn-on.

She was panting hard now, each out-breath a soft vocalisation. And then, much sooner than she'd expected, the feelings peaked and her hips twisted up and off the fur of the rug, her hands pushing his head away from her as she became momentarily too sensitive for his touch.

He looked up, eyes asking if he'd done something wrong, but her glazed, satiated expression must have given him his answer because he relaxed and knelt back on his haunches, finally undoing his own pants, releasing the flesh which was straining hard against them. Not bothering to undress any further, he just lowered himself back over her, weight supported on his tree-trunk arms, and pushed straight in.

She was still oversensitive from the sharp relief of her orgasm, and she let out a cry that was as much pleasure as pain when he entered her, but he was too far gone in his own desire to notice, and very soon the hard strokes of his body into hers began to build something inside her that gradually took shape as another orgasm, harder, less forgiving than the first. This time when she came he was right there with her, but her eyes were shut, all her senses focused on the fierce sensations in her sex, and all she heard was his gasping cry and then the sudden weight of his body as his arms collapsed and he fell on top of her.

After a few seconds, just as his weight was beginning to become a problem, he rolled off her, and they lay gasping side by side for a good five minutes. Tabitha turned her head to smile at him and found that he was already looking her, the lust in his face transmuted now into a sort of shy tenderness.

'Thanks,' he said.

Her smile widened. 'Oh, don't thank me yet.'

Chapter Two

Girl Least Likely To

Tabitha drifted out of sleep with a vague but growing awareness of being both sore and happy. She kept her eyes shut as her mind cleared, enjoying the play of sunshine across her eyelids and the peaceful chirrup of birdsong.

Not to mention the very raucous sound of too many young people with too much energy far too early in the morning. When Gerry had finally brought her back last night, it had been to find her roomie already asleep and the window wide open. She'd been far too tired to try to figure out how to shut it, and just collapsed on top of the bed, shedding clothes as she went, before drifting off into the sound sleep of the thoroughly satiated.

She had a sudden, slightly alarmed thought and ran her hands down her body, but she still appeared to be wearing panties and bra, so she'd obviously been *compos mentis* enough not to strip completely. Fiona just didn't strike her as the sort who'd enjoy a full-frontal view of her roommate first thing in the morning.

Tabitha smiled, reliving again the events of last night, one of those islands of fun which was enjoyed precisely because it was isolated, not to be revisited. But it gave her some hope that there might be compensatory pleasures to be found here in Crystal Lake. If nothing else, she'd have a few good stories for her friends back in LA when the sentence was up.

Finally, she opened her eyes to find Fiona staring at her from her own bed. The other girl was already dressed, slacks and a white dress shirt that would have looked better on a guy and had probably been made for one.

Tabitha found herself mentally making the other girl over, figuring out what could be done with the less than promising raw materials. De-emphasise the strong jaw, obviously, with a softer haircut than the current unruly brown fizz. Make-up would help too – Fiona didn't seem to be wearing any and had the unhealthy pallor of someone who'd spent most of what had been a glorious summer indoors. Most of all, clothes. Fiona's outfit was the epitome of unisex student grunge. Put her in something by a design house other than Fruit of the Loom and she might start to look faintly appealing.

She was so engrossed in these thoughts that it took her a moment to realise that Fiona had spoken. 'Sorry, what was that?' she asked, eyes refocusing on her roomie's real plain face rather than the fantasy made-over version in her head.

'I *said*, you've got five minutes before Professor O'Grady's lecture class starts and she really hates people who show up late.'

But Tabitha *did* show up late – nearly fifteen minutes. She might have got there a little quicker, but she'd stopped for a few moments in the central square to enjoy the view. In the daylight, the placed looked far less grim, pretty even. The red brick softened to rose in the gentle Fall sunshine, and the grass sparkled with the droplets of an earlier rainfall.

At her previous school, English had been a big subject, and her lectures – those of them she attended, anyway – had been so oversubscribed that late-comers had been able to sneak in and hide at the back without anyone being the wiser.

Tabitha was expecting the same here, so flung open the door of the classroom with blithe abandon.

Twenty pairs of eyes turned to stare at her in the sudden silence, the most disapproving from the front of the class. Professor O'Grady looked barely into her thirties, and glamorous enough to slot right into Tabitha's

LA life. Her hair was long, thick and dark, though not quite as dark or as thick as her eyelashes, and her eyes beneath them were a startling green, so pale they almost looked blank when the light caught them. They glared at Tabitha.

'So pleased you could join us.' Professor O'Grady's voice was as elegant as her clothes, deep and a little husky.

'The pleasure's all mine,' Tabith said coolly. She didn't know why, but there was something about this woman she just didn't like.

She felt several indrawn breaths of shock around her as she seated herself in the one free desk – which was, of course, right at the front.

The professor smiled back at her, unperturbed, before turning to the rest of the class. 'This is our transfer student, Tabitha Stone,' she told them. 'She's six years into her degree and still hasn't built up enough credit to graduate, so I guess she must really like school. Is that right, Tabitha?'

Tabitha was annoyed to find herself blushing, and she saw a few smirks from those around her.

'We're studying the English Romantics at the moment, Tabitha. Perhaps you could tell us what you know about them?'

Tabitha shrugged. 'Well, Duran Duran are OK, I guess, but I never got the big deal about Spandau Ballet.'

That got a big laugh from the class, and she swung round to give them a small ironic bow. As she did, her eye suddenly caught one guy, whose expression of sardonic amusement seemed more knowing than the rest, as if just he and Tabitha were in on some private joke. When he saw her looking he winked, an almost imperceptible flicker of his eyelid, then looked away.

O'Grady smiled too, but it wasn't pleasant. 'That's very funny, Tabitha. I hope you'll be bringing the same wit to the essay you'll be writing for the next class on the role of the pathetic fallacy in the poetry of the Romantics. Just to prove to me that you were, in fact, joking, and do know everything you should about a subject you've probably studied three separate times by now.'

With an effort, Tabitha managed not to let her annoyance show, just took out her notebook and scribbled down the title of the essay. When she looked back up, O'Grady had resumed her teaching, flicking through a PowerPoint presentation on Wordsworth and Byron which meant almost nothing to Tabitha. Her eyes drifted away from the screen and found themselves being almost magnetically drawn to the young man. His gaze was fixed on Professor O'Grady but somehow Tabitha was sure that his attention was still on her.

She could tell instantly that he wasn't her type. Her dating history had consisted of a stream of – in retrospect – near interchangeable clean-cut jock types with square jaws and trustworthy straight noses. This guy wasn't anything like that. His hair – sandy brown with golden highlights which were either natural or the work of a very expensive colourist – was cut rough and spiky on top of his head. The style was almost punky, but what it really made Tabitha think of was a character in that Manga DVD that Brad had once made her watch.

Maybe it wasn't the hair that made her think that, maybe it was something about the mouth. Mobile and expressive, it was a little too wide for his face, but combined with his thin sharp nose and startlingly high cheekbones the effect was not unattractive. His eyes were hidden behind his lashes, long for a man, but from his earlier glance at her she knew them to be an unusually pale, almost golden brown.

His wide mouth turned down at the corners and he leaned back in a long lazy stretch. She made an effort not to watch too obviously, keeping him in the corner of her eye, but she couldn't help noticing the muscle definition revealed as the thin material of his T-shirt was pulled tight against his chest. His hands were large but fine boned, an artist's or a musician's. If they hadn't caught her attention she might not have noticed that, when he brought them back down from behind his head, he placed only one of them on his desk. The other he slid lower, at the same time flicking her a glance she could only read as challenging. The hand settled, curled on his lap, fingers lightly tapping against his thigh.

He couldn't possibly mean what she thought he did – could he? Experimentally, she brought her own hand up to scratch her nose, then let it drop back down to sit on her thigh. She wasn't imagining his smile this time, or the air of conspiracy about it. He didn't look at her again, but she knew he was damn sure that she was watching him watching his hand.

Tabitha was hyper-conscious of the fact that, a mere ten feet away from both of them, Professor O'Grady was continuing with her lecture, and that she was shooting regular penetrating looks around the room to make sure everyone was paying attention. Tabitha knew all that but, when she saw the guy's hand tighten around the sharp bulge in the front of his jeans, she felt a warm flush spreading out from her chest to her extremities, and unconsciously moistened her lips with her tongue.

But this was ridiculous. She couldn't possibly do this – she'd be thrown off the course before she'd even started and her father would disinherit her. Only, the guy seemed aware that she hadn't joined him in this game, and his own hand had stilled and loosened and she knew, madly, that it was very important to her that he carried on.

'Next, I'd like to turn our attention to the influence of Dorothy on her brother,' Professor O'Grady said, and Tabitha very slowly curled her hand round the hem of her short skirt, sliding her fingers in over the tender flesh of her inner thighs. She couldn't move her hand much further without revealing to the entire class what she was doing, and only the tips of her index and ring finger brushed against the thin silk covering her sex. Even so, she felt how moist she was already, and the brief butterfly-soft brush of her fingers was enough to send a pulse of hard pleasure up into her belly. She'd never done anything like this before, had never even considered it as something she might *like* to do. Maybe it was something about being so far away from home that made it seem possible. Or maybe it was him, the fierce mischief glittering in his strange pale eyes.

Terrified to even look at him now, she nevertheless felt his approving gaze on her like a warm caress. She was so close already that she knew it would only take a few more strokes across that super-sensitive flesh to make her come, and it would be crazy to do that in here, to risk someone hearing or seeing, but nevertheless she flicked her fingers out once, twice, carefully controlling the sound of her speeding breath.

Hovering on the brink now, she risked another glimpse at her partner in this dangerous double-act. His face was flushed, highlights of red in his pale cheeks, and when she looked down she saw that his hand was squeezed tight enough to whiten his knuckles.

Watching him openly now, knowing that this would be too intense an orgasm to fully disguise, she flicked her fingers one last time against her swollen flesh. The shock of it was sharp and she let out a helpless gasp of pleasure that she only just managed to disguise as a cough.

He must have been at the same place himself, perhaps waiting for her to reach it first, because he let out a rough groan and shuddered, making no effort at all to disguise it.

Professor O'Grady broke off mid-sentence to study him, one eyebrow raised in sardonic query.

'Sorry,' he said, grinning unrepentantly, his cheeks still flushed. 'Old war wound playing up.'

After that, the lesson continued uninterrupted, Tabitha afraid to so much as glance at him again. When, finally, O'Grady dismissed them with an extra assignment on top of the one Tabitha had already been given, she rushed out of the class as quickly as she could, hoping to corner and at least identify the mystery man. But her bag snagged on the corner of her desk as she rose, and by the time she'd made it to the door he was nowhere in sight.

Chapter Three

Born Slippy

It wasn't until lunch break that Tabitha was able to start looking for him again. There'd been another class – Composition 101, a course she'd failed four times already and, judging by today's performance, looked set for a fifth – and then she'd been cornered by the admissions tutor and given a lecture about the strings her father had pulled to get her here and what a great place this was to learn and he really hoped she was going to use rather than squander this opportunity to study at their beautiful college.

Tabitha had already noticed the lack of cooking facilities in her dorm and resigned herself to a meal in the canteen, no doubt a haven for overcooked vegetables, carbtastic potatoes and low-GI meat. When she entered, the wave of noise hit her just before the smell – as she'd suspected of overcooked cabbage and stringy pot roast – and she paused in the doorway, wondering if it really was worth braving the place just in case he might be around. But after a morning of studying – hell, after a morning of being awake – she was starving, and she might as well get used to the place sooner rather than later.

She amused herself in the line, tray in hand, by mentally composing a letter to Jessica describing the whole experience, and managed not to wince too visibly when a woman almost as broad as she was tall deposited a sticky mess of mashed potatoes and a few dried-up slices of pork on her plate.

'Thanks, that looks really great,' Tabitha said.

The woman squinted at her through bloodshot eyes, but didn't seem to detect any irony. 'You're welcome, honey.'

She scanned the room as she paid up, but she couldn't see the man in question anywhere. The only person she recognised was Fiona, sitting at a table with a group of what Tabitha assumed were her friends. They exchanged a look which communicated quite clearly that Tabitha had no desire to join them and Fiona was very pleased that was the case.

The guy just didn't seem to be here. For a brief panicked moment she had start-of-Junior-High flashbacks, that horrible outcast feeling of being a stranger in a strange land. She looked around for an uninhabited table, but the place was packed and she'd have to sit with *someone*. Then she noticed a guy waving at her, not the ne she was looking for but definitely a face she recognised from her English class, lean and stubbled, surrounded by ringlets of long dirty-blond hair. Surfer wannabe, she guessed, probably a stoner too. But it wasn't like there were any other offers.

She slipped into the seat opposite him, and the girl to her left slid her chair aside to make room.

'Hey, Tabitha, you scored a home run in O'Grady's class,' the guy said.

Tabitha's breath caught and a hot blush crept up her neck as she realised that her secret little pleasure hadn't been as secret as she'd thought. But then the guy added, 'Duran Duran, good call,' and she realised that he wasn't talking about that at all.

He stuck his hand across the table, offering her knobbly fingers and ragged nails chewed to the quick. 'I'm Bramble. Yeah, I know, hippy parents, what you gonna do?'

Bramble introduced her to Keith, a short Asian-American with a diamond in his front tooth and a hip-hop attitude. Rounding out the group were Jade, a strawberry-blonde British exchange student who'd either had no sleep last night, or was strung out on something, or both, and Carter, a motor-mouthed punk with bad skin and a worse attitude.

Introductions over, they returned to what was clearly a long-running discussion of the merits of bud versus solid, and she let it all wash over her, concentrating on swallowing her food without gagging.

She was so lost in her own thoughts that she didn't realise someone had come over to speak to her until Bramble kicked her sharply in the shin. 'Hey, Tabby, you're supposed to zone out *during* classes, not afterwards.'

She looked up to see a trim athletic-looking guy standing beside her. For a moment she thought it was him, the man from class, but this guy was both more handsome and less attractive.

'Tabitha, right?' he said.

She nodded.

'Jake sent me, thought you might be looking for him.' He handed her a folded-over scrap of paper. 'He wanted me to give you this.'

'Jake?' she asked, but he'd already sauntered back to his own table, mission accomplished.

'In our class,' Jade told her, 'tall, big mouth – literally and metaphorically. Good-looking, I suppose, if you like that sort of thing.'

Tabitha felt a buzz of excitement, like a mild electric shock administered somewhere near her belly. 'Yeah, got you.'

'Passing notes in class?' Carter asked. 'What are we, in high school?'

Tabitha gave the note a cursory glance, then slipped it into her pocket.

Bramble stared at her. 'Aren't you going to read it?'

'It's the reading list from O'Grady. I would have thrown it straight in the trash but that just seemed rude.'

The others laughed, seeming to accept her explanation, and returned to their previous conversation. Tabitha remained with them long enough to avoid suspicion, then disposed of what remained of her lunch – nearly all of it – and strolled out into the heat of the sun. She looked around to make sure she wasn't being watched, then read the note again: *Let's meet in the church, by George.*

The white clapboard building was deserted at this time of the day, but she found that the door was unlocked and it was easy enough to slip in unnoticed. The dark of the interior foxed her eyes after the yellow-gold sunshine outside and she blinked for a few seconds, blinded. Once the interior began to swim into dim focus, she saw it: there, by the altar, an old-fashioned painting of St George, slaying the dragon.

She strode up to it, grinning broadly, expecting a figure to step out of the shadows to greet her. But when she reached the painting she found that she was still alone, the hushed interior of the building disturbed only by the sound of her own breathing.

'Bastard!' she said. Then she saw it, another small piece of paper shoved into a crack at the bottom of the picture's frame. She smiled and used her fingernail to prise it out.

This one was longer: *Sorry – got tired of waiting. Try the big tree in the small place. Before you go, leave an offering for St George. Any item of clothing will do.*

Tabitha debated for a second but, whatever game he was playing, she knew she wanted to join in. She'd dressed lightly that morning, a dark-green dress and the elegant Christian Louboutin sandals which had been her last purchase before her father cut off her supply of designer clothing for good. She was damned if she was going to lose those, and she could hardly leave her bra or panties in the house of God. Which meant only one thing – the dress.

She flicked a nervous glance back into the body of the church, though she knew that no one had entered since she'd been in, and even if they did now it would take their eyes a few minutes to adjust to the gloom. Was she really going to do this? She couldn't quite believe it but, almost without her conscious volition, she was lifting the dress up and over her head. The chill air inside the church brought out goosebumps on her exposed flesh, but her body felt as if it was burning up from the inside.

She had known instantly what he meant by 'the big tree in the small place'. She'd noticed it on the guided tour she'd been given earlier, as he'd probably realised she would, a tiny walled garden at the back of the college almost entirely taken up with one enormous apple tree. It was relatively quiet and secluded, possible to reach from here without being observed. Possible – but by no means certain.

She dropped her dress underneath one of the pews where it was unlikely to be seen and she could pick it up later – $2,000 Marc Jacobs didn't grow on trees – then, hugging the wall, flicking nervous glances back to the main entrance, she made her way to a side door she'd noticed earlier, the one which let out near the entrance to the walled garden. At the door itself she paused for a good thirty seconds, breathing deeply, not sure she could actually go through with it, but at the same time knowing that she wanted to, that she'd regret it if she didn't. Knowing, without knowing how, that the intriguing young man would rapidly lose interest in her if she proved unable to meet his challenge.

She wasn't sure why it mattered so much, but she was certain that she *had* to see him again. So she took a deep breath, stood as far to one side of the door as the tight space would allow, and eased it open.

The view outside was clear, nothing in sight through the narrow crack but carefully mown grass and a sliver of sky. Still, that left about eighty per cent of the view unaccounted for, and Tabitha couldn't see if there was anyone to witness her exposing herself without opening the door further and exposing herself anyway.

She realised that she was having fun, more of it than

she'd managed in a long time, even at all those high-end parties with all those dedicated party-goers she hung out with back in LA. They had liked to think of themselves as rule-breakers but they'd never taken any real risks because they all had too much to lose. Now Tabitha's father had already taken away all the things that mattered to her, what was the point of worrying? And with that thought she flung open the door and sprinted towards the suddenly very distant archway leading to the walled garden.

She didn't take the time to look around to see if anyone had observed her, just slammed the wooden door of the garden behind her and leant against it, panting. From the lack of wolf-whistles and shouting she guessed she'd gotten away with it, as everyone else was probably back in classes by now. After a while, she started laughing, thinking: I wonder if this was what Daddy had in mind when he sent me here?

The tree was in fruit, beautiful rosy apples which looked so tantalising she just had to pick one, despite the sign telling her not to. She wasn't surprised, this time, to find a note rather than a person sitting in a crook of the tree's branches. *Like Eve*, it said, *I hope you'll enjoy some forbidden fruit. And in homage to your ancestor, another tribute must be left.* She'd been expecting that too, of course. *Now it's time to see where Adam leads*, the note finished.

That one stumped her for a second, until she remembered the small lane she'd passed on her arrival leading out from the college grounds and into the surrounding woods. Adam's Lane. She'd wondered at the time where it ended, and now it looked like she was going to find out.

She slipped her bra off, and hung it from the apple tree by one blue strap, then let herself out of the back gate and into the overgrown wilderness outside where, away from the many-windowed gaze of the college, the forest seemed to be quietly reclaiming the land which had been stolen from it. One arm clasped across her exposed breasts, the rosy peaks of her nipples erect, chafing pleasantly against her skin, Tabitha picked her way carefully through the trees that bordered Adam's Lane, keeping the path in sight through the sparse underbrush. Twice, she had to duck down and hide as cars drove past, but the engine noise gave her plenty of warning and she felt far safer here out in the trees than she had in the college grounds. She knew that she was taking a big risk by coming here, but she'd always been someone to trust her instincts, and every instinct she had told her that Jake was trouble – but not more than she could handle.

Eventually, the road petered out and, at its end, she saw a surprisingly golden beach, only twenty or so feet long, and then the long calm waters of a large lake. The Crystal Lake of the town's name, she assumed.

It was very beautiful. The cars which had passed her on the way were parked up on the sand, so she didn't dare approach too closely, but the blue of the lake was a dark mirror of the blue of the sky, and the furthest shore lapped against the stark grey shoulder of a mountain, its head lost in gathering cloud.

She didn't know how she was going to find the clue here without revealing herself to the students who were tossing a ball idly back and forth on the beach. Where had he left it, anyway? If it was hanging on one of the trees, there was little chance that she'd ever find it. The answer, she thought, was to think the way he did. And the minute she did that, she knew what he'd want: he'd want her to get into the water, use it to hide herself from the other people there, her modesty preserved by only a few inches of liquid.

She wondered if he'd join her in there, but someone knew that he wouldn't, that he hadn't quite finished his game yet.

Very carefully, she crept further away from the beach, skirting the lake's edge but remaining in the trees. When she'd put at least thirty feet between her and the other students, she made her way down to the water, stopped to take off her sandals, placed them lovingly out of harm's way on a convenient rock, then dove in, her slender body barely making a splash.

The water was shiveringly cold against her bare skin. Her nipples tightened still further, pulling into aching tips that seemed to stream sensation straight down the centre line of her body. She saw the students glance over at her, and one of them raised his arm in a lazy wave, but none of them came any closer. It was an amazing feeling, that they were looking at her, naked save for a scrap of lace panties, and they didn't even realise it.

More daring now, she stroked confidently towards the centre of the lake, swimming almost as natural as walking to her, a skill she'd learnt in her parents' pool when she was too young even to talk. And there ahead of her she saw what must be the site of the next message: a red buoy bobbing with the motion of the waves.

The sun came out from the clouds as she swam towards it, sending sharp lances of light from the water, and she heard the students on the beach shout and laugh. For a moment she thought that the sunlight had somehow revealed her to them, but when she trod water to look back at them she saw that they were half the lake away still, just sharing a joke, not even looking in her direction.

The note had been taped to the side of the buoy, carefully sealed in a waterproof baggie. It was simpler this time, the end of the quest: *Room 3E. You know the drill by now.* She did. Without any hesitation at all this time, she hooked a finger through the waist of her panties, kicked her legs up and out, then let the silk drift gently to the bottom of the lake.

Jake must have swum out to this place himself, she knew, sometime between that first class and lunch. She liked the amount of effort he'd put into setting this up, the fact that he must have been thinking about her all morning as he did it. Somehow, the thought that he'd been here, in this same water, seemed very intimate to her. It was almost as if the water was an extension of him, as if the gentle waves lapping against her were *his*, a part of his body. Her hand drifted down, slowly, through the yielding resistance of the water, and she brushed her fingers against the knot of nerves at her core, letting out a breathy sigh at the sensation.

She wanted to carry on, but at the same time she wanted to wait. The next time she came, it would be with him, touching him, together. As she thought that, she had the sudden strong conviction that he *was* with her – somewhere near by, watching. Her gaze was drawn to the shoreline, and she thought she caught a brief flash of movement in the trees, the white flicker of teeth in a wide smile. But then it was gone and she was alone, on the lake, only the water on her skin, nothing but the distant shouts of the students and the lonely cries of seabirds around her.

She smiled and flipped herself round to head back to shore.

The first second Mark saw the girl, he thought he was imagining it, that she must be wearing some kind of flesh-coloured dress. But then he saw the nervous glances she was darting all around her, the way she clung to the shadows against the wall, and when she looked back in his direction he slipped back into the shadows himself – because he realised that she really was naked. He wondered if he ought to call out, if she'd perhaps locked herself out of her room while in the shower and might need his help, but she clearly didn't want anyone to see her, and besides, if she'd locked herself out of her room, what was she doing out here in the courtyard?

She was moving slowly, creeping forwards one careful step at a time, so he had plenty of time to study her. She was barely five-five, but her lean toned physique made her look taller. He found his eyes drawn irresistibly to his favourite part of a woman's body, the elegant curve of thigh into the swell of her buttocks. The skin there was much paler, denied the tan which had darkened the rest of her body. It was the vulnerable whiteness of that tender flesh which turned him on the most.

The pink tips of her nipples swung into view when she jerked another look behind her. Like a teenager, he felt himself hardening, unable to control it, overcome with an intense animal desire which had nothing at all to do with the intellect on which he so prided himself. She was barely ten feet away from him. As she leant round, her face momentarily emerged from shadow into light.

She was very pretty, there was no doubt about that, loose dark curls of hair framing a heart-shaped face, jewel-blue eyes staring out of it. But it was the slight imperfections which attracted him most, the charming upturn to her nose, the light dusting of freckles which the sun had brought out on her high cheekbones. She was a student of course, strictly out of bounds, and that was a rule Mark never had, never would, break. But, though he knew he should stop looking, he just couldn't seem to drag his eyes away.

She was still wearing shoes, he suddenly realised, high-heeled sandals which were probably both very fashionable and very expensive. Who *was* she? She stopped by the entrance to one of the dorms and he saw her finger run up the list of numbers at the side and hover briefly on the one to the furthest right.

Mark shook his head. Room 3E – of course. That, he thought darkly, explained everything.

Chapter Four

Make it Mine

If Tabitha hadn't been completely naked she might have hesitated before knocking on the door, suddenly nervous about meeting the man with whom it already felt as if she was having an intimate relationship. But, though Jake's room was tucked away at the end of the third-floor corridor, she would still be giving quite a display if any of the nearby students left their rooms.

She knocked once, hesitantly, then a second time more firmly. He answered almost immediately, as if he'd been waiting for her, and she wondered if he'd only just got home himself, if perhaps he'd been watching her progress all afternoon, vicariously enjoying her exhibitionism.

He paused a minute to sweep her up and down with his eyes before smiling slowly and opening the door wide enough to admit her. She stepped deliberately closer to him as she entered, allowing her bare skin to brush against his arm, and was gratified when she saw the pupils of his unusual golden eyes dilate until there was almost nothing to them but blackness.

The room was the same as any other student dorm in size or shape, though it contained only one double bed rather than two singles – no roomie, obviously. She wondered how he had persuaded the university authorities to let him do this, when members of the opposite sex weren't even allowed in the dorms after ten at night. On each wall there was a richly patterned hanging, and the furniture looked old enough to be antique, cluttered with artefacts from a good five continents. It wasn't at all what she'd expected, but it just made him seem that much more intriguing.

She finally turned from her study of the room to its occupant. His eyes raised as she faced him and she knew with a warm flush of pleasure that he'd been looking at her, studying the lines and curves of her body.

He raised one eyebrow now, looking back down at her sandaled feet. 'Now how did I guess those would be the last things a girl like you wanted to lose?'

'A girl like me?' It was an unaccustomed sensation, standing so exposed in front of a man who was fully clothed, but she found that she liked it. She might have expected it to make her feel powerless, but she knew that she was the one with the power here, felt it in the over-fast sound of his breathing, the way his eyes kept returning again and again to her breasts, thighs, the thin strip of hair shading the flesh between her legs.

He licked his lips. 'An unusual one.'

She took her time to look *him* up and down. He was still wearing the same jeans and pale T-shirt he'd been wearing earlier, though she could now see a trace of leaf dust on his shoulders. She smiled as she realised that he *had* followed her into the woods and watched her from the shore. His face was flushed and his eyes hooded, as if he wasn't entirely sure he wanted her to be able to read them. 'I think one of us is unsuitably dressed for the occasion,' she said. 'Unless you just invited me over to be your study buddy?'

He grinned at that, a light open expression that made his face seem a whole lot younger. She wondered just how old he was – not a freshman, that was for sure, but probably no older than 21. Her toy boy, she thought, but that just didn't seem right. If anyone had been toyed with, it was her.

'No,' he said, 'that wasn't exactly what I had in mind. But you're right – it doesn't seem fair that I'm dressed and you're . . . not.'

He reached out a hand towards her and her breath caught raggedly as she realised that this would be the first time he'd ever touched her. Very gently, he touched just the tip of his finger to her lips, stroking it backwards and forwards as if learning their shape. After a moment he ran it down her chin, then further, along the tender curve of skin beneath, hesitating in the hollow of her throat, as if he could feel the wild beating of her pulse there, and then round to circle and finally touch each nipple in turn.

Tabitha had been with men who prided themselves on their technique before – men who seemed to pause after each act expecting marks for artistic interpretation. Jake wasn't like that at all. He was totally focused on what he was doing, doing it because it was exactly what *he* wanted to do. She could feel herself moistening, her core muscles contracting as if trying to will him into her.

When his eyes met hers again there was a fire in their golden-brown depths. She was so focused on them that for a moment she didn't notice what he was holding in his hand: a small blue scrap of material. Her bra.

'Souvenir?' she asked, surprised at how shaky her voice was.

'Like you said, one of us isn't dressed right.'

He lifted his hand towards her and, after a moment, she realised that he was asking for hers. Puzzled, she put it in his and watched as he raised it to his lips. For a moment she thought he was going to kiss it, a gesture that would have seemed uncharacteristically chivalrous, but instead he took each finger into his mouth in turn and ran his teeth gently up and down the length of it, his tongue swirling briefly against each sensitive pad.

Then, when her eyes had almost drifted shut to enjoy the sensation, he slipped the silk strap of her bra over her shoulder. She looked questioningly at him, but he just grinned. He took her other arm and repeated the move, biting down a little harder on each finger this time, hard enough to hurt a little, but the pain turned to pleasure somewhere on its journey down her arm and arrived as a sharp jolt of lust in her centre.

When both arms were through, he reached between her breasts to fasten the centre clasp with practised ease. Only when her breasts were covered in the lacy scraps of silk did he drop to his knees and take each in turn into his mouth. Tabitha let her arms drop down to run them through his hair, not guiding him, just enjoying touching him, anchoring herself to the concrete reality of his body as the sensations he was causing threatened to float her away.

His mouth was very hot against the skin of her breasts, still chilled from the water and their long exposure to the cooling afternoon air. She could feel his breath pant out rapidly against them, a flush of sensation every time, but he didn't seem to be in any hurry. She traced the outline of his head beneath his hair, the firm bones of his skull, then the delicate cheekbones and the slender arch of his nose. She rested a finger against his mouth and he alternated between sucking that and sucking the proud flesh of her nipple.

When he finally stood up, she wasn't surprised to see him reach behind and bring out her blue summer dress. He slipped it over her head, following its flowing path down her body with his mouth so that she wasn't sure which touch was the material's and which was his. He was gently pushing her backwards, pressing her towards his big double bed, and when her knees hit the mattress she allowed herself to sit down, and he knelt in front of her.

The dress hung down just past her knees, hiding everything from his view, and he watched her face, daring her to look away as he pushed his hands up out of sight, fingers skimming along the baby-soft skin of her inner thighs, pausing as they felt the stickiness there, the evidence of just how much he'd turned her on.

When he reached the centre, he ran his fingers gently

through the curls there, feeling their outline, as if he hadn't already seen them. Almost against her will, she felt herself pushing down towards him, desperate to feel him touching her sex, knowing it wouldn't take much at all to push her over the edge. But, as she pushed down, he pulled back and she saw him frown and knew that he wanted to control this.

Then, finally, his fingers reached up and brushed against her, circling gently around the epicentre of her pleasure.

'Is this how you did it?' he asked. 'In class, with all those other people around and me watching, is this how you touched yourself?'

She nodded. 'But just a little harder.' Her voice was a husk of its usual rich alto.

He increased the pressure a little, circling inwards in spirals until he touched her *there*, and the moment he did she came, her muscles clutching hard against air when really they wanted to be clutching against him.

'Sorry I didn't manage to get your panties back,' he said, but though his tone tried for nonchalance she could hear the tightness in his voice, the effort it was costing him to draw this out.

'That's OK.' Her voice had recovered a little, though she still felt weak and languorous. She scooted back on the bed, knelt back and held out her arms to him. 'You can go fetch them after.'

She pulled him to her then pushed him down till he was lying prone, suddenly willing to follow *her* lead, confident it would take him somewhere he liked. She realised, shocked, that they still hadn't kissed, and she decided that they wouldn't, not until they'd done everything else. She liked the back-to-front start, the way she'd started naked and ended up dressed, the fact that they hadn't even been introduced, hadn't said each other's name yet.

His arousal was pushing hard against his jeans, hard enough to hurt, the essence of him wanting to find its home in her. She liked that about men, the primal nature of their desire, how simple it was, how basic a thing it came down to in the end. She didn't feel she understood much, had certainly never grasped all the things she'd spent the last six years studying, but she understood *this*.

The button slipped out of his fly as if it was in as much of a hurry as he was but she took her time pushing the material aside, easing him out of his grey boxers, because she didn't want to hurt him, and because she wanted to tease him, just a little, the way he'd teased her.

When he was free, she ran her fingers up the length of him a few times, looking in his eyes, challenging him to look away the way he'd challenged her. He held her gaze as she eased herself down, guiding him in with her hand. She could tell that he wanted to arch up into her, saw it in the strain on his face, the tight white line of his mobile mouth, but he let her set the pace, obeying her rules as she'd obeyed his. She reached her hands behind her, leaning back to allow herself more leverage, pumping faster, knowing that she'd have to work hard to come again but that it could happen, and it would, because he was waiting for her, gasping with the effort, and then it *was* happening, her clenching around him, him spilling into her, both of them finally shutting their eyes, the joining giving way to the intensely private sensation of orgasm.

Afterwards, she lay on top of him, her ear against the hard thump of his heart, but she didn't stay there for long. Normally she loved the cuddling, basking in the afterglow and the blurring of boundaries that only seemed to take place after great sex, but that just didn't seem right here. They'd started this as strangers, and it seemed very important that they end it that way.

When she pushed herself to her feet, he didn't seem offended, just watched her with an amused expression as she brushed a hand down her dress to smooth out the wrinkles, the other working out the tangles in her hair.

'I guess I'll see you in psychology tomorrow,' he said finally, his tone businesslike, no trace of what they'd just done in his voice.

She nodded, her hand already on the doorknob. 'Yeah. Maybe someone there can introduce us.'

On the way back to her room she passed Bramble and Carter, and when Bramble gave her a grin and an ironic V sign she felt content enough to smile and wave back, almost fond of them in a way that had seemed inconceivable earlier. She felt the same warm flush of emotion when she returned to her room to find Fiona sitting at her desk, books open in front of her and the curtains closed. The girl couldn't help it if she had grown up in the back of beyond, far from the life-giving designer boutiques Tabitha had taken for granted all her life. She wasn't hopeless, she'd just got off to a bad start. And Tabitha felt, for the first time, that life at Adirondacks U needn't be hopeless either.

Didn't her dad always say that life was what you made of it? It seemed to Tabitha that she might be able to make something halfway decent out of her time here. She could build an existence which might not quite be the equivalent of her one back in LA, but might still have ... rewards of its own.

Shame about all the damn work she was expected to do. But, looking at Fiona, studiously ignoring her as she bent over her books, her hand occasionally flicking her thick brown hair out of her eyes, Tabitha had a sudden excited thought.

'Hey, Fiona,' she said, perching on the edge of her roommate's desk. It occurred to her that she hadn't yet washed and that Jake's smell must be all over her, but the other woman didn't seem to notice, just frowned up at her in annoyance. 'Yeah?'

'I've got a proposition for you.'

Fiona leant back, brows raised. 'Why don't I think I'm going to like it?'

Tabitha shrugged. 'Because you've got a suspicious mind? It's more an exchange of services really. The thing is, I need some help with the work here – studying just isn't my forte.'

'Really? I never would have guessed.' Her tone was bland, but the sarcasm was unmistakeable.

'I mean, it's not like I want to be here.'

'So why *are* you here?' Fiona's eyes flicked to the neat line of designer shoes Tabitha had laid out by her bed. 'You don't seem like someone who's going to be held back in life by a lack of qualifications.'

'Yeah, well, normally you'd be right. But my dad's taken it into his head that I need to graduate. And, if I don't, he's going to cut me off without a cent.'

'Good Lord,' Fiona said, sounding genuinely interested for the first time. 'How amazingly Victorian.'

Tabitha nodded. 'Victorian. Yeah, that's my dad all over.'

'So, what? You need my help with your next paper?'

'And the one after that.'

Fiona pursed her lips. 'And what do I get in return?'

Tabitha bowed theatrically. 'Your own personal shopper.'

'But I thought you said you didn't have any money.'

'I don't,' Tabitha said. 'I'm not going to buy your clothes for you – just pick them out. I'll be your own individual style guru.'

But Fiona's expression had hardened, the momentary human interest she'd shown in Tabitha gone. 'So,' she said bitingly, 'this is your way of saying I need to dress better.'

Tabitha realised she'd made a mistake, but smiled through it, hoping she could win the other woman over. 'You know what they say – you can never be too young, too rich or too stylish.'

Fiona stood up and begun stuffing her books into her bag with short angry motions before stalking to the door 'Well, believe it or not, I'm happy the way I am, stylish or not. And you can do your own damn work like everyone else,' she said and slammed the door behind her.

'Shit.' Tabitha sat down hard on the bed, her earlier good mood evaporated. She'd only meant to help – what was the *matter* with some people?

Chapter Five

King of Snake

She was in his psychology class. Mark had only seen her briefly the day before, but had found himself unable to shift the image from his mind, little details of it – the swell of her breast, the little crease beneath her buttocks – popping into his head at the most inappropriate moments.

Jake was already in the class, loitering near the door as usual, legs crossed at the ankle in a posture of easy arrogance that stopped just short of outright insolence. When she came in, dark curls falling across her eyes, Mark expected her to head straight to Jake, but she just glanced in his direction with almost convincing casualness, then sauntered to the front of the room and sat directly in front of Mark. But when her eyes glanced over him he could tell that they didn't see him and he knew that all her attention was still focused on Jake. This was an act for Jake's benefit, or perhaps some game the two of them were playing together. Jake was very good at getting other people to join in his mischief; it was probably his greatest skill.

When the class had settled down, Mark turned to her. 'You're new in this class, aren't you?'

She nodded. 'Tabitha Stone, I'm a transfer student from LA.' Her voice was a clear alto, but there was something about the tone that spoke of a secret amusement that she didn't plan on sharing with the world.

'You know this is *advanced* cognitive psychology? You need to have passed the introductory courses to be taking this one.'

Tabitha smiled, and Mark realised for the first time that she was a little older than Jake, maybe in her mid-twenties, no hint of age yet in her face but a confidence in her bearing that most college students lacked. 'I've done the courses,' she said. 'I'm a psychology major.'

There was something about the way she said it, a hint of mockery, that made him push her further. 'So you'll know all about Baddeley and Hitch's working model of memory.'

'Yeah.'

After a second he realised that was all she was going to say. 'Care to give the class a brief summary?'

Her eyes narrowed slightly. 'Isn't that your job?'

He folded his arms and looked down his nose at her, a forbidding expression on his face which had put the fear of God into many a student before her. Her smile broadened, as if she held him and the entire class in mild contempt.

He thought he had her pegged now. She was the kind of woman who'd coasted by on looks and money her whole life and had every chance of continuing to do so for years to come. Utterly selfish, because the world had never taught her not to be. No wonder Jake was attracted to her – they were two of a kind.

Mark sighed and turned to the rest of the class, dismissing her from his thoughts. Jake would soon tire of her, and he wasn't prepared to waste time on a student who didn't want to learn. Or thinking about a woman who was strictly out of bounds – even if he had been prepared to take Jake's leavings, which of course he wasn't.

But he found his eyes straying back to her helplessly as the class progressed, tracing the shape of her breasts through her light cotton top. And, when at the end of the lesson she approached Jake and shook his hand as if they'd never met, Mark watched and wondered.

* * *

Jake invited Tabitha to join him for lunch after the psychology class, but she declined, instinctively knowing that he would lose interest if she made this too easy for him. Instead she went back to her room to study, picking up one of the recommended psychology books from the library along the way.

Fiona was in the room, already hard at work. She didn't look up to acknowledge Tabitha's presence when she entered. The other woman had barely spoken two words to her since their conversation the day before. Tabitha had intended to apologise, attempt to build some bridges, but something about Fiona's stony demeanour stopped her, indicating that any attempt at reconciliation would be rebuffed. So that, thought Tabitha, made it her roommate *and* Professor O'Grady who seemed to have taken an instant and violent dislike to her. She didn't think her psychology teacher Professor Sinclair was her biggest fan, either. His eyes – a startling blue almost violent in their intensity – had drifted to her a few times during the course of the class, but they'd been cold, as if he was summing her up and didn't like his conclusion.

She thought she knew his type – no sense of humour, no understanding of anyone who didn't find his subject as fascinating as he did. He couldn't have been much more than thirty but he acted like he was a decade older. His face was, she supposed, reasonably handsome, but he held it in such a rigidly controlled way that it looked like a mask, the sharp cheekbones and deep eye-sockets hiding his real emotions behind them. Which meant it was probably best that she make some sort of effort to actually get the work done for him. He didn't look the sort to be amenable to the kind of sob story which had always – previously – been able to get her out of trouble, even with her father.

Two hours later, she'd barely managed to get through one chapter, the words swimming in front of her eyes as she reread one paragraph for the fourth time. It was true, as she'd told Sinclair, that she had been a psychology major back in LA, but that was like saying that grass was more edible than wood. It had simply been her least bad subject. And she supposed it was kind of interesting, except that everyone teaching it – Sinclair included – seemed determined to suck the joy out of it, talking about neural networks and the computational theory of mind when, really, didn't people study psychology because that was what they were interested in: people?

Jake didn't bother to knock when he came round, just sauntered in as if he had a standing invitation. Fiona's head jerked up, ready to snap at him, but then she noticed Tabitha's smile and returned her attention to her books, mouth set in a thin irritated line.

'I told you I didn't want lunch,' Tabitha said, turning *her* head back to her books as if she'd dismissed him from her mind.

He walked over to her desk and leant behind her, chest pressed against her back, breath hot against her cheek, to look at her workbook. She'd written a total of three lines in it. 'Yeah, I can see you've made good use of the time you saved.'

She saw that his hair was wet, darker with the moisture in it, little beads of it dripping down on to his brow. She guessed he'd gone to the school's gym since she'd last seen him. She could smell the faint fresh aroma of his sweat. With his hair plastered back, the outline of his face was clearer, strong definite lines as if they'd been painted by an artist who was very sure of his strokes and knew exactly the effect he was aiming for.

He stood back and folded his arms, forcing her to twist round in her seat to face him. 'Just thought you might want to drop in at our party tonight. If you've got space in your busy social calendar.' He handed over an invitation, colour printed on copy paper, just a picture of Russell Crowe in gladiatorial costume and the phrase 'Prepare to Unleash Hell' with Greek letters and an off-campus address.

'Gladiator and slave-girl theme,' he said. 'I'm told it's ironic, but personally I think I could manage to unironically appreciate the sight of you in a skimpy dress. I guess I'm just not very sophisticated.'

Tabitha thought there was a genuine compliment somewhere beneath the banter. 'Didn't know you were a frat boy.'

'Me neither,' Fiona said dryly, without looking up from her books. 'It seems so out of character.'

Tabitha and Jake both ignored her. 'I'm not,' Jake told her. 'But they were the first people I got to know when I transferred here from Columbia.'

'You're a transfer student too?' She looked up at him and saw a sudden slight guardedness in his eyes, as if this was touching on territory he wanted to shield with more than a joke. But he just shrugged.

'Managed to get here for the start of classes, unlike some people.'

Tabitha turned round in her chair, straddling it so that she was facing him full on. 'All good things are worth waiting for.'

He nodded seriously, as if she'd made a good point. The fading sunlight struggling through the window glowed only faintly on his cheekbones and forehead, leaving the rest of his face in shadow. 'So, does that mean you'll come?' He sounded suddenly serious, as if this actually did matter to him. Or maybe it was just another role he was playing.

Tabitha had a sudden thought. 'Exactly how long have you been planning this party?'

He smiled at that, light glimmering on his straight white teeth. 'Since you said you didn't want to come to lunch with me.'

'Well, I guess I could make it,' Tabitha said. She looked at Fiona, head still down over her work, though Tabitha was sure she hadn't written anything for the last five minutes. 'Fiona, want to come to a party?'

Fiona glared at her, though Tabitha hadn't meant the

invitation mockingly. 'Aren't you a little old to be going to a kegger?' she said with contempt.

Tabitha felt her temper snapping, another overture of friendship summarily rejected. 'Aren't you a little young *not* to be going?'

Jake backed away, hands up, wanting no part of the argument. 'It starts at eight – don't be late,' he said, taking in both women with the statement. But his eyes held Tabitha's all the way to the door, the same golden colour as the dying sunlight.

Tabitha would normally have spent far longer preparing for the party, making sure that her make-up and clothes were just so, but the glowering presence of Fiona, watching her preparations with a jaundiced eye, drove her out of the room by nine o'clock. She was glad, at least, that her first major social outing was so early into the semester, before all her best outfits fell seriously out of fashion. She'd chosen a floral print Dolce & Gabbana mini-skirt on the bottom, a vintage lace-up leather shirt on top. It wasn't exactly Roman slave-girl, but she knew it showed off her body to its best advantage and it was skimpy enough that she didn't think any of the frat boys was likely to complain. She hoped Jake wouldn't, anyway.

She decided to walk, knowing she'd likely be over the limit by the time the party was over and glad of a little fresh air to clear her head. She still couldn't believe how little she and Jake had actually said to each other. The flirtation was fun, but she wanted to know more about him. Maybe tonight they'd have a real conversation. It would be their third time, if you counted the encounter in Professor O'Grady's class, surely it was time. But she knew, too, that he was enjoying the strange game they were playing, and she wasn't sure that personal revelations were in the rules.

The party was being held a good twenty-minute walk away from the school, in one of the big dark houses that lurked on the outskirts of Crystal Lake. Once she'd found the right street it wasn't hard to locate the actual building, hip hop pumping out of it at volumes loud enough to wake the neighbourhood. Through the front window she could see a crowd of people dancing hard and, yes, a large keg. The turnout looked impressive for an event whose invites had only gone out five hours before. Clearly Jake's parties were well known. It didn't surprise her.

Jake himself was waiting for her as soon as she stepped through the door, bare arms folded above a leather kilt and what looked like a real sword strapped over his shoulders. He looked her up and down and frowned slightly. 'The slave-girls are supposed to be Roman – not Princess Leia in *Return of the Jedi.*'

Tabitha shrugged, knowing that the gesture would pull the paper-thin leather of her top tight against her breasts. 'I guess I flunked history. Is that a problem?'

He didn't reply, just eyed her up and down again, much more slowly this time, studying every detail as if she really were a slave he was contemplating buying. Then he shook his head and held out his hand, taking hers to lead her through into the main room.

Tabitha had only gone to one or two frat parties when she first started school. Having already spent two years hitting the LA club scene by the time she started university, she wasn't impressed with the sight of inexperienced drinkers getting out of control on cheap beer and bad drugs. But now, as she took a few drinks, enjoyed the music and nodded her head at the people Jake introduced her to, unable to hear anything much beyond their names, she wondered if she'd missed out. She'd been acting like a twenty-year-old in her teens, maybe in her twenties it was time to start reverting.

Somewhere in her head she heard Fiona's voice telling her that people generally tried to move forwards rather than backwards, but she ignored it. People who grew up ended up like Fiona, and who wanted that?

As if to illustrate her thought, she suddenly noticed

Fiona standing uncomfortably against a wall, her idea of a slave-girl outfit seemingly a skirt that fell to just below her knees and a crop-top that rose to a little above her belly button. The other woman, Tabitha saw, had a reasonable body, but she held it so rigidly that it was as if she had an invisible barrier around her. She had a drink in her hand, a fruit punch that Tabitha had already ascertained was frighteningly alcoholic. As Tabitha watched, she knocked it back in a few gulps, glaring round her as she did, as if daring anyone to speak to her. Tabitha guessed that Fiona had come to prove some kind of point, but she didn't look like she had any intention of enjoying it.

Tabitha just didn't get that attitude at all. Before Tabitha's mother had walked out on them back when Tabitha was ten, she'd told her daughter that she needed to find herself, that she'd given up her life for her little girl and only now realised what a mistake that was. Tabitha didn't intend to make the same mistake. She wasn't going to reach her thirties tied to a husband and child she suddenly realised she didn't want. Tabitha intended never to give up anything for anybody. But then Jake smiled at her across the dance floor, and she knew that there were some things, at least, that she would give up for this young man about whom she knew little more than a name.

The evening went on. She drank, she danced – and she watched Jake. He watched her back, but they never touched and they barely even spoke. Jake's friends were happy to fill in for him, asking Tabitha about herself and the life she'd led back in LA. She knew this kind of crowd, a party crowd ready to adopt anyone who wanted their kind of good time. As the light alcohol buzz grew, she found conversations melting and flowing into each other, more and more people joining the party in this strange large house that didn't seem to belong to anyone there.

'Whose place is this, anyway?' she asked, looking round at the careful display of herbs and spices on one wall of the large kitchen, the rack of cooking utensils, its tidiness a contrast to the wreckage of the party strewn on the work surfaces below.

'Professor Sinclair,' a dark-haired girl told her, Jackie, or maybe Jamie – Tabitha couldn't remember.

Tabitha raised an eyebrow. 'What – this is *his* party?'

'No, Jake said he's out of town. Jake said we may as well use the place while he's gone.'

Tabitha laughed, not quite believing it but liking the idea of Jake pulling off something so crazy for her sake. It seemed to fit with the atmosphere of the evening, that dreamlike quality that all the best parties developed as the hours wore on, irrationality ruling the night.

It felt like part of the same dream logic when she saw a girl lying prone on one of the long benches against the kitchen wall and a crowd of jocks around her taking body shots from the exposed skin of her throat and shoulders. But then her eyes focused on the girl's face, the square jaw and heavy eyebrows, and she realised that it was Fiona. Closer up, she could see how glazed her eyes were, senses hazy with too much alcohol drunk far too quickly. Her skirt had ridden up over her knees, and one of the boys was reaching up further, laughing as he ran his fingers up her leg.

Tabitha shoved him away, face flushed with anger. 'Leave her alone.'

The guy looked at her, his hollow-cheeked face startled. 'I don't see her complaining.'

'Yeah, and you don't see her consenting, either. Or was date rape the plan for the evening?'

He backed away at that, shooting a remark at his friends which she couldn't hear but was sure wasn't flattering.

Tabitha ignored them, hooked Fiona's arm over her shoulder and helped her to stagger to her feet.

Fiona muttered something that sounded like, 'What are you doing?'

'Taking you away from these assholes,' Tabitha said,

as she led her out of the kitchen and up the central stairs, a grand sweep big enough to accommodate five people abreast. 'You know, drinking punch like it's lemonade isn't the world's best idea,' she added, but Fiona was too far gone to pay attention, stumbling hard against Tabitha as she lost her balance on the top stair.

Tabitha sighed and concentrated on getting the other woman into one of the many bedrooms, one which wasn't occupied either by couples petting or stoners sharing a joint. She laid Fiona as gently as she could on the bed, head carefully to one side in case some of the alcohol she'd consumed decided to come back up again. As Tabitha was pulling the sheets up over her, Fiona's eyes sprang open, a momentary clarity in them. 'Am I drunk?' she asked.

Tabitha nodded. 'Yeah, but you can sleep it off up here.'

Fiona's eyes had already closed, though, so Tabitha left her in peace, closing the door of the room behind her and hoping that no one else found her and tried to take further advantage.

On the way back out she took some time to study the house she was walking through. It must have cost enough to bankrupt a small nation, she thought. There were at least seven bedrooms that she'd seen and there was a third floor somewhere above. It wasn't what Tabitha would have expected. If she'd put any thought into where Professor Sinclair might live, she guessed she would have suggested somewhere very modern with a minimalist clinical design. This was just the opposite, filled with incongruous clutter. The furniture was solid and old, probably antique, but a small number of the paintings on the walls were modern, some abstracts, one a startling primitive picture of man, etched into paint so thick Tabitha itched to reach out and feel its texture.

One wall was covered in nothing but masks, about twenty of them staring out at her with blank expressionless eyes. She couldn't imagine walking past them every day, or sitting downstairs knowing that they were here, blind faces that still felt as if they could somehow see her. Another wall was covered in a large tapestry, a scene of knights and dragons which had to be several hundred years old.

She saw a far smaller stairway leading up from the end of the longest corridor and peered up it, wondering whether to explore further or return to the party below.

'Nothing but the master bedroom up there,' Jake's voice said from very close behind her. 'Want to take a look?'

She smiled and turned to look at him. 'Do I sense a theme?'

His answering grin was rakish. 'Well, you definitely sense an ulterior motive.'

He gestured upwards with his arm, urging her on and after a second she went, even though she'd intended to actually talk to him tonight, hoping to meet him on something more than a purely physical level.

The third floor was smaller, more intimate. There were only two doors off a central landing and Jake led her to the furthest, opening it to reveal a bedroom bigger than some apartments. One side of the room was given over to the sleeping arrangements, a king-size bed covered in what looked like Egyptian cotton sheets, a vast wooden wardrobe intricately carved with plants and flowers and a full-length mirror in an elegant art deco silver frame. The other half looked like it had been moved wholesale from a library: two big overstuffed armchairs and four ceiling-high bookshelves. As Jake switched on the few lamps dotting the room, Tabitha walked over to inspect the bookshelves more closely. She saw that many of the books were very old and probably very valuable. Although she'd never been a big reader, she felt an urge to pick them up, something about their antiquity drawing her like an unsolved mystery.

'Welcome to Professor Sinclair's love nest,' Jake said, with heavy mockery in his voice.

Tabitha thought again how mismatched they were: the cold haughty man and this lived-in cluttered home. 'He must be worth a fortune,' she said, the part of her that came from her lawyer father instinctively trying to work out the value of the place and its contents, the income which would be required to support it. She didn't know exactly how much, but it must be way more than a university professor earned, especially at a backwoods place like Adirondacks U.

Jake shrugged, uninterested. 'Family inheritance.' Then he grinned.

With the lamps alight, the room was a patchwork of light and shadow. Jake stood half in one, half in the other, only one eye gleaming wickedly at her. It was more than enough for her to read his intent.

She sauntered over to him, slowly undoing her leather shirt. 'Think we could get thrown off the course for using the professor's bed without permission?'

He pretended to consider it, brow creased in a theatrical frown. 'It's a risk, isn't it? Maybe we should reconsider our options.'

She prepared to pull her shirt apart but his hands stilled hers and he shook his head. When she looked questioningly at him, he took her gently by the shoulders and turned her round so that her back was flush against his chest, both of them facing the long art deco mirror. She tried to turn back towards him and ask what he wanted. He held her head gently but firmly in place, forcing her to look only at their reflections. As she watched, he reached up and pulled her shirt apart then eased it gently from her shoulders. She hadn't worn a bra under the top and now she saw her breasts standing proud, nipples already erect, cherry pink against her light tan. His hand drifted up lazily to circle then pinch the nipple.

She let her head fall back against his shoulder, but kept her eyes forward now, understanding his game. This time, though, she didn't want to let him set all the rules. When his hand moved to her other breast, she placed hers over it, holding him in place.

'Hi,' she said. 'I'm Tabitha. I'm a senior here at Adirondacks U, all the way over from LA.'

She saw his reflection smile, amused, but accepting her new rules.

He moved his hands from her to himself, pulling his T-shirt up and over his head then tossing it into a darkened corner of the room. 'I'm Jake,' he told her. 'I'm a senior too, born in Boston. I studied at Columbia before I transferred here.'

She was only giving half her attention to his words, fascinated by the glimpses she got of his bare chest hidden behind hers, the first time she'd seen him undressed. His shoulders were strong, layered with muscles, and she could see the ridges of his abs where the breadth of his chest exposed him behind her. His body didn't look pumped, just perfectly toned, like a well-tuned engine.

'I don't want to be here,' she told him, hands moving to the little silver buttons running down the side of her skirt, undoing them one by one. 'I've been at school in LA and picked up some credits, but a month ago my father decided that wasn't good enough. He cut off my allowance, got me a place here and told me if I didn't graduate by my next birthday I'd be out on the streets.'

He was watching the movements of her fingers intently, mouth parted slightly as if breathing was becoming more difficult for him, but she could tell that he was listening, saw it in the subtle shifts of his facial expression.

As soon as she'd kicked her skirt away, leaving herself wearing nothing but bikini-cut panties hardly more substantial than a thong, he began to work on the fly of his own pants. 'I'm not here by choice either,' he told her. 'My – my family live round here, and all my money's in trust until I'm twenty-five. I was flunking out at Columbia so they made me come here.'

His legs were free too now, the firm length of them

dusted with light-brown hairs. She could feel his erection pressing hard into her buttocks, pushing against her through two flimsy layers of material.

She looked back up, studied his face as her hands eased her panties from her thighs. She let them slide down her legs before kicking them away. 'My mother walked out when I was ten,' she said, and she saw the way his mouth kinked slightly, as if he wanted to say something and then thought better of it. Just one upright frown line appeared between his eyes.

He had to lift each leg in turn to free them from his black briefs, gently running his toes along her calves on the journey back down. 'I've been with a lot of women,' he said, not a hint of the normal mocking humour in his voice, 'but I've never been with anyone as beautiful as you. The second you walked into that class, I knew I had to have you. I knew it would be different with you – and it was.'

He ran his hands gently up and down her sides, just his fingers, a tickling caress that made her shiver, and in the mirror she saw the motion travel the length of her body, like a wave passing through water.

'I've been with a few men,' she told him. 'But I've never had as much fun as I'm having with you.'

His mouth dropped to her shoulder, dotting a series of biting kisses up her throat, across to her ear. She watched her reflection's skin redden and blush. When she reached back behind her to touch the hard rod of flesh pressing into her buttocks, she saw his reflection buck into her hand, his mouth opening into a perfect black circle.

He used his feet to edge hers apart and eased her forwards until she was supporting her weight against the mirror with her hands, staring into the dilated pupils of her own eyes. She saw them widen as he pressed himself against then into her. The penetration was deep at that angle and he went hard, pistoning himself into her so that she had to press back against him to fight being crushed to the mirror.

After a few minutes he reached round, pressed his fingers between her legs with rough urgency. She moaned, then again, as he plunged back into her, the sensation and her cries growing in strength as he kept up the relentless rhythm so that she felt entirely surrounded by him.

When she came the sensation was like a beautiful weakness. She felt her legs buckling but he wouldn't let her fall and her ears were ringing as he pounded into her with no control or finesse. Her eyes were shut but she knew if they'd been open she would have seen a wild expression on his face, and then his legs gave way too and they collapsed together on to the soft Persian rug.

Except that her ears *weren't* ringing. The sound she could hear was police sirens, and they were right outside the house.

Chapter Six

The Law Won

Tabitha dived straight for her clothes. She'd been at parties broken up by the police before, and she knew the drill: get out before they got in. And those parties had been in houses owned by at least one of the people present. She didn't like to think what would happen to anyone caught breaking and entering Professor Sinclair's house.

She'd just managed to locate her panties – which had, somehow, become lodged underneath the enormous wardrobe – when she remembered Fiona. The other girl was probably still asleep in the bedroom downstairs, too far gone to hear the commotion outside or understand what it meant.

Tabitha hesitated for just a moment, but she couldn't leave the other girl to face the music. It just didn't seem like the kind of thing Fiona would cope with well. She gave up trying to inch her finger underneath the wardrobe and hook her panties out and got to her feet, still completely naked. She found Jake equally naked, arms crossed, staring at her with a broad grin on his face as if he personally had not a care in the world about getting caught.

'Fiona,' she told him. 'She's out cold downstairs. We've got to get her out of here.'

'Who's Fiona? And why should you care?'

Tabitha had to think about that for a moment. 'Because it's my fault she's here, I guess. And she'll never get over it if she gets caught.'

She didn't have time to argue further, the sounds of

fleeing party-goers and pursuing lawmen already drifting up to her. No time to get dressed, either, but at least she could be fairly certain there'd be no other students left upstairs to see her reveal all. She was surprised to find Jake following her out the door then downstairs and into the bedroom where she'd laid the other girl out.

As she'd suspected, Fiona was still on the bed, her eyes only just beginning to blink groggily open.

Tabitha shook her roughly, then began trying to roll her off the bed and on to her feet. After a moment, Jake joined in. It occurred to Tabitha that her roommate wasn't going to react well to finding two naked people manhandling her, but Fiona just looked her in the face and slurred, 'What are you doing?'

'Cops are here,' Tabitha told her. 'Get out before they catch you.'

That seemed to wake the other woman up a little, and she managed to support herself on her own two feet. Tabitha cautiously let go of her and Fiona stayed upright, swaying only a little.

'Where's the exit?' Fiona asked.

Jake pointed down the opposite end of the corridor from the main stairs. 'There's another door out of the kitchen. You can get out of the yard at the back.'

Fiona seemed finally to have noticed that both the people talking to her were entirely naked and that one of them was a man. Her eyes widened. 'What the hell's going on?' she asked Tabitha indignantly, her voice an alcohol-roughened rasp.

'There's no time,' Tabitha told her. 'If you don't get out now, you're going to get caught.'

Fiona looked – typically – like she was going to argue some more. But then she too must have registered the sounds of the police sirens, still screeching outside, because an alarmed expression came over her face and without another word she stumbled away down the corridor.

Tabitha would have dearly liked to follow her, but she

knew she had to get her clothes first – it wouldn't be too difficult to trace their owner if they were found in Professor Sinclair's bedroom, and she didn't think he'd fail to notice her leather shirt draped over his antique lamp, or the panties wedged under his wardrobe. So instead she turned back round and ran for the stairs leading to the third floor. She could hear Jake following behind her, much slower, as if he really wasn't worried that the sheriff and what sounded like every deputy in town were rapidly closing in on them.

She was just two feet away from the door when she felt a hand on her shoulder that she knew instinctively wasn't Jake's.

Tabitha wrapped one arm around her breasts, another held low to cover as much of her modesty as was possible, but she felt a rosy blush start in her cheeks and spread out across her neck and chest. The deputy – a stocky man in his thirties with an ill-judged moustache – took his time looking her up and down before drawling, 'Well, you sure as hell ain't Professor Sinclair.'

An older man she guessed must be the sheriff followed them up the stairs. He spared Tabitha only one contemptuous glance before pulling off his long windbreaker and throwing it to her. 'Cover yourself up,' he barked.

Downstairs, she could see Jake wrapped in a sheet from one of the bedrooms, feet poking out of the bottom. With his sandy hair tousled from their love-making he looked like a little boy dressing up as a ghost for Halloween. His eyes caught hers and she suddenly found herself struggling not to laugh, even though another part of her knew that she'd just got herself into a whole heap of trouble.

The sheriff turned to Jake, folding his meaty arms across his chest. 'Care to explain what's going on?'

Jake shrugged, the movement rippling the sheet. 'You look a bit old for that talk about the birds and the bees.'

Tabitha winced and tried to say something more conciliatory but it was already too late. The sheriff ignored her, stalking down the stairs until he was right in Jake's face, his nose less than an inch from the other man's. Jake didn't turn away and even Tabitha could see the look of barely disguised amusement on his face.

It infuriated the sheriff. 'You think this is funny, boy?' he roared.

Jake didn't even flinch. 'I think it's mildly amusing, yeah.'

After that, there was no way they weren't getting taken down to the station.

Jake and Tabitha were driven in different cars, so Tabitha didn't get a chance to ask him just what the hell he thought he was doing. Her earlier slightly hysterical amusement had given way to worry and a slowly simmering anger. Jake might not care about getting into trouble, but if Tabitha got kicked off this course she'd lose everything. Not to mention the possibility of actual prison time. They were, after all, guilty of breaking and entering.

She became conscious of eyes studying her, and pulled the windbreaker hastily closed, shielding her breasts from the avid gaze of the deputy sitting in the back of the car beside her. His eyes just slid lower, to the long legs which the garment barely began to cover. Tabitha clenched her fists and looked out of the window, willing herself to ignore him. They could have given her something more substantial to wear, or allowed her to retrieve her own clothes, but had deliberately chosen not to. No doubt something else she had to thank Jake for.

The countryside slid by outside the window, the endless gloomy pillars of trees and beyond them a blot of darkness against the stars, the outline of mountains. Tabitha felt a sudden hot stab of homesickness for LA and its ceaseless noise, a city blind to the mass of stars she could see above them now, its own light too fierce to accommodate any competition.

The car drew into the station house. Tabitha found her fingerprints being taken and a mugshot being snapped, but it was all a bit of a daze, perhaps shock or just the alcohol she'd consumed during the night finally catching up with her. They asked her if there was anyone she wanted to call, perhaps someone who could bail her out, but the only person she could think of was her father. She told them there was no one.

Jake must have done the same, because he was waiting in the station's one small holding cell when they brought her there, the sheet still wrapped around him.

'Professor Sinclair's been called,' the sheriff said as he locked the metal bars behind her. 'He's on his way back to check out the damage to his house.' Then he left them alone, although Tabitha could see the winking eye of a CCTV camera looking down at them from the far-left corner of the room.

She hunched on a bench as far away from Jake as she could get, drawing her knees up into her chest and pulling the windbreaker down over them until she was wrapped in a tight angry ball.

'You're pissed at me,' Jake said.

She glanced up quickly to see that he had settled himself on a bench opposite her, leaning back with his arms folded behind his head as if he didn't have a care in the world.

She looked away again without replying.

'You know, we would have gotten away if *you* hadn't insisted on going back for that roomie of yours,' he said after a moment

'And we might have gotten away with a warning if *you* hadn't pissed the sheriff off!' she snapped back, instantly annoyed with herself for allowing him to provoke her into responding.

Now he'd drawn her attention he leant forward, elbows on his knees. 'You've got to admit I know how to show a girl a good time.'

She couldn't help smiling a little at that. But she wasn't willing to let go of her anger just yet. 'So just how much trouble do you think you've got us into?'

He shrugged. 'We're both legal, so they can't get us on the booze. It's no big deal – they break up student parties all the time.'

'Yeah, but not ones that are taking place in one of the professors' houses.'

'That was what made it so much fun.'

She looked at him to see if there was even a hint of remorse or worry in his face, but his wide mouth was grinning, his expression animated and happy. He meant it, she realised. And she had to admit, she'd enjoyed the risk of the little striptease game he'd set her in the college. When he'd made love to her in Professor Sinclair's bedroom, part of the reason it had been so exciting was that it *was* Professor Sinclair's. She'd enjoyed playing with fire, so she shouldn't complain if she'd been burnt.

She sighed, not letting him off the hook, but not ready to carry on the argument just now. 'I'm going to try to get some rest,' she told him. 'My head's starting to feel like a moose crapped in it.'

He laughed and she lay down along the bench, making sure the windbreaker hid her from the camera's view. She didn't think she'd actually be able to sleep, her hipbone digging into the hard wood of the bench and the events of the night hanging over her, but she must have been more exhausted than she realised because, almost as soon as she lay down, she felt herself drifting into unconsciousness.

His voice woke her some time later, still disoriented from her light sleep. The lights in the holding cell had been dimmed but not put out, and she could see him lying on the bench opposite, his body a mirror of her own.

'Do you want to know what my favourite part of you is?' he asked, looking straight at her, his body entirely motionless.

She glanced up nervously at the camera, but he just smiled. 'No sound,' he said.

She relaxed a little, though she didn't know how he could be so sure. 'Don't tell me it's my sparkling personality.'

His smile widened. 'Well ... that's certainly a contender. But I was thinking about your fingers.'

'My *fingers*?' She wasn't sure if she was flattered.

He nodded, his expression serious again. 'You've got very elegant fingers, very delicate. But they look competent, too, like you know exactly what you're doing with them. I look at them and I think about them touching me. And then I think about them touching you, and that turns me on even more.' He paused a moment, and when he continued his voice was softer, more intimate. 'In O'Grady's class, I hardly needed to touch myself to make myself come. Just watching you, it was almost like when you stroked yourself you were stroking me. Do you get what I'm saying?'

'Yeah,' Tabitha said huskily, through a suddenly dry throat. 'When I was in the water, picking up your last message, I felt like the water was ... I don't know – like it was a part of you, somehow.'

'Like I was touching you all over, inside and out?'

She could see that the idea excited him. His chest rose and fell with his speeding breaths, his gaze intent and unwavering on her.

'Exactly. And when we made love looking in the mirror, when I saw my own body, I loved that what I was seeing was what you were seeing. I didn't have to imagine how I looked to you.' There was a deep pleasurable ache in her centre, but she didn't make any move to touch herself there, not just because the camera was watching but because that wasn't the way this game was supposed to be played. She could see that he remained equally still, hands still cushioning his head.

'You looked incredible. Your eyes are the most amazing blue – so bright you almost think they must be emitting light. And your lips. I guess some guys might call them blow-job lips, but that's not what I think about when I look at them – though, don't get me wrong, they'd be perfect for that too. But I don't just want to feel them there. Your lips are so soft, and that perfect little bow in them. They need to be sucking on my fingers, and my ear, and the tip of my nose and most of all they need to be kissing my mouth, because we haven't done that yet, and I can't help feeling that's a massive oversight.'

'Your own mouth is kind of strange,' she told him, and he raised an eyebrow but she carried on. 'It's too wide, you know, almost too big for your face. It means you're not pin-up good looking, but it's a mouth that's just made for being bad. It's just about the most *expressive* mouth I've ever seen. There's all kinds of places I'd like that mouth to be.'

'I'd like it to be there too,' he whispered, his voice rough with passion. 'I'd like to taste your breasts again, because I just can't get enough of them. They're the perfect size, and the feeling of your nipples against my lips . . . I'd like to taste you all over, find out the different flavours and textures of your skin. Some men, they only concentrate on the obvious parts, but it's all the secret bits of you that interest me, the bits you don't share with just anyone – like the skin in the crook of your knee, or that little soft bit behind your ear where you're so incredibly sensitive . . .'

Tabitha was astonished to realise that she was close to coming just from his words. She squeezed her knees together, pushed herself down against the bench, enjoying that feeling of completion being almost but not quite in reach. 'I want to taste your cock,' she told him, bolder now that her orgasm was approaching. 'I love to see you lose control. You're so in command of yourself, most of the time, but when you're really excited. When *I* excite you – you can't help letting yourself go.'

He let out a small groan of excitement, as if merely

talking about losing control was making it happen. Suddenly, she wanted that more than anything.

'I want to watch it happen.' All her attention was focused on his face, the sharp cliffs of his cheekbones beneath the vivid gold of his eyes, darkened to amber by his desire. 'I want to have my mouth around you, gently at first, just a tease, and I want to look up at you and see you trying to hold on. Maybe biting your lip when I'm increasing the pressure, making sure I put my tongue against that sensitive place right where the head meets the stalk. You're biting your lip because you don't want to make a sound –'

He let out another groan, louder this time, and she saw his hips buck, helplessly, outward.

'But you can't help yourself, because it feels so good – and your fingers are caught up in my hair but you don't try to force me because I'm going just the right speed, fast and hard as you get nearer, and –'

'Would it be terribly rude of me to interrupt?' a cold voice said, and Tabitha was so startled she almost screamed, because the voice had come from inside the room. She sat up, wrapping her arms defensively around her, and saw that Professor Sinclair was standing only a few feet away, his eyes boring into her. She didn't know how long he'd been there, or how much he'd heard but, from his arctic expression, it was more than either she or Jake would have wanted.

Jake stood up, wrapping the sheet around him. 'You took your time,' he said.

Sinclair's eyes shifted from Tabitha to Jake, and she felt a palpable relief as if a physical weight had been lifted off her. Sinclair stared at him for what felt like an age, expressionless, then turned away in disgust. 'I've told them they can let you go.'

'You *have*?' Tabitha exclaimed. 'I mean, thanks. We're really, you know – sorry about the –'

He turned back to look at her again and the words

froze in her mouth. 'I didn't have much choice. I can hardly accuse my brother of breaking and entering.'

'Your *brother*?' Tabitha said, thrown. And then she saw the way Jake was looking at Sinclair. She saw the identical cowslicks each had in his hair, though Sinclair's was far fairer than Jake's. The wide mouths, Jake's generous and laughing, Sinclair's hard and unforgiving. She saw their eyes, both pairs looking at her now, one golden, the other blue, but both burning with the same bright light. 'Your brother,' she repeated.

The drive back to campus took place in one of the most uncomfortable silences Tabitha had ever experienced. Jake had taken the front seat next to his brother, but neither seemed to have anything to say to the other. She stared resolutely out of the window, the same trees passing by as on her way to the station, like a video being played in reverse, except that now the first glimmer of dawn was lightening the horizon, sketching the outline of the forest in pale blue.

Every so often she would flick her eyes to the front mirror. Whenever she did, she seemed to find Sinclair's eyes studying her like a biologist looking at a bug on a slide.

The car pulled up in front of Sinclair's house. Jake's house too, she supposed, though obviously he spent most of his time in his place on campus. 'You can stay here for what's left of the night,' Sinclair told Jake when he made no move to get out of the car. 'That way, you can start cleaning up the mess you've made as soon as you get up. I'll drive your . . . friend back to her room.'

Jake hesitated, looking back questioningly at Tabitha, but she didn't have anything to say to him and after a second he got out without a word.

Sinclair watched him walk into the house in silence. Then he turned round to Tabitha. 'Get in the front. I'm not driving you around like a damn chauffeur.'

Tabitha obliged. He remained parked, looking at her,

and after a moment she realised that he was waiting for her to do up her seatbelt. She saw that her hand was shaking when she did it. There was something about this man that put her on edge. He and his brother both, she realised, disturbed her equilibrium, but at least with Jake it was in a pleasant way.

It was only a five-minute drive back to campus, but it felt like an eternity. The security guard at the gate waved them through, gazing into Tabitha's window curiously as she went past, clearly wondering what exactly Professor Sinclair was doing driving one of his students around at this time of the morning.

When at long last the car stopped outside her dorm building, she fumbled with the handle, wanting to get out as quickly as possible. She realised after a second that the door was locked and turned to look questioningly at Sinclair.

'I want you to stay away from my brother,' he said.

Tabitha knew she should just agree and get out of the car, get this interminable night over with, but his insufferable arrogance, the automatic assumption that she would obey his orders without question, infuriated her. 'Believe it or not, *he* seduced *me*.'

'Really?' His cold blue eyes seemed to be looking right through her. 'It didn't look like you were putting up much of a fight.'

She blushed at that, wondering again just how much of their conversation in the holding cell he had overheard. 'So what?' she said defiantly. 'Last time I checked we were both consenting adults. You might take an unhealthy interest in your brother's sex life but I don't see that it's any of your business.'

He drew in a breath, a flush of anger in his cheeks, but when he spoke his voice was tightly controlled. 'That's true. It's also true that you're my student, and your ability to graduate this school depends on the grades *I* give you.'

'Are you blackmailing me?' Tabitha asked indignantly.

But on the inside she was wilting. She wondered if Sinclair knew just how very much her future depended on his good will.

He reached over to click open the lock on her door. 'My brother's been going through a bad time recently, he's been going off the rails. I brought him here to help him pull himself together, and I'm damned if I'm going to let some airhead LA heiress with nothing better to do with her time drag him down to her level. So, no, Tabitha, I'm not blackmailing you, I'm telling you that the first time you put a foot wrong I'm going to make sure this school kicks you out so hard you won't *need* to book a flight back to California.'

As soon as she was out of the car he drove off, the wheels throwing up a curve of gravel. Tabitha watched the car receding into the distance, knowing that she'd made a very dangerous enemy. And wondering if she really should stay away from Jake – and more importantly, if she *could*.

Chapter Seven

Demon Days

Tabitha managed to sleep for two or three hours, but woke up shortly after nine with a pounding head and eyes which felt like they'd been rubbed with coarse grit. When she dragged herself out of bed, she saw that Fiona was still lying in hers, staring blankly at the ceiling. The other woman had dark shadows under her eyes and a pallor that could best be described as deathly.

'You know,' Tabitha said, sitting on the edge of her bed, head resting gingerly in her hands, 'an isotonic sports drink and two Advil would probably help.'

Fiona groaned. 'I think only decapitation could help at the moment. Why the *hell* did I let you talk me into going to that party?' Tabitha didn't have much she wanted to say to that, but after a moment Fiona rolled over to face her. 'Thanks,' she said gruffly. 'For getting me out of there, I mean. And for – well, I don't really remember much about the earlier part of the evening, but I think you got me out of trouble there too.'

'That's OK.' Tabitha shrugged. 'You would have done the same for me. And those guys were jerks.'

Fiona started to nod, then seemed to think better of it as her complexion went from white to green. She swallowed convulsively for a few moments before speaking. 'So did you and Jake get away OK?'

'No, we spent the night in a cell in the sheriff's office before Jake's brother Professor Sinclair came and got us out.'

Fiona stared at her, dumbfounded. 'You got arrested?'

Tabitha nodded.

'Hang on – Jake is Sinclair's *brother*?'

'Yeah,' Tabitha said, 'that was exactly my reaction.'

They proceeded to wash and dress – gingerly, in Fiona's case – in a silence that was for once companionable. Tabitha hesitated to break this new truce, but she wanted to clear the air entirely between them. She felt for the first time that she and Fiona might become real friends, but only if all their outstanding issues were resolved.

'Fiona,' she said cautiously. 'I'm sorry for what I said earlier. Yesterday, I mean.'

Fiona paused, toothbrush halfway to her mouth. 'What, that I've got no sense of style and I'm in serious need of a make-over?'

'I didn't say that!' Tabitha protested.

To her surprise, Fiona smiled. 'No – but you were thinking it.'

Tabitha opened her mouth to protest and then realised that it would be pointless. 'I just think – you know, if you're on the market, you need to advertise the goods.'

'And what makes you think I'm on the market?' Fiona held out her left hand, and Tabitha realised that she was sporting a tasteful solitaire diamond ring.

'You're engaged?' Tabitha asked.

Fiona laughed. 'It would be more tactful to sound less surprised.'

After a moment, Tabitha laughed too. Then, after a nod of permission from Fiona, she perched herself on the end of the other girl's bed.

'So?'

Fiona frowned. 'So what?'

'So I want to hear all about him.'

Tabitha didn't catch up with Jake until they were both heading to their psychology class. The class which would be taken by his brother. The good mood she'd developed while gossiping with Fiona faded slightly, but then she saw the smile he sent her way, the expression in his eyes that said it was just for her, and she couldn't hold on to her anger.

She fell into step beside him across the shorn grass of the courtyard. 'When exactly were you thinking of mentioning that Professor Sinclair is your brother?'

'Mark,' he said.

She raised an eyebrow.

'He's called Mark,' he clarified. 'I don't know, in between watching you touch yourself in class, and then you running around the college naked, and then us making love, and then us making love again in Mark's bedroom, there just didn't seem a good moment. Oh hi, Mark,' he said before Tabitha had begun to frame a reply, and she snapped her head around to see that Professor Sinclair was right behind them and had probably heard every word that Jake had been saying – which had no doubt been Jake's intention.

Mark's face remained impassive but his eyes burnt into her, as if holding her personally responsible for his brother's behaviour.

Jake, it was clear, was unrepentant and incorrigible. But then, wasn't that what had attracted her to him in the first place?

It was a lecture on Attentional Biases, usually a subject Mark enjoyed teaching, but he found himself unable to concentrate. Jake and Tabitha were sitting together, directly in front of him. It had been his brother's decision – the girl had seemed less than willing, hanging back when Jake walked forward, but after a second she had followed him. It was quite clear that she was entirely under his spell.

Not that she seemed in any way an unwilling participant. Whenever he looked at her, Mark found the words he'd overheard in the holding cells replaying in his head. He hadn't needed his brother to tell him that they'd made love in his bedroom. He'd found the debris from their union strewn around the room – her leather shirt hanging from a Tiffany lamp, his briefs beside the mirror. Mark hadn't slept easy last night, unable to rid himself of mental images of their coupling.

He wasn't sure why the two of them together bothered him so much. He'd seen his little brother with plenty of women and had long ago accepted that the charming eight-year-old he'd once known was long gone. His brother was a man, or well on his way to being one, and he was entitled to choose his partners for himself.

Except that, damn it, he wasn't! This girl was trouble, Mark could see it even if Jake couldn't, and the two of them together were a recipe for disaster. As Mark carried on with his lecture, his gaze flicked to them and he saw their heads angled towards each other, as if an invisible force drew them. She was dangerous.

Looking at her, he had a sudden flash of how she'd appeared at the station, the sheriff's windbreaker barely stretching beneath her buttocks, one half fallen open to expose the contour of her breast. Most clearly of all he could see her cupid's bow mouth, the slight smile it had worn when she'd described the blow-job she wanted to give Jake. No doubt later today she'd be delivering on the promise. The idea made Mark feel physically ill.

Things are going good, Daddy. So, I got a C minus in my mid-term for Professor Sinclair, but that's still a pass, right? And I'm going to all my classes like I promised, and handing in my assignments.

So now you've made your point by sending me here, and I'm keeping up my side of the bargain – for nearly two whole months now – how about letting me have my credit cards back? Or maybe just one of them. You can keep the limit low, if you like, maybe only $20,000 or so, just enough to let me buy some new clothes and upgrade from this rustbucket of a car you got for me.

I know you think none of that stuff matters, and I get that you were angry with me because you thought I'd gotten my priorities wrong, but the thing is – I've met this guy. It's almost like I can see your face as I write that because I know exactly what you'll be thinking. But he's not like the others. He's called Jake, he's a student here, and his brother's one of the professors.

We hooked up together the first week here, and he's been a really good influence on me. I mean, I felt like I'd been sentenced to prison when you sent me here, but thanks to him I can see an upside. And I think you'd like him. He kind of reminds me of you – only miles better looking, obviously.

Love you, Daddy,

Tabitha

Tabitha finished the last flourish of her signature as Jake leant his head round the door. Fiona, typing an assignment at the cranky old computer on her desk, waved him in, her eyebrows raised as she saw what he was carrying in his arms.

'Ready?' he asked Tabitha.

'Give me a minute.' She sealed the letter in an envelope, scrawled a quick address then handed it over to Fiona. 'You can borrow my iPod for tonight if you mail that for me.'

'Why can't you mail it yourself?' Fiona asked irritably, but she took the letter anyway.

Tabitha lifted the gauzy white dress from Jake's arms, leaving him holding the demonic mask and sacrificial knife. 'Because it's Halloween, and we've got other plans.'

Jake drove a pick-up, an ugly battered-up monster of a vehicle that looked as if it had been dredged from the bottom of a lake. Tabitha hated riding in the thing, but Jake loved it, loved the way it stood out among the sensible Fords and gas-guzzling SUVs of the other students.

'Is this really going to work?' she asked him as he put the pick-up in drive and took the road out of the college.

He turned and grinned at her, the dying sunlight

bringing out the planes and shadows of his face, rendering it as demonic as the mask which sat at his feet. 'Trust me – it's perfect.'

'And they'll definitely be there?'

He nodded. 'Every year, it's their little ritual – a test to frighten the pledges. Only this time, it won't just be the pledges getting scared.'

They'd been over this already, and when Tabitha had found out that the students involved were the same ones who'd been taking body shots off the unconscious Fiona at that disastrous party she'd been glad of the chance to pay them back. Not to mention that frat boys just irritated her on principle. Still ... She looked down at the long curved knife sitting beside the mask. 'And what if they decide they want to join in?'

'I don't like to share,' Jake told her.

In the weeks since she'd first met him their relationship had settled into, if not quite a routine, at least something that bore a close resemblance to it. Sure, they still had fun, but the wild excitement of the early days had inevitably dissipated, and though they spent a good amount of time together, at least a couple of days a week, she still didn't feel that she knew Jake very much better than when she'd first met him. He intrigued her still but in many ways he remained a stranger.

So, when he'd suggested this little practical joke, she'd leapt at the chance, hoping that a return to their earlier game-playing might also push their relationship forwards. She'd been seeing no one else since she'd arrived at Adirondacks U, yet she still didn't refer to Jake as her boyfriend and she'd never asked how he described her. She liked the fact that he didn't try to tie her down, and that he never made any promises he wouldn't keep. She didn't need any promises. But she did want a sense that she meant something to him, at least in this time they were together.

She studied him now as he concentrated on navigating the winding road into the mountains, college rock playing on the radio. She might not have come to know the real him, but she'd learnt some of his tells, and she knew that he was excited. He'd told her that nothing could go wrong, but she knew that part of the draw for him was that it *might* – that the frat boys they were planning to haze might not be such easy marks, and that they might end up being the ones having a not so pleasant night in the woods. She guessed that was part of the draw for her too, or why would she be going along with him?

She'd elected not to change into her virginal white outfit until they were nearer their destination, but he was already wearing the black robe he'd chosen. It had fallen open as he drove and, slightly absurdly, the black boxers he wore underneath were showing through.

It was only a fifteen-minute drive, but that was plenty of time to have a bit of preliminary fun. She reached a hand across and slipped it inside the robe, enjoying the feel of his bare muscular chest beneath. He smiled slightly, keeping his eyes on the road, but when she tweaked his nipple she saw the material of his boxers twitch.

She raked her fingers down his chest, allowing the nails to scrape through the light hairs there, then rested her hand on its real target, already hardening beneath the silk.

Jake brushed her hand away. 'Later.' His eyes were still on the road, face perfectly controlled.

That's just like him, she thought irritably – loves to go over the line, but only he gets to decide how far. Well, not tonight. Snapping her seat free, she leant over until her mouth was resting over the rigid flesh at his groin, her breath a hot caress over it.

To her amazement, he grabbed her shoulder and yanked her back hard, slamming on the brakes at the same time. The pick-up screeched to a halt. 'Don't be so fucking stupid! Do you want to get us both killed?' His face was flushed, his mouth hard and tight, more furious than she'd ever seen him.

She leant away from him, holding her hands up as if to physically ward off his anger, though he made no move towards her. 'I just thought you might like it,' she said placatingly.

'Well, I wouldn't,' he said curtly. 'And keep your damn seatbelt fastened.'

The rest of the journey passed in silence, his brooding and hers hurt. She had half a mind to tell him to take her back to college and forget the whole thing, but in a bizarre way she was pleased that she'd seen him react that way – displaying, for once, some spontaneous uncensored emotion.

When they reached their destination, a remote hiking trail far up in the Northern Mountains, he put the pick-up into park, switched off the lights, then sat staring into the darkness of the woods around them. After a few seconds he let out a rough sigh and turned to face her. 'I'm sorry,' he said quietly. 'I overreacted.'

She shrugged. 'I guess it was a pretty stupid thing to do.'

'Yeah,' he said – and then he grinned, suddenly back to the Jake she'd known all these weeks. 'But not as stupid as what we're about to do.'

They set themselves up in a small clearing in the trees, about fifty feet from where the pledges and their frat-boy minders had pitched their tents. The sacrificial slab that Jake had gotten the drama club to make up for him out of Styrofoam looked surprisingly realistic, and they'd put the four metal bolts into the corners, just as he'd asked. They'd even added blood spatters, also alarmingly realistic.

In the distance, she could hear the sound of their marks settling down for the night. She couldn't put off changing her clothes any longer, although there was an icy nip in the air which made her reluctant to wear nothing but the flimsy silk shift the set-up required.

Before she could think better of it, she pulled her sweater up and off, taking her T-shirt with it. She didn't bother folding them, just laid them behind a convenient tree, following them with her jeans. Her bra was black, she realised, so she took that off too – if it showed up under the shift it would spoil the illusion.

She looked up to find Jake watching her, a familiar heat in his eyes. It pleased her that she still excited him, that he'd take time out just to watch her get naked – though she knew the joke they had planned had something to do with it. Jake was never more turned on than when he was getting into trouble. Her nipples were already erect in the cold night air and they hardened still further as he watched. His mobile mouth gave a predatory smile. Then, very slowly, she slipped the white shift over her head. From his expression, she knew that it did little to maintain her modesty.

She lay down on the fake slab, then sat back up, supporting herself on her elbows. 'OK, before I do this, I want you to promise it's not me who's the butt of the joke. You're not going to just tie me here and run off, are you?'

Jake rested his chin on his fist, as if seriously considering the question. 'Well, let's see – I've got a beautiful nearly naked woman tied up and helpless, and I'm just going to walk away. Does that sound like me?'

She laughed and lay back without another word, stretching out her arms and legs so he could tie them to the corners of the slab. The ties were silk, comfortable on her arms, but he pulled them tight and she found that she had very little movement. Only her head was free, and she tipped it to one side to watch him preparing himself.

The demonic mask, which had look faintly absurd in the shop, looked far more real in the pale moonlight. The horns were sharp and red and the eyes were dark and unreadable, no hint of gold in their depths. When he pulled out the long curved knife and a calf's heart they'd obtained from a local butcher, Tabitha shuddered, but her body felt energised, excited by this hint of danger.

She knew he wouldn't hurt her, he just didn't have it in him. But she'd never let him bind her in this way before. She'd never been entirely powerless when she was with him. He could do absolutely anything he wanted, and she wouldn't be able to stop him. She watched as he lit the tall black candles they'd had to order over the internet from some terrible goth website. There were five of them, one at each corner of a pentagram he drew in the leaf-mulch with his heel. The soft golden light flickered over the mask he wore, seeming to draw human expressions out of it. It was as if Jake's personality was so strong it was reaching through the plastic, animating it. When he looked at her she thought she could see a fierce desire written in the red snarling face.

Then he started the CD player they'd brought with them along with the big battery-powered speakers, and an unearthly wailing echoed through the forest. There was an agitated rustling of leaves, the sound of small frightened animals fleeing.

Then, faintly, she heard the sound of human voices – male but high pitched. Scared out of their wits. She traded a look with Jake and this time she could read his barely suppressed amusement in the light way he held his body. She grinned back, but quickly schooled the expression into a frown.

When she heard the first cautious footsteps approaching through the trees, she let loose with a piercing scream. It had occurred to her, and she had suggested to Jake, that if the pledges thought they were interrupting a human sacrifice they might leap to the rescue and Jake might get hurt in the process.

She needn't have worried. The pledges stumbled through the trees, night-blinded and wearing only their jockstraps. That, Jake had ascertained, was one of the requirements of this particular hazing ritual. She got one very brief look at their faces as Jake turned towards them, knife held high in one hand and calf's heart in the other. She didn't think she'd ever seen human beings look so terrified.

Then, as one, they turned and ran.

Jake held the heart a moment longer. When it was clear that they weren't returning, he shrugged and threw it into the bushes, letting the knife drop to his side. The candlelight still flickered around him.

Tabitha looked away, up at the thin sliver of starlit sky above her. The joke had been played, but it felt like a beginning, not an ending. She heard Jake step closer, his feet crunching in the fallen leaves. She pulled against the ties that were binding her, but they remained as firm as ever. She was entirely helpless.

One more stride, and the stars were blotted out by the dark outline of Jake's face. He was still wearing the mask, the horns two jagged peaks of darkness above her. He looked taller from that angle, as tall as the sky. Unconsciously, her hands reached up to touch him, but they were impotent to move.

He eased himself down, his knees either side of her, his weight resting back against her thighs, so that she was pinned by his body, held down as well as tied down. The material of his black robe was rough against the bare skin of her legs, and she could see his erection already, pressing urgently through the robe. With deliberate slowness, he eased the thin material of her shift up and over her belly. She watched him in silence. Even the creatures of the night seemed to have retreated to their beds. It felt, suddenly, as if the world was holding its breath.

Then he brought the knife up and cut through her panties, one quick cut at each side before tossing the knife aside. She lifted her buttocks to allow him to remove the material. He threw it into the undergrowth as carelessly as he'd thrown the calf's heart, then pressed down against her thighs, pushing her back down, his fingers going to the centre of her, opening her to his eyes. She felt more vulnerable then she'd ever felt in her life. She strained against the bonds, not sure what she wanted to do, scared of the arousal she was feeling.

She thought that he'd take the mask off then, but he didn't, just lowered his head to her. She saw his tongue flick out, shockingly pink against the scarlet of the mask. Then it touched her, and she took one last look at him bent over her, the black robe and the plastic mask, and then she closed her eyes to concentrate on the sensations. He circled her slowly at first, just flicking occasionally against her clitoris, then more rapidly, building up the tension inside her. His eased one, then two, then three fingers inside her, pumping them in time with the movements of his tongue. Finally, he bit down lightly and her back arched helplessly, pushing him away from her as an orgasm of shocking intensity rippled through her.

When she opened her eyes a few seconds later, it was to find him crouched over her, his cock millimetres from her lips. She flicked her tongue out against the tip, tasting the salty pre-come which was already gathering there. He made an animal sound and lowered himself further, thrusting into her mouth. Hands tied, body prone, she was unable to control the act in any way. She'd always hated, before, when men tried to take control during oral sex, making her feel like a vessel, something that was being used. But this was different. She *liked* the fact that he was using her, and he never thrust too hard or too deep, but it didn't feel like he was being careful, just that there was a natural rhythm between them, in this dark strange night, and that it was guiding them both, him rising above her, thrusting into her mouth, her moving her tongue, pressing it against all the most sensitive parts of him.

She sensed when he was close from the jagged rhythm of his thrusts, but he pulled out before he could finish, then swiftly slid back down her body and buried himself inside her, continuing the tempo. His hands were to either side of her head, supporting his weight, his masked face just a few inches from her, staring at her. This close, she could see his eyes, the golden light of them.

Another climax hit her, unexpected and strong, and she shut her eyes and felt him collapse on top of her, holding her as close to him as her bonds would allow as he emptied himself inside her.

He untied her after a few moments, gently pulling the knots loose, before removing his mask. His face beneath was slick with sweat and raw with an emotion she didn't fully understand. Her wrists were sore and she realised that she'd been pulling against the bonds, chafing them. He gently took each one in his hand and kissed it, then put his arms around her and nestled into her chest.

They lay in silence as their breathing evened out and the forest came slowly back to life around them. Then he reached out a hand and gently brushed a lock of her hair out of her eyes. 'My parents died when I was eight,' he said softly, looking past her into the trees.

Tabitha stared at him, shocked, and his eyes met hers, more naked than she'd ever seen them.

'They were killed in a car crash. Mark's looked after me ever since.' He shrugged. 'So that's me, the big secret.'

She felt a lance of empathetic pain, but she didn't say anything. She knew there was nothing she could say. She just hugged him tight, holding his face to her body and pressing her mouth against his hair.

After a few minutes he drew back and dropped a soft kiss on to her cheek. 'I'm glad I met you, Tabitha.'

PART TWO
Christmas

Chapter Eight

Do They Know it's Christmas?

'You've got to be kidding me!' Tabitha would have hurled her cellphone across the room, but some small part of her was worried that she wouldn't be able to afford another one. 'This is a school, not a prison camp. I'm allowed out for Christmas!'

'You're welcome to buy your own flight home, if you've got enough money saved from your allowance.' Her father's voice was calm and measured. She recognised it. It was the voice he used during a difficult contract negotiation when he knew exactly how much he was prepared to offer and wasn't going to budge an inch.

Tabitha left a fuming silence.

'Alternatively,' her father said after a moment, 'you can do what every other student does during vacation and get yourself a job.'

'But, Daddy,' she wheedled, trying a different tack. 'I was really looking forward to seeing you.'

'No, you weren't,' he said crisply. 'You were looking forward to partying with your friends. I'd have seen you for two hours over Christmas dinner if I was lucky. But if you save enough money from your job, you can always come visit for New Year.' He hung up before she could say anything further.

'Shit!' Tabitha *did* throw her mobile phone this time – though she aimed it carefully at the bed. It hadn't even occurred to her that she wouldn't be going home for the next three weeks. That, and Jake, were what had been sustaining her through the hard academic grind of the semester. She couldn't believe that her father would forgo their traditional Christmas morning, the dinner they always cooked together and ate around a fake log fire he hired specially for the occasion, just to make a point. A small guilty part of her remembered that for the last three years she'd found excuses to cut their celebrations short, but she dismissed it. *He* was the one being unreasonable, not her. She sat down on her bed and rested her head in her hands, embarrassed to realise that she was on the point of crying.

Fiona looked at her sympathetically as she packed her own bags for the vacation. 'Problems?'

Tabitha shrugged, still struggling to hold back tears. 'Just my dad being a horse's ass.'

'I've got to say, condemning an LA girl to a New York winter does seem a little harsh.' Fiona hesitated a minute, then continued cautiously, 'You know, you could always come back, spend the vacation with my family. The house isn't big but you'd be made welcome, and my mom always likes to check out my friends, make sure they're not a bad influence.'

Tabitha managed a smile at that. 'But I *am* a bad influence.'

Fiona finished stuffing the last of her sweaters into the large black suitcase and struggled to zip it shut. 'That's OK, she's always been a lousy judge of character.'

Tabitha could see that the invitation was genuine, and was touched that the other woman would ask her, but she shook her head. She knew that Fiona's fiancé was home from sea for the vacation and even the stoic Fiona had been unable to hide her excitement at being reunited with him for a couple of weeks. 'Thanks, but you haven't seen Adam all semester, the last thing you want is me hanging around while you're with him.'

Fiona made to protest, but Tabitha held up her hand. 'Honestly, I'll be fine. I'll get a job like my dad said. And maybe on my own here I'll be able to concentrate on my studies better. I might even be able to scale the heights of a C plus in my next paper.'

The other woman looked at her shrewdly. 'Jake not going to be around, then?'

'Haven't asked him,' Tabitha said as nonchalantly as possible.

But it turned out that he wouldn't. 'I'll be skiing in Hamilton. Mark's paying me to get out of his hair for the vacation,' he told her as they lay curled up together in his double bed. He turned his head sideways to look at her. 'You could always ditch California and come along too – he'd never know.'

She studied his face, but it was impossible to tell if he really wanted her company or was making the offer because he knew it would be turned down. She pulled his head towards her for a slow kiss, then got out of bed and began to pull her clothes on. 'No can do,' she said. 'Parties to attend, people to see. Besides, I'd freeze my ass off in Canada – I'm a hothouse flower.'

He shrugged, accepting it, and she thought that perhaps he was relieved she wasn't going. She didn't ask who else would be there, not wanting to know if there'd be any other women present. She and Jake had never promised to be exclusive, but she found the idea of him with anyone else increasingly difficult to accept. Best to operate a 'don't ask, don't tell' policy in the whole area.

'So, when are you flying out?' she asked him.

He looked at his watch. 'In around two hours. You?'

She shrugged, and carefully didn't look at him. 'I don't know – I might hang around for a few days first, maybe even get some studying done.'

He laughed as he swung his legs over the side of the bed and stood, the firm muscles of his stomach bunching. 'Yeah, I guess there's some strange alternative universe where that's possible.' He leant down, still naked, to bite and then suckle her lips. 'Have a good Christmas, Tabby.'

She realised that she'd been dismissed and struggled not to feel hurt, aware that he'd need to start packing if he was leaving so soon. At the door, she turned round and smiled at him. 'Don't do anything I wouldn't do.'

He smiled back. 'That doesn't rule much out.'

On the walk back to her dorm Tabitha felt like she was walking through some kind of refugee clearing centre. The entire student body was deserting Adirondacks U *en masse*. Most of the faculty seemed to be heading for the hills too, as if they all knew something Tabitha didn't.

Her room seemed very empty without Fiona in it. She hadn't imagine she'd ever find the place too big, but now she felt like she was rattling around in there. She decided that she might as well use the time productively, but when she opened her psychology textbook on her desk she found that she didn't know where to start. At least when Fiona was around she would answer Tabitha's questions, summarise the key points she needed to know and generally save her from having to do too much reading of her own. And, when she *did* have to do some reading, she always knew that Jake might arrive at any moment to distract her from it.

Now there was no one for company but herself and *Cognitive Psychology: A Student's Handbook*. She spent fifteen more fruitless minutes trying to work out exactly why you were supposed to turn over the E and the 7 in the Wason Card Selection Task and not the 4 or the K, then sat back and closed the book with a thump.

'OK, first things first,' she told herself, speaking out loud to fill the lonely silence. 'If I get a job that will give me something to do.'

She was halfway down the corridor before she realised that getting work generally involved handing out a resume, and that she didn't have one on her – or, indeed, at all. She returned to her desk and spent an hour on her laptop, one of the few things her father had let her bring, trying to put one together. After she'd printed out ten copies she sat back and admired her handiwork. She was quite proud of the design: simple, clean and all on one page, as she had vague memories of being told was best in some long-ago life-skills class.

On the other hand, the reason she'd managed to fit it all on one page was that there was very little to it. When she was fourteen her father had forced her to spend one evening a week helping out at the local homeless shelter, but shortly after that he'd lost what little control he ever had over his wayward daughter and since then she hadn't worked a day in her life. Tabitha fought down a hot flush of shame, determined not to see her father's side in this. If she hadn't worked, it was because she didn't need to, and where was the justice in a rich girl taking jobs away from people who really needed them?

Still, she could see that it didn't look good, so hurriedly added a couple more imaginary summer jobs – waiting tables at Denny's and working the till at a bookstore – then printed the document again and strode out the door.

The cold air hit her as soon as she stepped outside, as if it had just been waiting for the other students to depart before it pounced. She pulled her brown satin Marc Jacobs jacket tighter around her, but it had been designed for the mild chill of a Californian winter, not the arctic wind which was currently slicing into her skin. The sky was a steely grey and Tabitha realised that it was going to snow.

Town was strangely soulless, as if when the students left they'd taken the spirit of the place with them. Half the stores were shut, and there was a sign on Fat Sam's Pizza Palace which told her he'd gone to visit his folks for the holiday and hoped they all had a great festive season.

The mini-mart was open, shoppers scuttling through its overlit aisles like rats in a maze. She stopped a moment outside to look at the staff, drones dressed in the red and green corporate colours of the chain. She tried to picture herself in the uniform and found that she just couldn't. The green would clash horribly with her complexion.

But it wasn't as if there would be anyone around she knew to see her, she reminded herself, and pushed her way through the big glass doors before she could change her mind. Smiling her best smile, she approached a slouching teenager with a shock of bright-orange hair who was wearing a supervisor's badge.

'Hi,' she said brightly.

He looked at her with guarded washed-out blue eyes.

When, thirty seconds later he still hadn't responded, she held out her resume. He made no move to take it. 'I'm looking for work,' she told him. 'I was hoping you might be hiring for Christmas.'

'Hiring?' he said.

She nodded.

'For Christmas?'

She nodded again, wondering if he was wearing the supervisor's badge by mistake.

But then he seemed to come to life. He laughed, displaying a startling array of bright-white teeth. They looked like he spent his entire wage packet and then some on them. 'We ain't hiring – we're laying off.'

Tabitha let the arm holding her resume drop to her side. 'Why?

He jerked his head towards the window, where a single car could be seen crawling down the main road in the growing gloom. 'Nobody much around this time of year. Nobody who can afford to get out, anyway.'

'OK,' Tabitha said. 'Well, do you know any other places which might be hiring?'

'There's Radio Shack,' he told her. 'But they're not taking anyone on either.'

He was right, she discovered, even though she trekked out to the edge of town just to make sure. The assistant in Radio Shack was a lot more pleasant, but no more helpful; he thought her chances of finding work in Crystal

Lake at this time of year were zero to none. The two other stores she made herself go into after that proved that he was right.

The walk back to the school seemed to take a lot longer than the walk out, and with even the meagre heat of the sun now hidden behind the mountains it was seriously cold. She hung her head and tried to come up with alternative plans, wondering if she might have to commute further, perhaps to Lake Placid, to have any chance of finding employment. She didn't notice the security guard in her path until she'd almost walked right into him. She stepped back, startled, when she realised that he was blocking the way back into the campus.

He frowned at her. 'Where do you think you're going?' he asked her.

Tabitha was at snapping point by now, but Jake had told her long ago that security – frustrated cops with access to heavy ordnance – were the last people you wanted to piss off, so she managed a polite smile. 'Heading back to my room. Why, is there a problem?'

She could tell he was looking to see if she was joking. When he realised she wasn't, he shook his head sympathetically. 'Dorms are shut for the vacation,' he told her. 'Didn't anybody tell you?'

'Shut?' Tabitha looked at him carefully to see if *he* was joking.

'Yeah – no point keeping 'em open with nobody in 'em. Waste of heat and electricity.'

'But *I'm* in them!' Tabitha protested.

He shook his head. 'Sorry – rules are rules. There's a few places in town hiring out rooms, if you want to stay on in Crystal Lake.' He made it sound like it was very unlikely that anyone sane would.

I can't afford a room! Tabitha wanted to tell him, but she didn't. Her pride wouldn't let her.

She half-thought about ignoring him, just going back up to her room and staying there anyway. Even if they switched off the power, it had to be better than the alternative. She didn't get the chance, though. The security guard walked beside her all the way to her room, only stopping outside the door when she shot him a venomous look. She tried to take her time packing, but all the time she could hear his foot tapping impatiently outside her door, so in the end she just shoved her clothes, books and laptop into any bag she could find handy and dragged them outside the door. He didn't offer to help carry them, just watched in amusement as she made three staggering trips down to the car with the bags balanced precariously in her arms.

When the car was packed he stood with folded arms at the gates, waiting for her to leave. Then he shut the gate behind her with a terminal clunk.

Tabitha didn't slow down until she was out of sight, determined not to let him think he'd got to her in any way. But once the school campus had disappeared from her rearview mirror she slowed to a halt at the side of the street, rested her arms against the steering wheel and her head on top of them.

What the hell was she going to do?

After a moment she pulled herself together. He'd said there were rooms for hire in the town – she'd get one for tonight, then worry about looking for work in Lake Placid tomorrow. Except that, when she asked the Crystal Guest House whether they had any rooms free, she was told that the cheapest was sixty dollars plus tax. When she pulled out her purse, she discovered that she had a grand total of fifty-three dollars and twenty cents to her name. It hadn't occurred to her to save any of her allowance for the vacation – she'd assumed she'd be back home and living off her father's largesse for the duration.

Tabitha looked at the woman behind the reception desk, a motherly type with blue-rinse hair and over-large pearl earrings, and knew that if she broke down and cried – as she was feeling a very strong urge to do – the woman would drop the rate for her, maybe even let her stay for free.

But it would be too humiliating. Putting on a bright social smile, Tabitha asked if there was anywhere a little cheaper. The woman hesitated a moment, then told her that the Crystal Lake Motel might have something but that, well, she didn't like to think of a nice girl like her in a place like that.

Five minutes later, Tabitha sat outside the Crystal Lake Motel and realised that there were certain depths she just couldn't sink to. The beam of her headlights had caught the dark scurrying form of what she was sure was a rat as she'd pulled into the parking lot, and the two men she could see letting themselves into one of the rooms were accompanied by a barely legal girl who could only be a hooker, and not an expensive one.

Tabitha carefully reversed the car out of the lot, then drove back to Adirondacks U. She was quite prepared to throw herself on the security guard's mercy, such as it was, but there was no sign of him when she arrived and his hut was locked and dark. The temperature had slid down another few notches as twilight deepened into full darkness, and even though she cranked the car's heating up to full she could feel the cold pressing in around her.

She knew that she ought to call her dad. He'd give her a lecture, then phone up the Crystal Guest House and book her a room on his credit card. But this was *his* fault, and she was damned if she'd give him the satisfaction of proving everything he said about her right. Instead, she drove away from the dorms and into the parking lot by the main teaching building, in whose windows a few lonely lights were still shining.

She had a car, she could stay in it for the night, then figure out what the hell she was going to do in the morning. It wouldn't be the first time she'd slept in a car. But as soon as she turned the engine off the temperature plummeted, icy air leaking in through the edges of the doors. It didn't matter, she told herself stubbornly. She had her clothes with her – she'd make a nest of them and sleep in the back. It ought to be plenty warm enough.

Except that the back was so small that she was only able to lay down with her back flat out if her legs were squashed upright against the far door. And she had plenty of clothes, but none of them was designed for this kind of weather, and most of them were little more than scraps of cotton or silk. After trying to arrange them into some sort of organised layers, she gave up and just tipped out her whole suitcase on top of herself, lacy panties and light summer dresses showering around her.

It was still painfully cold. She closed her eyes, determined to sleep though it, but after half an hour of hopeless wakefulness she started shivering, hard whole-body convulsions which felt like they were tying her muscles in knots. *Just sleep, sleep*, she told herself, trying to count the shivers, work out if they were getting faster or slower. She curled herself into as tight a ball as possible, fingers tucked into the marginal warmth of her armpits, anything to distract herself from the slow freezing numbness that was creeping through her body. Only now the numbness was staring to transform into a blessed welcome warmth, and she thought that the sun must somehow have emerged again, though when she opened her eyes and squinted dazedly out she could see the mercury shimmer of moonlight on snow. But it didn't matter because she felt so much better. And then, finally, she closed her eyes and drifted off into a dangerous sleep.

It was gone eleven by the time Mark finished up in his office, locking the door behind him out of habit, even though there were unlikely to be spies from other universities wandering the corridors, determined to steal the rough draft of his latest paper for the *Journal of American Psychology*.

He always got the most done at this time of year,

when the undergraduates had left the college and his teaching duties eased off, aside from the doctoral students he supervised, leaving him free to concentrate on his research. Sometimes, when he was explaining for the tenth or eleventh time to an uncomprehending class of eighteen-year-olds why retrograde and anterograde amnesia really were quite different things, he found it hard to understand why he'd chosen to pursue this course in life. When he could get stuck into a good piece of empirical research, it was easier to remember.

And easier to distract himself from the gathering evidence that Christmas was approaching. That, all around him, families were gathering around their Christmas trees or Menorahs, opening presents or eating Chanukka gelt or lighting lamps for Diwali. Jake had been dropping heavy hints all semester about how good the snow was looking up in Hamilton and two weeks ago Mark had caved in and bought him the tickets. It wasn't as if he and his brother ever made much of Christmas when they were together. And without Jake around it was easier to pretend that it wasn't happening. Besides, if Jake had wanted to stay in town, he might have wanted to keep Tabitha with him.

Mark locked the front door of the building behind him too, confident that no one else would have been working as late as him. A heavy snowfall had started, early but not unexpected, and he turned his collar up against it. Visibility was little more than two feet, so he didn't notice the other car until he was almost on top of it.

It was parked just ten feet from his own and he assumed that it must belong to another faculty member also burning the midnight oil. He sighed and prepared to head back through the bitter cold to the building and open the door again. But then he caught a flicker of what looked like movement inside the car through the heavy coating of snow on the windows and he realised that the vehicle wasn't one he remembered seeing in the faculty car park before.

Frowning, he used a gloved hand to brush the snow off the window and peered inside. Someone seemed to have tipped out a suitcase full of clothes on to the back seat, and for some reason the clothes seemed to be moving. Then he saw the face peeking out from beneath a pile of T-shirts and the hand that was flung out, palm open, motionless. The hand that was so pale in the moonlight it looked blue.

Cursing, he wrenched open the door and pushed the seat forward to give him access to the body in the back. The hand was icily cold in his own, but after a few seconds of panic he felt a faint thready pulse. A pair of thin silk pants were covering the figure's face. When he brushed them away, he immediately saw two things: that this was Jake's girlfriend, Tabitha, and that she seemed to be suffering from hypothermia.

Tabitha woke groggily to a rocking sensation and thought in confusion that she must be on a boat somewhere, maybe on the yacht her father had hired one summer to take her and her mother round the Islands. He'd stayed back in Los Angeles, too busy negotiating some A-list contract to join them.

Except if this was the Caribbean it was awfully cold. And the noise she could hear sounded more like a car's engine. She tried to sit up, but her arms seemed to be tied down to her sides and she let out a cry of mingled pain and fear as agonising pins and needles shot through her.

'Just stay still,' a voice said from somewhere ahead of her. 'I'm trying to get you warmed back up.'

She forced herself to stay still and instead eased her eyes slowly open, though they felt painfully swollen, her eyelids almost gummed shut. It was dark wherever she was, but her vision gradually acclimatised and she saw that the thing round her arms was just a blanket and that she was being driven along on the back seat of a car much larger than her own.

'How are you feeling?' the voice asked and she finally recognised it as belonging to Professor Sinclair. But that couldn't be right, because what the hell was she doing in a blanket in the back of his car?

'What's happening?' she tried to ask, only her voice came out as little more than a dry croak.

He seemed to understand it. 'As far as I could tell, you were attempting to get yourself killed.' She heard the crunch of gravel beneath the car's wheels and then a gentle rock forward and back as it stopped. 'You ought to be in hospital but the nearest one's a good hour's drive away, and I thought it would be better to get you warmed up as soon as possible.'

She tried to say something in response to that, but her eyelids felt unnaturally heavy and they drifted shut again as he reached into the back and pulled her effortlessly into his arms, so that the protest she tried to make died on her lips and everything faded to black once again.

When she next regained consciousness, probably only a few minutes later, it was to find Professor Sinclair kneeling beside her, undoing the buttons of her blouse.

She made a protesting noise and batted his hand away, though her arm felt like it had no strength in it at all, and the small motion wrenched a further cry of startled pain from her.

'I need to get you in a warm bath,' he explained, his face expressionless. 'Your body temperature's far too low and that's the fastest way of warming you up.'

She tried to speak, coughed, then tried again. 'I can undress myself,' she managed eventually.

He pursed his lips and leant back, as if inviting her to try. She lifted her hands up to her blouse, but though feeling was rushing painfully back into them it was as if they were covered in large oven mitts. She couldn't seem to get her fingers to do what she wanted and after three fumbling attempts to undo the same button she dropped them to her side and turned her head away, cheeks flushed with shame.

Without comment, he resumed undressing her himself. Her thinking was still fuzzy, and for a few moments his face blurred out of focus and Jake's seemed to blur back in, so that it was the other brother who was taking her clothes off one by one, as he'd done many times before. She thought she might have said his name and she sensed a stiffness in the figure by her side as she did, but then she drifted out of consciousness entirely and when she drifted back in she was completely naked and the arms which were lifting her up could have been Jake's but the chest she felt herself pressed against was broader and the smell of the man was wrong, a different cologne from the one she was used to and the underlying masculine scent of the flesh unfamiliar too.

She closed her eyes, not sure how she could look at her professor, her lover's brother, as he touched her so intimately. But the shock of warm water hitting her chilled body forced her eyes open and she saw that Sinclair's face was distant, his eyes focused elsewhere as if he too was willing himself as far away from this uncomfortable situation as possible.

As soon as she was fully submerged he turned away, leaving her her privacy. 'Are you awake enough for me to leave you?' He sounded like he passionately hoped that she was.

'Yeah.' Tabitha still felt woozy, but she didn't think she'd drift into unconsciousness again. 'Thanks,' she added awkwardly, realising for the first time that he had probably saved her life.

She saw his shoulders lift in a shrug. 'There's a robe by the door, put it on and come downstairs when you're done.'

She stayed in the bath as long as she could, occasionally topping up the hot water from the big silver faucets. But she knew that she couldn't put off facing him forever, so when the water had begun to chill after its third refill she climbed out, slipped the big white robe around her shoulders and headed down the stairs. She noticed that he hadn't told her where to go, confident that she'd be able to navigate the house after her first uninvited visit.

The place looked much bigger when it wasn't filled with partying students. She took time to study some of the ornaments as she descended the stairs, partly as a delaying tactic, partly out of genuine fascination: Japanese swords, scowling African masks, grinning gargoyles chipped from European churches. It looked like the collection of a particularly eccentric Victorian explorer. And yet here Professor Sinclair was, locked away in a backwater corner of a vast continent, with no evidence that he ever intended to go anywhere. The parts of him didn't seem to match up.

She found him waiting for her in the smaller living room. He'd started a log fire, and was sitting in an armchair in front of it, staring unseeingly into the flames.

'Hi,' she said from the doorway.

He started, then gestured her in. She settled into the chair opposite, drawing her knees up to her stomach and wrapping her arms around them, unconsciously curling her body into a protective ball.

He looked at her for a moment, his blue eyes expressionless. She realised that they were almost the same colour as her own, the one small point of similarity between them. 'So,' he said eventually, 'do I want to know why you were freezing to death in a car outside the faculty building?'

'To get out of Christmas shopping?' she suggested, but she could see from his expression that she wouldn't be able to joke her way out of this. She shrugged. 'I didn't have anywhere to stay, and I didn't realise it was going to get so cold. It wasn't a bizarre suicide attempt, if that's what you were thinking.'

He smiled very slightly. 'No. You don't seem the type to deprive the world of your presence.'

Tabitha could tell there was an insult buried in there somewhere, but couldn't quite figure it out.

He leant forward, chin resting against his elbows, thumbs against his lips. 'I know the dorms are closed, but didn't you consider renting a hotel in town? There's no way they'd be fully booked at this time of year.'

Tabitha looked away, staring into the heart of the fire rather than face his scrutiny. 'I couldn't afford it.'

'Really? That's not the impression I got from Jake. Or from your wardrobe.'

'But that's my dad's money, not mine,' she said quietly. 'And he's cut me off. He told me I had to find a job and support myself over the vacation. Only there *are* no jobs in this frozen hellhole.' She looked briefly up at him, then back down at the fire, not wanting to read the expression on his face, whether it was contempt or pity.

'Does Jake know about this?' he asked, his voice carefully bland.

When she looked at the flames long enough, she found that she could see shapes in them, faces. She shook her head. 'I didn't want to spoil his skiing trip. And, anyway, it's not like there's anything he could do. He told me you control the trust fund till he's twenty-five and you don't exactly shower him with money.'

He ignored that, just folded his arms and leant back in the chair. 'Well, you'll have to stay here tonight. I've put your things in the bedroom at the far end of the second floor.'

She finally met his eyes. 'Thanks, Professor.'

He frowned. 'Mark will do.'

'Mark,' she said awkwardly. 'You know, you don't have to do this. I could have phoned my dad. It was dumb of me not to.'

'Yes, and so very out of character,' he said dryly, then held up a hand to stop any protest or come-back. 'Just go to bed, Tabitha. You've put your body under a lot of strain tonight and it needs the rest.'

She had no energy to argue with him, and little will

either. If she didn't stay here tonight, where *would* she go? The bedroom he'd directed her to was small and bare compared to the rest of the house. He definitely doesn't trust me with the family silver, she thought. But she wasn't in much of a position to get on her high horse about that.

She didn't think she'd be able to sleep, the social discomfort of the evening coupled with the residual ache of deep cold in her limbs too distracting. But the instant she shut her eyes, huddled under a thick goose-down comforter, she found herself sinking into unconsciousness. Her mind was a jumbled confusion of images: Jake's expression when she told him she wouldn't come skiing, his brother's face when he'd found them together in the cells right back at the beginning of semester, and then again, looking at her in the car's mirror, telling her she'd nearly died. Her last waking thought was that the brothers were less alike than she'd thought, but she couldn't work out exactly what that meant.

Chapter Nine

Nine Till Five

When she came down to breakfast the next morning, Tabitha saw no sign of Professor Sinclair. She was starving, though, as if her body realised that it had used up all its stored reserves of energy last night and needed to replenish. A quick rummage through kitchen cupboards revealed nothing resembling her usual pop tart, so she had to settle for some disgustingly healthy bran flakes and Greek yoghurt.

She was polishing off her third bowl when Mark came through the back door. He was wearing loose sweats and breathing heavily, a light sheen of exertion on his face. His hair was damp and dark with sweat, ringlets of it plastered to his head, and she could smell the musky odour of his exertions from the run. She was surprised to learn he was an exercise nut. He had a good body, what little she'd seen of it, but he'd never given the impression of caring very much about it.

'You must be crazy,' she said. 'It's got to be ten below out there.'

He leant over the kitchen sink to splash water on his face. 'It's warmed up since last night. And, unlike you, I *do* own clothes which cover more than twenty per cent of my body.'

She looked up to find that he was half-smiling at her, and realised that she was being teased rather than criticised. She flipped him the bird and he shook his head in mock affront, but his smile widened slightly. For just a second, he looked startlingly like Jake.

Then his expression closed down, shutters falling over

his emotions, and he came to sit opposite her at the long oak breakfast bar. 'You can stay here for the rest of the vacation,' he told her without preamble, 'but I expect you to sing for your supper.'

She stared at him, wrong footed. 'What?'

'You need somewhere to stay and you need a job,' he explained impatiently. 'I've got a house with too many rooms and I'm short a research assistant for the next couple of weeks.' At her continued silence, he added, 'Alternatively, you could try sleeping out on the street again.'

'But I suck at psychology,' Tabitha protested. 'What kind of use would I be as an assistant?'

He poured himself his own bowl of bran flakes. 'You'll be slightly better than useless. Which is why I'm only going to be paying you minimum wage.'

He parked beside her car outside the faculty, then told her he had to meet with the accounts department to let them know he was taking her on, but that he'd be back in fifteen minutes' time. It took her a little time to locate his office, the faculty building a warren of interconnected corridors and tiny windowless rooms. His, when she finally found it, did have a window, offering an uninspiring view of the parking lot, but it wasn't much bigger than a cupboard. It occurred to her to wonder why someone with his obvious money would choose to work in a place like this. Why, in fact, he would choose to work at all.

She wondered if he expected her to get on with some work while she waited, but the place was spotlessly tidy and she couldn't imagine what he would want her to do, so instead she made herself a mug of coffee and sat in his chair – the more comfortable of the two in the room – resting her feet on his desk and flicking desultorily through the journals piled on one corner.

'Nice to see you start as you mean to go on,' he said when he entered the room. He stood at the door, arms folded, until she got up from his chair and sat in the wooden one at the other side of his desk.

'Don't sit down,' he said as soon as she had. 'There's some filing for you to do.'

'Some' proved to mean two whole rooms of it, each stacked with teetering piles of paperwork.

She turned to face him in the doorway. 'I thought you said I was supposed to be helping you research?'

'You are,' he said blandly. 'You'll be helping me research by getting this done and leaving me free to get on with it.'

'But this could take days!' she protested.

'Sooner you get started, sooner it will be done,' he said, then shut the door behind him, leaving her surrounded by walls of paper. She sighed and picked the top folder off the pile.

She didn't see him for four hours, when he came in to tell her that it was lunchtime, there was a dispenser downstairs for sandwiches, but he expected her to be back at work in half an hour. He took a look at the hundred-odd files she'd managed to sort into alphabetical order – then took them out of the cabinet and tossed them back on to the floor.

'What the hell are you doing? That took me all morning!'

'Yes,' he said, 'I can tell you've really been pushing yourself to the limit. But, in the normal world, files are organised alphabetically by family name, not first name. So start again and do it right this time.'

She opened her mouth to shout at him that he could have told her that four hours ago, but he'd already shut the door behind him and she was left, fuming, to contemplate the vast stacks of paper. Her mobile was in her bag, and she seriously considered phoning her father and explaining exactly why he *had* to send her some money. Except that would be handing him a victory she wasn't prepared to give. And, she somehow felt, handing Professor Sinclair a victory too.

She sighed and picked up the top file, putting it under T for 'Thompson' rather than J for 'Justine' this time.

She expected him to return at half-five and tell her the day was finished, but when he still hadn't shown up at six she was forced to track him down in his own office. He was sitting at his desk, head down over a stack of term papers, reading glasses sliding down the arch of his nose, and she stopped a moment in the doorway, hesitant to disturb him. She could tell that he was entirely lost in his work, two neat creases in his forehead as he circled a word in red pen. The only time she ever saw Jake so lost to the world was when they were making love. The rest of the time his attention was like a lightning bug, settling brightly but briefly on everything around him.

Mark suddenly sensed her presence. He looked up, cold blue eyes refocusing on her through his glasses. 'What do you want?'

'It's six o'clock. I want to go home.'

He shrugged. 'I'm not stopping you. You'll find a duplicate of the key under the mat at the back door. I guess you might as well keep it for now.'

'And when are you going to be home?'

'When I finish up here.' He leant back, stretching out the bones in his neck with an audible crack.

'And when will that be?'

'I don't know!' he snapped. 'I didn't realise there was a curfew.'

She drove home furious, wondering exactly why he insisted on being so obnoxious to her. She didn't have any money for groceries – he'd told her she wouldn't get paid till she'd worked a full week – but the house turned out to contain a bare minimum of food so she made herself a Spanish omelette and took it into the smaller of the three living rooms to eat in front of the TV, sure that Mark would object strenuously if he could see her doing it.

He still hadn't returned by eight and, with the television schedule filled almost entirely with reruns of *Law and Order*, she eventually brought her laptop down and made a start on her English paper in between figuring out if the guy being charged with murder on the TV looked familiar because she'd seen him around the club scene in LA or because he'd been in ten other episodes of *Law and Order* already. She'd discovered the wine cellar while she was looking for ingredients for her dinner, far better stocked than the refrigerator, so at nine she opened a bottle of Pinot Noir and poured a generous glass.

At ten o'clock Mark finally returned. His glance took in the television, the opened bottle of wine and the detritus of her make-shift dinner. 'No, really, make yourself at home,' he said dryly, then headed into the kitchen with what she saw was a take-out bag from the local Thai. That, she soon discovered, was to be the extent of their conversation for the night.

They settled into a kind of uncomfortable routine. Mark rose for a run before she was out of bed, then they shared breakfast in near silence before driving separately to work. He always left several hours after her but the second day he gave her some cash to buy food. She cooked lasagne, something her mom had taught her before she walked out, and left a portion on the side for Mark, for which she got a muttered thanks.

On the third day, she finally finished the filing. He had her working in the office with him after that, data entering into the computer, which meant that they *had* to talk, or the silence really would have been too painful. Talking, it turned out, meant him giving her pop quizzes on all the psychology classes she'd skipped during the semester and sighing at her answers.

On the fourth day she walked into the office and said, 'Baddeley and Hitch's Working Model of Memory was a refinement of Atkinson and Shiffrin's 1968 Modal Model; Wernicke-Korsakoff Syndrome leads to retrograde amnesia with a negative temporal gradient and it was Bruce and Young who said there's an entirely different brain system for processing faces. Now can we please talk about something else?'

Mark, she wasn't surprised to discover, didn't have much of a talent for small talk, but he asked her a few neutral questions about her life back in LA. As she talked about it – probably in far greater detail than he'd wanted – she was overcome with a strange mixture of homesickness and nostalgia. She was, she realised, starting to think about it as if it was part of her past.

Attempts to question Mark about his own past yielded little more than the information that he'd studied for his doctorate at Harvard and that he'd never been south of the Mason-Dixon line but had travelled over most of Europe.

'Is that how you picked up all that stuff in your house?' she asked.

'Some of it,' he replied. After a moment he added stiffly, 'Some of it was inherited.' And that was the end of that conversation.

On Friday, they ate together for the first time – Mark grudgingly accepting that it was his turn to cook, something he turned out to be surprisingly good at – and even found a topic it seemed they could have a safe and reasonably normal conversation about: film. Unlike most people Tabitha met back in LA, Mark seemed utterly unimpressed by her father's Hollywood connections, but he was deeply interested in the way power and money were traded in a town where they were the only things which really mattered. And, for once, it was a subject she knew more about than him.

In the middle of a particularly detailed explanation of why back-end points were valueless, she noticed that he was leaning back, smiling.

She broke off. 'What?'

He shook his head. 'Just impressed with the depth of your knowledge.'

'That's like being impressed that a fish knows about water. I've been around this stuff all my life. And before you start wondering why I don't apply the same degree of thought to my studies, yadda, yadda, yadda, psychology's never going to be a day's use to me as long as I live.'

'So why exactly *are* you studying it?'

Tabitha couldn't tell if he was pissed or amused. She shrugged. 'I had to study something – dad didn't want a high-school-educated daughter. And I thought psychology would be about people, so it ought to be kind of interesting. Only what I knew about psychology was what my friends told me about their therapy sessions, which it turns out isn't the same thing at all.'

'So, if you didn't want to go to school,' he said, 'what did you want to do with your life? What *do* you want to do?'

She was saved from having to answer by the telephone ringing. Mark picked it up and snapped, 'Yes?' into the receiver with his usual impatience. Then his expression shifted slightly. 'Jake,' he said, 'I wasn't expecting you to call.'

Tabitha tensed. She didn't know why, but she very strongly didn't want Jake to know that she was there. She couldn't begin to imagine what he'd make of it, but she was sure it wouldn't be anything good.

Mark, fortunately, seemed equally unwilling for his brother to find out. As he talked, he kept sending quick edgy glances in her direction, but he said nothing about it to Jake. Though Tabitha couldn't hear the words, the cadences of Jake's voice echoing tinnily through the receiver made her miss him, suddenly. She remembered how easy it was to be with him, conversations flowing, not usually about anything very important, but not delicately negotiated minefields like talks with his brother.

The call finished, and she could sense immediately from Mark's stiff bearing that the goodwill they'd spent the last few days building up had dissipated.

'Didn't think to mention I was staying here, then?' she asked, knowing as she said it that she was being totally unreasonable since she herself had wanted it kept a secret.

His mouth tightened but he didn't respond directly, just got up from the table and carried his still half-full plate over to the kitchen sink. 'I need to finish grading some papers,' he said. 'You can load the dishwasher, can't you?' He didn't stop to hear her response, just locked himself in the study, leaving her with a half-finished dinner and the sour feeling that she'd done something wrong, but wasn't quite sure what.

As usual, she brought her laptop down to do a little studying in front of the TV – it was amazing how much more interesting psychology was when accompanied by the latest episode of *Lost* – but her mind kept returning to Jake's call and eventually she gave up on working altogether and decided to turn in for an early night.

Mark must have decided the same thing, because when she reached the top of the stairs she saw him emerge from the bathroom, naked aside from a small towel round his waist and the other one he was using to dry his hair. She wasn't surprised to see that he had a good body. She knew he went running every morning and she'd seen the shape of his muscles through the sloppy T-shirts and jeans he habitually wore. But she paused a moment, taken aback, to see how much it was a *man*'s body, sturdy and definite. It made Jake seem almost fragile by comparison.

When Mark's head emerged from the towel he was looking straight at her, and she realised that she was staring at him. She gestured at his bare chest. 'Dinner and a show. Must be my lucky night.'

He frowned but said nothing, just walking past her to mount the stairs to his room.

She went to her own room, quickly changing then slipping into bed. Sleep didn't come easy, though. There was an edgy, itchy feeling in her body that wouldn't let her rest. She guessed it wasn't surprising she was feeling horny – the last few days had been the longest she'd gone without sex in the last three months. Cold turkey. But then it occurred to her that there was no reason she couldn't at least speak to Jake – if she called on her cell, he'd have no way of knowing where she was calling *from*. The possibility that he'd be with another woman crossed her mind, but if he was he simply wouldn't answer and she'd be none the wiser – the way she wanted to remain.

He did answer, though, on the second ring, almost as if he'd been waiting for it. 'Hey, Tabby – missing me?'

For the first time, she realised how much he and Mark sounded alike, the same faint Boston accent to both their voices, both deep and melodic.

'Haven't spared you a thought,' she said.

'So you just pressed speed dial by mistake?'

'Uh-huh.' She lay back down on the bed, phone resting between her ear and the pillow. 'Still, now you're here . . .'

He laughed. 'How's the land of eternal sunshine?'

She looked out of the window, where a grim grey drizzle was falling, as it had been all day. 'Same as ever. How's the Great White North?'

'Kind of dull.' There was a pause, during which she knew they were both thinking exactly the same thing. 'I'm trying to come up with an original way of asking what you're wearing,' he said eventually.

She looked down her body and thought about lying, but she wanted *him* to tell her the truth so that she could imagine him as he actually was, and it seemed only fair that she should do the same. 'Blue and white PJs,' she told him.

'Hmm. Sounds hot.'

'Not yet,' she said, 'but it's getting there. You?'

'Just navy boxers. The cabin's got a big double bed and I'm curled up in the middle of it, looking at the snow falling outside, the way the light from the window's shining through it. I haven't closed the blinds – I like to be woken up by the sun in the mornings. It's real bright up here, brighter than you'd think.'

Tabitha slid her hand down and under her top, letting her fingers trail gently over her stomach, just a glimmer of sensation. 'Have I ever told you what a great cock you've got?'

'No.' She could hear the smile in his voice at the abrupt change of topic, along was a hint of something else.

'Well, you have. It's not the largest I've seen, but it's perfect, straight and thick. I love the way it gets so hard for me.'

'It's hard for you now,' he told her. 'Are you wet for me?'

She trailed her hand lower, dipped it into herself. 'Oh yeah. You know, there's only one problem with your cock.'

'What's that?' She could tell from the light strain in his voice that he was already touching himself.

'That you're always the one who decides what to do with it.'

He laughed, surprised. 'Yeah, I can see how that might be a problem.'

'Not tonight,' she told him. 'Tonight you're going to do *exactly* what I say, when I say it. Are you touching yourself right now?'

'Yeah,' he said. 'Does that make me a bad person?' But the joke was only half-hearted, and underneath it she could hear his real excitement. She pictured him, lying on his back, one arm flung behind his head in that easy way he had, the other firmly round his cock, fingers squeezing just below the head where she knew he was most sensitive.

'I want you to take your hand away from yourself,' she said. 'I don't want you to be touching any part of you.'

'You know, that wasn't the way I imagined this conversation going,' he said.

'I mean it!' she snapped. 'You don't touch yourself unless *I* tell you to.'

'OK, I get it.' The roughness of lust was back in his voice. He understood the game now.

'Now take your finger, your index finger,' she told him. 'I want you to run it round the head, as gently as you can. Very slowly. However slowly you're doing it now, I want you to do it slower.' There was a brief silence during which she could hear nothing but his breathing down the phone, a little fast, but not ragged with excitement as it got at the peak of his passion. 'How does that feel?'

'It's not enough.'

She smiled at the frustration in his voice. 'Well, you know what you have to do if you want more.'

'What?'

'Beg.'

There was another silence. She knew that he was struggling with himself, that the part of him which enjoyed letting go was warring with the other inner core of him which never did and hated ceding control to anyone else. But in the end, as she'd known it would, lust won out. 'Please, Tabitha.'

'Please what?'

He laughed, a strained sound. 'Please, Tabitha, I want to touch my cock harder.'

'All right then, you can use two fingers. A little more pressure, if you need to, but I want you to run your fingers up and down this time – and you're still going to keep it real slow.'

He groaned, and she could tell that the pressure still wasn't quite enough. 'Shit, Tabitha.'

'Keep going,' she said, remorseless. 'Up and down, just two fingers, keep stroking, keep teasing yourself.'

'You're the tease,' he said, his teeth gritted. She could hear his breathing take up the rhythm of her voice, in time with the slow steady stroking of his fingers.

'Not enough sensation?' she asked with mock sympathy.

Her only response was a low groan.

'OK then, take your other hand, and curl it round your balls.' She waited a moment then said, 'Have you done that?'

'Yeah.'

'And you're still stroking your cock?'

'Oh yeah.'

'OK, with the hand around your balls I want you to squeeze gently. Tell me how that feels.'

He gave a breathy laugh. 'How do you think it feels?'

'I ask the questions!' she said sharply.

'It feels ... it feels good, but it's not gonna get me there.'

'Not enough? Then squeeze your balls harder.'

'I don't –'

'Just do it!'

She heard the change in his breathing, the way it caught on each in-breath as if it was having to work past an obstruction.

'Harder,' she said again.

He didn't protest this time, but she heard the slight gasp he let out as he complied. She could see his face as clearly as if it was in front of her, the way his wide mouth would be drawn into a tight line, the topography of the muscles in his chest and arms. The compelling golden eyes.

'Too much?'

'That fucking hurts,' he said, but she knew it turned him on too.

'Well ... I guess you can ease off a little. Why don't you let go of your balls for now and take your nipple instead, your left one, and I want you to pinch it between your nails, and then I want you to do the same on the right.' She knew that, unlike some men, he was very sensitive there. He made a sound that was almost a whimper as he obeyed her.

Her own hand was doing to her nipples what she'd told him to do with his, twisting and pinching the delicate tips. A sharp sensation shot straight down to her core but she didn't touch herself there yet. She knew she'd come almost as soon as she did.

'Want to keep on doing that?' she asked him.

'Yes please.' His voice had deepened as his excitement mounted, and she realised that he sounded more like his brother than ever. For a dizzying moment she thought that she'd dialled the wrong number, that it *was* Mark she was playing this game with. But, of course, this was a game Mark would never play. Still, the lingering thought of him remained. His image, ghostlike, overlaid Jake's in her mind.

'Good boy,' she told Jake after a moment. 'As your reward, I want you to make a circle of your thumb and index finger and wrap it around the base of your cock. And then I want you to move it up and down, just those two fingers, as hard as you like but as slow as you can.' She'd seen him masturbating, not just the first time they'd met, when she hadn't really seen that much – she'd watched him several other times as part of their foreplay. So she knew this wasn't how he liked to do it. She was making him behave in ways he wouldn't normally do, and the erotic charge of that was like a jolt of electricity through her.

His low groans told her that he was feeling the same charge.

Finally, unable to resist, she slipped her right hand down to her sex, her left still twisting and tormenting her nipples. She touched herself there as slowly and delicately as she had told him to touch himself, but for her it was just the right pressure and she let out a groan of her own.

'Are you touching yourself?' he asked.

'Yes,' she told him. 'I'm touching myself and I'm picturing your hand moving up and down on your cock. Only now I want you to stop, just under the head, the place where you're most sensitive. Have you done that?'

He let out a grunt that she took as an affirmative.

'Now I want you to circle, right there, keeping the pressure on as hard as you like.'

Her own finger speeded up, circling but never quite touching her clitoris.

He seemed beyond words now, all his attention focused on what she was making him do to himself. Her own attention seemed strangely divided, like an out-of-body experience, half of her concentrating on her own fingers and what they were doing, while the other half watched him and what he was doing, the two creating a positive feedback loop of pleasure which mounted higher and higher.

'Oh God, Tabitha,' she heard him gasp as he came, and she was coming too, hard, even though she'd yet to touch her most sensitive places. As she came, she tried to keep the image of him in her head, his face and body as he reached his own climax. But in the relaxation of after-glow the image subtly changed, and she found herself imagining Mark, how *he* would look as he came.

She ended the conversation with Jake soon afterwards, neither of them with much energy left for talking. Besides, there were too many lies Tabitha would have had to tell if she'd let him ask her any questions. But the biggest lie she was telling right now was to herself: that she hadn't seen Mark's face, rather than Jake's, as their game had ended. And that she hadn't liked it.

Chapter Ten

Torn

Tabitha was uncomfortable around Mark the next day, unable to look at him without remembering the image of him that was burnt into her mind from the night before. She kept reminding herself that he wasn't actually telepathic and would have no way of knowing what she was thinking, but whenever he turned towards her she found herself turning away, fidgeting uncomfortably with her stainless-steel Raymond Weil watch or jumping up and offering to make coffee. What was the matter with her? It had been an idle thought at a moment when she wasn't exactly in full control of her mind. It didn't mean anything. But, every time he looked at her, she looked away.

At lunchtime Mark seemed to finally lose patience with her twitchy behaviour. He took off his glasses and thumped them down on the desk. 'If you look at your watch one more time I may have to kill you,' he said.

She shrugged, hoping she didn't look as guilty as she felt. 'Sorry if I'm finding entering three jillion numbers into a computer less than exhilarating.'

He sighed. 'Fine, go home. Take the rest of the day off.'

'I can't, I need the money,' she told him, unsure why she was arguing since getting away was exactly what she wanted to do.

'Don't worry – I'll pay you for the full day. In fact, it's about time I paid you for your work so far. Including today, I make that five hundred dollars total. I guess cash would be best?' He opened his wallet and counted out a small stack of notes.

'Last of the big spenders,' Tabitha muttered, but she took the money gladly. 'What happened – get visited by the ghost of Christmas past?'

'I'll give it to a more deserving cause if you want,' he said dryly.

She closed her fist around the money.

He waved at the door. 'Then get out before I change my mind. Oh, and happy Christmas.'

It was only as he said it that she realised what day it was: Christmas Eve. She couldn't believe that this hadn't occurred to her before, but she'd been too distracted all morning to think straight.

She wandered out of the ghost-town of the college into the barely more lively streets of Crystal Lake. A thick layer of snow covered everything, deadening sound. When a car drove past her it felt like an intrusion, its tyres marring the perfect white blankness of the world.

It was very pretty, she had to admit, the image of small-town life she'd carried unexamined in her head since childhood viewings of *It's a Wonderful Life*. The stores seemed to have conspired to buy only the most delicate white lights and they glittered tastefully along the awnings of every building. Only the mini-mart had bucked the prevailing understated trend and placed a twenty-foot-high inflatable Santa on their front step, his big beaming bearded face already half-deflated, looking a little sinister, like a wino wearing fancy dress in the hope it would help him bum a cigarette.

A portly middle-aged man she vaguely recognised as a janitor at the college passed by on the other side of the street and raised a gloved hand in a friendly wave. Tabitha waved back, suddenly feeling like it really was Christmas. And, to add to the festive spirit, she had more than five hundred dollars burning a hole in her pocket. The voice of caution told her that she ought to use it as a deposit on somewhere to stay for the rest of the vacation – but it was never a voice she'd paid very much attention to.

The two clothing stores in town weren't even worth looking in, but there was a music shop, a little independent place which sold instruments too and was the hangout for all the local goths. Tabitha suddenly felt the urge to treat herself to something other than the mix CDs which were all she'd been able to fit in her suitcase when she came.

The interior of the shop was gloomy and almost unbearably noisy. Even on this day of the year, a group of three black-clothed, eye-linered teenagers was clustered around an electric guitar, blasting out what they probably thought were rocking power chords. Tabitha winced and tried to concentrate on the CD selection. She'd heard that Franz Ferdinand's latest was worth listening to, but even as she browsed she found her eyes drawn outside. Across the street was a parking lot which had begun the month filled to overflowing with Norwegian pines and was now down to a few sad-looking specimens, orphans in need of a good home.

Mark didn't own a Christmas tree, not even one of those pale synthetic imitations which Tabitha had always scorned. There were no decorations in his home either. Which was, she thought now, a shame – it was just the sort of house which would look absolutely amazing if someone put some festive spirit into it. It even had an open log fire.

She put the Gorillaz CD she'd been about to purchase back in its rack and instead headed over to the Christmas music section.

It took three trips to bring everything she'd bought back to Mark's house, including the large ham which, she'd ascertained, was missing from his refrigerator. The fourth and final trip was for the tree she'd already reserved. She'd intended to take the biggest and least mangy of those remaining, but instead had picked the most forlorn. With its runt-of-the-litter look it had seemed appropriately like the Tiny Tim of Christmas trees.

The sun had already set by the time she made it back to the parking lot. Most of the shops had shut down too, only the twinkle of the fairy lights left to lighten the darkness. It was bitterly cold, but her one purchase for herself, an enveloping woollen coat, kept her insulated. Clothes had never been something she'd previously considered as having any purpose other than decorative. Living out here, she was beginning to understand the utilitarian way Fiona dressed.

The snow made a sound under her shoes which was halfway between a crunch and a squelch. The line of her footprints stretched back into the distance, crossed only now and then by those of another living human. She'd considered bringing her car, but it wasn't big enough to hold the tree, and she wouldn't know how to begin tying it to the roof. Of course, the idea of dragging it home had felt a lot more feasible before she was standing next to the thing, which was no giant but was still much taller than she was.

'You sure you're gonna be OK with that?' the beefy young man who'd sold her the tree asked.

She examined him rather than the tree, appreciating the strong square line of his jaw and the thick blond hair which tumbled artlessly over his forehead. 'I guess if there's anyone who can give me a helping hand . . .'

He smiled, no doubt aware of where her eyes had been. 'I'm shutting down for the day anyway. Reckon you're the last sale I'm likely to make. Why don't you give me thirty seconds, and I'll help you carry that home. I'm Joel, by the way.'

'Tabitha.' She smiled her gratitude at him. When he emerged from the small office a few minutes later, she saw that his unruly blond hair had been hurriedly brushed, and she smiled again. It was nice to know some men still found her attractive even in a coat so shapeless it was barely possible to be sure she was a woman.

'Moved here recently?' he asked as they walked down

the street together. Helping her turned out to mean him carrying the tree on his own, its branches tied to its side and the thick trunk tucked under his equally thick arm.

'September,' she told him. 'I'm a student.'

He turned his head to look at her, surprised. 'You don't seem –' He cut off, seeming to realise that she might not be pleased to be told she looked too old to be a student. 'You don't look the type,' he amended.

She smiled. 'I'm twenty-four. Came here to finish my course.'

'How come you're not back home for the vacation?'

'Needed to earn some money. Besides, home is LA, and who wants sunshine for Christmas when you can have snow?' She realised there was a certain amount of truth in this. Back home the festival had always had an unreal suspended quality for her, as if she was somehow missing the point. Out here she could see exactly what it was all about – even if she was spending it with a man who seemed intent on pretending it wasn't happening.

Mark's house was on the edge of town, but at the brisk pace Joel set it took them less than ten minutes to reach it. Tabitha enjoyed the walk, the harmless flirtation. When they reached their destination, Joel hefted the tree on to his shoulder. 'Want me to help you put this up?' he asked, asking a different question with his eyes.

Tabitha had already seen the lights on in the house and the dark silhouette of a man in the window. 'That's OK – I think I can take it from this point on.'

'If you're sure,' he said, but then he too noticed the lights and the occupant. He put the tree to the ground and backed off. 'Well, it was nice meeting you.' There was a note of irritation in his voice, as if he felt she'd been leading him on. *It's not what you think*, she wanted to say, except she didn't because, well, it wasn't like she actually wanted to invite him in.

As soon as Joel was gone, Mark came outside. He folded his arms and gave both her and the Norwegian pine a jaundiced look. Then, without a word, he lifted the tree and carried it inside, placing it beside the huge pile of decorations in the living room.

He took a moment to survey it all, then raised an eyebrow at her. 'My house seems to have had an early visit from Santa.' He picked up a garish garland of gold, green and red tinsel. 'And he appears to be colour blind.'

She laughed. 'If you leave things last minute, you don't get the pick of the range.'

He put the tinsel back beside the tree. '"Last minute" implies that I was, at some point, intending to do this myself.'

'You weren't going to buy any Christmas decorations? But wouldn't that make you some kind of killjoy?' She widened her eyes in pretend astonishment.

'There is also,' he said, 'a ham in my kitchen large enough to feed the entire Marine Corp.'

She squatted on her haunches and began to unbind the branches of the tree. 'Wow, Santa must really have been feeling generous.'

At first, Mark just sat back and watched as she raised the tree and hung baubles from its branches, a motley and ill-matched selection ranging from silver plastic stars to chocolate snowmen. The only ornament of any quality was the delicate filigree angel she'd found for the top – but when she came to put it in place, she realised she couldn't reach. She didn't hear Mark come to stand behind her and jumped when she felt his hand reach over her shoulder to take the angel.

'Let me,' he said.

She turned her head to look at him and suddenly realised how close he was standing, his chest nearly pressed to her back, his chin brushing the top of her head. His fingers touched hers as he took the ornament and she felt the contact with an intensity disproportionate to its duration. Their eyes met and held – until he dropped his and concentrated on placing the angel on top of the tree.

'I'll put these outside,' Tabitha said awkwardly, picking up one of the several strings of icicle lights she'd also bought.

'You'll need a ladder,' he told her, his face again wearing its usual impassive mask. 'And, knowing you, you'll probably fall off. I'll do it.'

They ended up doing it together, Tabitha holding the ladder while he strung the lights under the eaves. 'My neighbours will think I've been abducted by aliens,' he told her as he flicked the switch and the bulbs started to flicker epileptically.

'And replaced by a human being?' she asked. The earlier awkwardness between them had eased and she realised that she was having a good time.

It was too cold outside to stand and admire the lights for long, though Tabitha took a moment to appreciate the way the Christmas tree glittered enticingly in the window. Once they were back indoors, Mark offered to cook her dinner, since she'd be in charge of cooking tomorrow's Christmas dinner if she was going to insist on having it.

While he retreated to the kitchen, she headed upstairs to freshen up. She'd intended only to change her T-shirt, but after she'd showered she found herself standing in front of the closet and studying all the available clothes critically. It seemed very important to her that she looked good that evening. She told herself that she always dressed up for Christmas and that there was no point going to all the effort of decorating the house if she wasn't going to decorate herself. Still, as she tried on and then rejected first a chiffon and lace sky-blue Versace dress that had been a birthday present from Jessica, then an appliquéd silk Miu Miu and finally a classic black Burberry, she found that she was imagining how Mark would react to them, whether he'd think the first was too slutty, the second too formal and the third too flattening of her already less than ample chest.

When she realised that she'd been agonising for more

than half an hour, she finally settled on an elegant pink Rick Owens three-quarter length. The sheer material of the dress clung to the right parts of her body and draped over the others, and she knew that the colour set off her skin tone fantastically. It also allowed her to wear her Christian Louboutin sandals, something for which she never passed up an opportunity.

Mark watched her in silence as she walked all the way down the sweeping central staircase, making her feel like a fifties movie actress making her grand entrance. She was surprised to see that he'd changed his clothes too, swapping his faded Henley for a maroon dress shirt which made his skin look translucent, like a very ancient ivory carving. She realised how fine his bone structure was, the perfect arch of his brows and the high cheekbones. She thought for a moment that he ought to be wrapped in cotton wool and kept somewhere safe, and it was the first time that she'd thought of him as in any way breakable, as if the dry unyielding surface of him was something brittle which could crack to reveal the vulnerable softness beneath.

She blinked her eyes and the image was gone and it was just Professor Sinclair, holding his arm out ironically to escort her to the dining room. But, though he smiled and made a dry joke as he led her through, she could feel that the muscles of his arm beneath her hand were rigid and, beneath their long lashes, his blue eyes wouldn't quite meet hers.

The meal was simple but she could tell that he'd put some effort into preparing it. The zucchinis were lightly pan fried with garlic, and the steaks were beautifully tender and subtly seasoned. He'd also opened one of the better wines in his cellar and for the first time since she'd met him seemed prepared to treat her like an adult. They stayed away from painful subjects, and Tabitha was grateful that he didn't ask why she didn't phone her father, or where her mother might be. Still, conversation flowed better than she'd expected, touching on films, books and the European cities they'd both visited.

After the food she demanded a tour of some of the odder artefacts in the house. The masks, as she'd guessed, were African. She asked about one in particular, a pale mask with deeply scored groves running across its entire face and 'hair' made of knotted leather and wooden tubes which had always intrigued her.

'It's from the Chokwe people of Angola,' he told her. 'It represents a female ancestor spirit. You can tell from the closed eyes and the characteristically feminine facial decoration . . .' He trailed off as he realised that she was staring at him.

'Is there anything you *don't* know about?' she asked.

'My particle physics could do with some brushing up,' he said with a straight face.

She pointed to another mask, this one with sunken cheeks and a short prominent beard. 'And this is by the same people, right? Maybe that other one's husband.'

He raised his eyebrows. 'How did you know that?'

She shrugged. 'The same way I can tell a Stella McCartney from an Alexander McQueen at fifty paces. You can see if something's been made by the same person. It's like . . . you can work out what kind of mind came up with it.'

She caught a glimmer of something unexpected in his expression, but he quickly turned away to show her a Louis Quinze table and she decided that she must have imagined it.

Later, they retired to the living room to enjoy basking in the light of the tree. Tabitha insisted that they watch the late showing of *It's a Wonderful Life*, a Christmas tradition she wasn't prepared to abandon just because she was on the East Coast.

She found herself watching him as much as the film. It was strange. As the emotions of the film played out across his face, she caught glimpses of a different younger man. She might have expected this man to remind her of Jake, but looking at him now she didn't really think they were that alike. They both closed parts of themselves off to the world, but she wondered if they were the same parts, or for the same reasons.

When the film was finished, Tabitha sighed. 'I always forget what a sad movie that is.'

Mark leant back, arms folded behind his head. 'Do you think so?'

'Don't you? He gives up everything he wants to take care of other people. He's made a difference to their lives, but what about his? In a lot of ways, he's wasted it.'

'I don't call a life spent looking after other people a waste.'

Tabitha couldn't read his voice or his face at all, the dying embers of the fire lighting him in sombre shades of amber.

'A waste is a life spent looking out for no one but yourself.'

'Yeah, that's what we're supposed to believe, but really – do you think anyone lies on their deathbed thinking, Gee, I wish I'd spent just a bit less time having fun?'

'Is that the principle you've lived your life on?' he asked. 'Do what you want and damn everyone else?'

She knew the answer she ought to give, the one that would make her come across as a better person, but she was still filled with a warm wine buzz, and it suddenly seemed important to her to be honest. He was leaning towards her, his face and voice intense, a growing closeness between them. This didn't seem like the time for glibness or dishonesty, not if she wanted this thing that was growing between them – the thing she didn't even really want to acknowledge – to be real.

'Yeah, when it comes down to it, that is what I think,' she told him. 'Other people are never going to look out for you the way you look out for yourself. Take my mom. She spent ten years taking care of me, and what did she get out of it?'

He shook his head, as if he just couldn't understand her. 'She got a beautiful daughter.'

They were very close on the couch, although the only parts of them that were touching were their legs, her knee against his thigh, a deep warmth seeming to emanate from that one point of contact.

She slid her arm along the back of the couch so that her hand was almost brushing his hair and leant in towards him. 'But it wasn't enough, was it? Otherwise she would have stayed.'

She could see his eyes narrow as he realised what this meant. 'Your mother abandoned you when you were ten?'

She nodded, suddenly aware of just how much she was revealing to a man she still barely knew. 'Yeah, well, this was California. Everyone has to go and find themselves – leaving your daughter behind just gives you something extra to talk to your guru about.'

His mouth twisted into a sour shape, and she knew that he could keep on at this, keep picking at the scab until it came off entirely – but it seemed to her that it was time for him to reveal something about *himself*.

'But I guess you did give up your life for someone else,' she said. 'You've looked after Jake since he was eight, haven't you? How old were you then – twenty?'

'Eighteen,' he said in a flat voice, clearly trying to shut down the conversation.

But Tabitha didn't want it to be shut. 'You – you lost both your parents in a car crash, didn't you?'

He stood up and walked over to the fire. His back was to her, his face hidden, but she could read his mood in every tense inch of him. 'I don't want to talk about this, Tabitha.'

'What, I show you mine but you don't show me yours?' She softened her voice, a sudden insight coming to her. 'Did they die at Christmas? Is that why you don't like to celebrate it?'

He spun round to face her and she felt herself physically

pushed back into the couch by the force of his rage. 'Just because you're fucking my brother doesn't mean you get the right to ask that kind of question!'

There was a frozen moment as he stood there, fists clenched at his side, breath rasping out of him. She'd never seen anyone so furious, not even her father when he told her that he was sick of the way she was living her life. She thought about saying something, but couldn't think of a single thing that would make this any better and was afraid that anything she said might make it worse.

After a few unbearable seconds his fists unclenched and he let out a slow controlled breath. 'It's late – I'm going to bed,' he said. 'Turn the lights out before you come up.'

Tabitha realised that she was shaking as he left the room. In the doorway, he turned to face her. 'And, for your information, they were killed on New Year's Eve, not Christmas.'

After he'd gone, she felt the air rush back into the room, filling the vacuum left by his anger. Now that she'd had time to get over her initial shock, she was equally furious at him. How dare he react to a simple question like that? What was so damn special about him that no one was allowed to get close?

Underneath that, there was a simmering anger at herself. Because she'd known she was provoking him and persevered anyway. And now she felt that something important, but still only half-seen, was irrevocably damaged.

Chapter Eleven

Brothers in Arms

Tabitha woke early on Christmas morning, as she had done since she was a little kid. She lay curled up in bed, enjoying the warmth and the peace, letting her mind drift unconnected from the world. After a few minutes, though, the events of last night and the reality of where she was intruded. She sighed and rolled out of bed.

There was a small wrapped parcel on her dressing table, a silly little gift she'd bought for Mark yesterday in the middle of her shopping spree. She felt absolutely no desire to give it to him now.

It was still only six-thirty, but Mark was already in the kitchen when she went in there to get herself a pop tart and a hot chocolate. He barely acknowledged her presence, just glanced up briefly from the textbook he was reading as he ate his toast and jelly.

'Good morning,' she said brightly.

He stood up, as if her mere presence in the room was driving him out of it. 'I'm going to work – there's some grading I need to finish up. You can take the day off, but I expect you back in again nine o'clock sharp tomorrow.' He strode out of the room, book tucked beneath his arm, before she had a chance to reply.

'And a merry Christmas to you too,' she muttered sourly.

Hanging around the house just reminded Tabitha how alone she was, so she put on her new woollen coat and her least frivolous pair of shoes and went for a walk. It had snowed again during the night, a good seven inches of it. Most of it remained a pristine white, unmarred by footprints or tyre-tracks – no doubt because everyone else in the neighbourhood was sitting at home enjoying the holiday with their families, not freezing their nuts off outside.

Tabitha wondered whether she ought to call her father. He'd rung her cell a few times since the vacation had begun, but she hadn't returned his calls and after the first couple of days he'd stopped. She'd switched her phone off entirely this morning, just in case he was overcome by the holiday spirit and decided to try again. She didn't know what she'd say to him, but whatever it was she didn't think it was likely to improve their relationship.

She found that she missed him terribly, though. They'd never been exactly close but he'd always been *there*, a solid irascible but dependable presence in her life. The only one, really, who was always around.

She thought now that maybe she could call him, tell him that she was doing OK and wish him a happy Christmas. Where was the harm in that? Except that he'd want to know what she was doing and where she was, and she didn't want to talk about Mark. Besides, he'd left her to fend for herself without seeming to care very much whether she'd be able to – if he was worried about her now, perhaps that would teach him a lesson.

A path had taken her out of the town on to one of the back roads that snaked its way up into the surrounding mountains. Only one vehicle passed her in the entire time, a navy-blue SUV which hooted a greeting as it passed. She knew better now than to wander into the forest without a map, but there was a small footpath which led to a spectacular outlook north towards the Canadian border. In normal conditions, it took fifteen minutes, but trudging through six–inch-deep snow was more draining than she'd realised and by the time she reached the top her feet were soaked in ice-cold water and her thighs were burning from the exercise.

She'd never been much of a one for scenery. It was

things made by people which impressed her. Still, looking out over the snow-smothered peaks of the mountains, a vast whiteness broken only by the dark-green stains of forest, she felt a sort of wonder. The world was so large. Living in LA you felt it was everything that mattered, but out here you could see that there was more. LA's social system might be Byzantine in its complexity, but live with it long enough and you could figure it out and learn how to play it. The Adirondacks, on the other hand, seemed endlessly unknowable.

Thinking about things which were unknowable made her think about Mark again. Why couldn't he be more like Jake? They'd both been through the same tragedy, but in Jake it had just given him a philosophy of seizing the day. Tabitha could relate to that. And Jake had been far younger than Mark when they'd lost their parents – so it must have been worse for him, mustn't it? Plus he'd had to deal with being brought up by a tightass like Mark, who seemed to think that emotions were something to be rigidly policed and if possible utterly suppressed. When you thought about it, it was a wonder Jake had turned out as well as he had.

These thoughts banished the last residue of pastoral peace from her mind and she realised that her feet were beginning to go ominously numb. She took one last look at the view, grey clouds building in the distance that spoke of more snow to come, and then turned and headed back down the path.

It was quicker but if anything more unpleasant on the way back down and she gave up trying to retrace her own footsteps when she realised that the crushed snow had solidified into ice. She'd already lost her footing once, landing jarringly on her knees and hands, lucky not to have broken a wrist. By the time she reached the bottom she was shaking from the cold and the effort. And it was still morning – what was she going to do with the rest of what was turning out to be the worst Christmas she'd ever experienced?

Head down, thoughts churning, she didn't notice the new vehicle parked in Mark's drive until she'd walked past it. It took her a further second of confusion to recognise it – Jake's grubby pick-up. She felt an instant and intense mix of emotions: pleasure that Jake was here and she'd have some company at last, and apprehension as she realised she'd have to explain why she was here too.

She found him sitting in front of the TV with his feet on the antique coffee table – something which she knew would drive his brother absolutely crazy. He was watching a carol concert and drinking one of Mark's most expensive wines straight out of the bottle.

'Surprise,' Tabitha said expressionlessly.

He jerked his head round so fast that a fine spray of red liquid shot from the wine bottle to spatter the expensive Persian rug. 'Tabitha?'

She held her arms out in a *ta-da!* gesture.

'What in hell are you doing here?'

'I could ask you the same question.'

She saw a glint of suspicion in his eyes that she didn't entirely understand. He rose and walked to her, bottle still swinging from one hand. 'Yeah, but I actually live here, so I've got my answer pretty much covered. How about you?'

She shrugged, suddenly not quite sure where to begin. 'It's a long story.'

He gestured at the TV with the wine bottle. 'Do I look busy?'

They retreated to the kitchen where Tabitha scavenged bread and cheese to sate the appetite she'd worked up on her walk and Jake made a big bowl of mulled wine for both of them, seasoning it liberally with cinnamon and clove. Unlike his brother, he wasn't much of a cook, but he knew every way to prepare alcohol in existence.

'You nearly froze to death?' he said.

Tabitha nodded.

'And Mark saved your life?'

'Well, yeah, I guess. But not in what you'd call a particularly heroic way.'

Jake studied her face for a long moment as he poured out the wine, not seeming to like whatever he saw there. 'So why didn't you tell me you had nowhere to go?'

Tabitha looked away. 'It's not like you could have done anything about it. And I thought I'd be able to get a job – or at least have somewhere to stay.'

Unexpectedly, he started laughing. 'I bet you were pissed when you realised no one wanted to hire you and then they threw you out of the dorms.'

She started laughing too. 'Thanks for the sympathy!'

And after that the conversation seemed to be closed. Tabitha was grateful in a way – there were a whole bunch of things about the last few days she didn't want to talk to Jake, or anyone, about. But at the same time she noticed that he hadn't said 'you can always tell me when something's wrong' or 'if I'd known I would have come back and taken care of you'.

'How about you?' she asked him after she'd finished the bread and cheese and they were both settled back in the living room, their legs resting parallel to each other on the antique coffee table. 'I didn't think you'd be back for a week.'

'Ran out of money,' he said.

His voice told her that wasn't the whole story and dared her to ask more. She raised her eyebrow at him and, after a few seconds' silent staring, he caved.

'Big poker game with the boys. I was holding a king-high flush and Miguel had the ace-high – it was a bad beat, anyone would have lost their shirt on it.'

'Or, in your case, your brother's shirt,' she said.

His expression darkened briefly, but then he grinned.

'So what *are* you going to tell Mark?' she asked.

'Definitely something other than the truth. Maybe I broke my skis. Or maybe I was just missing the old home cooking. Where is he anyway?' He looked around the room, as if expecting his brother to be lurking behind a bookcase.

'At work,' Tabitha told him.

'Jesus, he's getting worse.'

Tabitha nodded, not wanting to give him any reason to ask exactly why his brother was working on Christmas Day. But when she risked a glance at him she saw that he had something entirely different on his mind. His wide mouth was quirked into a Mona Lisa smile, and his eyes were filled with mischief.

'So basically what you're saying is that we've got the whole house to ourselves and Mark probably won't be back for hours?'

Tabitha could feel the warmth of arousal in her belly, a fire his desire for her always lit. 'But there's so many rooms to choose from, I wouldn't know where to start.' She licked her lips, enjoying the way his gaze followed her tongue, the flutter of the pulse at his throat.

He stood up, holding his hand out to her in a courtly gesture that briefly reminded her of Mark before she quickly banished the thought. 'I have an idea,' he said.

She thought he'd lead her to one of the bedrooms, or maybe to the kitchen, where the many work surfaces seemed to be inviting a use other than culinary. But the room he took her to was the only one she'd never entered before.

'Mark's study?' She peered nervously round the door, even though she knew for sure that he wasn't home. Nearly every night she'd been staying he'd disappeared in here to work. He'd never told her that it was forbidden territory, but he hadn't needed to. The place was pretty much his inner sanctum.

'I'm not allowed in here,' Jake confirmed. 'He thinks I'll mess something up.' He pulled on her arm, drawing her inside.

'Now why would he think that?' she said.

The place was smaller than most of the other rooms in the house, dominated by a huge wooden desk, its top covered in worn-looking green leather. There was a computer in one corner, but also an expensive-looking fountain pen and a beautiful silk-covered notebook with a peacock feather print on its cover. There were shelves on every wall, filled with books, not just psychology textbooks but James Bond paperbacks, volumes of poetry and even some children's books. She guessed that many of them were first editions and wondered why Mark had chosen to keep those particular volumes around him while he worked. Sentimental value? It was hard to imagine Mark surrendering to sentiment.

Jake sat in the big leather swivel chair in front of the desk. When he spun it to face her, she saw that he was wearing a pair of Mark's reading glasses. For reasons she didn't want to examine too closely, she found that it made him look more attractive, lending his face an ersatz maturity. 'Do you think he ever puts it to his students in here?'

'I seriously doubt it,' Tabitha said through a suddenly dry throat.

'But I bet he fantasises about it, don't you?' Before she could respond his expression hardened, suddenly making him look even more like his brother. 'Your grades have been very poor, Miss Stone!' he snapped. 'What have you got to say for yourself?' His fingers drummed impatiently on his knee.

Tabitha knew the part she had to play. She dropped her head, lacing her fingers behind her back like a naughty schoolgirl. 'I'm sorry.'

'Not good enough!' He thumped his palm down on the leather surface of the desk, and even though Tabitha knew it was a game, she jumped nervously. 'Since you seem incapable of making up your credit academically, we're just going to have to find another way for you to do it. Aren't we?'

'Yes, Professor Sinclair,' she whispered, then realised a moment later what she'd said. Her eyes jerked guiltily up to Jake's but the words seemed to be just what he wanted. There was a charge in the air unlike anything she'd felt in their previous encounters. She knew that it was dangerous, and maybe unhealthy, but she could feel her centre warming with her excitement.

He let the silence rest for nearly a minute, an invisible tension stretching the air between them. 'Take your clothes off,' he said finally. 'And fold them neatly. I hate disorder.'

Tabitha almost smiled at that, because it was true – Mark was an obsessively tidy person. Except that nothing about this game was funny. It was too intense, too serious for that.

She took her blouse off first, kneeling on the floor to fold it as Jake had instructed. He stayed seated, face inscrutable, golden-brown eyes glittering behind Mark's glasses. She stayed kneeling to remove her bra, folded that too then placed both carefully to one side. Her breasts swung gently as she stood back up, the peaks standing achingly proud, evidence of her arousal.

'Come here,' he said.

When she approached he reached out and held her breasts, at first just weighing them, then delicately circling the nipples with his thumbs. The contrast between the gentleness of his touch and the harshness of his face and voice was unsettling, leaving her feeling off balance.

'You're not naked yet,' he said after a moment, so she stepped back and shucked her jeans and panties.

It felt odd to stand in front of him entirely exposed while he inspected her. It was nothing like that first time, when it had all been so light-hearted. She felt now that he was looking for something specific, searching for clues in her face and body, but she couldn't tell if he'd found them. He patted the desk and she understood what he wanted. She sat in front of him, legs splayed, entirely exposed to his eyes.

'You're very beautiful,' he told her quietly, but he wasn't looking at her face. Then he lowered his own and used his lips and tongue on her. She spread her legs wider, as wide as she could, leaning her weight back against her hands. Her head fell back, hair brushing her shoulders, lips dried by her panting breath.

He usually took this part of their love-making slowly. Unlike some men, it was something he enjoyed for its own sake, not just for its effect on her. But today he was unrelenting, seemingly intent on proving just how quickly he could make her come. It didn't take long. She let out three short gasping moans and then a loud cry as it felt as if every part of her body convulsed and then relaxed, leaving her to collapse backwards against the table.

When she opened her eyes it was to see him leaning over her, studying her face as if to memorise exactly how she looked in this moment.

'Say my name,' he said.

'Jake.'

'Again.'

'Jake.' She sat up and reached her arms around him to pull him into a kiss.

He allowed it a moment, tongue invading her mouth then inviting hers back into his. Then he pulled back, only an inch, so that their breath was still mingling in the air between them. 'Who am I?' he asked again. There was a darkness in his light eyes that drew her in, a vacuum desperate for something to fill it.

'Professor Sinclair,' she told him.

'And what do you want me to do to you?'

'Fuck me,' she said. 'Please.'

He didn't bother undressing, just unzipped his jeans and freed his cock. It was red and fiercely hard, jutting up from his groin like an irrefutable statement. She reached down, wanting to feel it, enjoying the length and heat of it beneath her fingers. Then she took him and guided him inside her. She was so slick from her earlier orgasm that he slid in smoothly, filling her entirely.

He paused a moment when he was all the way in. She

could see in his eyes the enjoyment he took in this possession, a pleasure quite separate from the raw animal satisfaction of fucking her. But he wanted that too. His hands grabbed her hips, hard enough to bruise, as he pumped in and out of her.

She groaned and leant back, bracing her hands on the desk behind her. He lifted a hand and cupped her head, forcing it back up so that she was looking directly into his eyes. 'Do you like this?' he asked.

'Yeah,' she whispered, the effort of forming sentences too much as his physical assault on her mounted.

'You like being fucked by me on my brother's desk?' He increased his pace, losing rhythm as he quickly neared his release.

'Yes.'

That final admission seemed to push him over the edge. His arms went around her, squeezing tight, and he grunted into her shoulder as he spent himself inside her. She was seconds from her own release. As the shudders of his orgasm subsided he brought his hand down between them, pressing against her clitoris without any finesse, but it was enough. She bit down hard into his shoulder to muffle her scream of pleasure.

After a few minutes their breathing subsided to a steady synchronised pace. Tabitha raised her head to look at him. His face was dripping with sweat, although their exertions had lasted only a few minutes, and there was still a wildness about him, as if some new creature had emerged inside him which wasn't yet fully tamed. Then he grinned his crooked wicked grin, and he was just Jake again. He looked down at the leather surface of the desk. 'Think it will stain?'

Mark didn't return till gone seven. Jake and Tabitha had made love once more, in Jake's bed this time, and now they were ready to go out to a party that one of Jake's less salubrious friends was throwing in his cabin out in the woods.

Tabitha had changed into a pair of micro-shorts and a crop-top, both of which revealed far more than they hid. She saw Mark's eyes flick very quickly over the ensemble, then move to his brother – who was wearing an almost identical outfit. Mark's mouth twisted into a grimace of disapproval.

'Costume party – clones,' Jake said to him, obviously enjoying the disapproval. 'Count yourself lucky we didn't go for the moustache and leather chaps option.'

'I wasn't expecting you home yet.'

'Yeah,' Jake drawled, 'otherwise you would have rolled out the red carpet. Don't worry, I won't be around enough to annoy you.'

Mark's mouth thinned still further. 'Nevertheless, the house isn't big enough for three.' Both Tabitha and Jake raised their eyebrows at this patent absurdity, but Mark ignored them. 'Since you've got some money now, Tabitha, I think it would be best if you rented a room in town for the next week. There should be plenty available.'

He walked upstairs without another word. Tabitha watched him go, feeling a stab of pain as sharp as betrayal, but she couldn't rationalise it. She'd hardly expected Mark to let her continue lodging with him: why would he allow a relationship he didn't approve of to continue under his own roof? She'd hoped, at one stage, that his getting to know her better might lessen his disapproval of her being with Jake, but their argument last night had put paid to that idea.

Jake was looking at her, a thoughtful expression on his face, but she just shrugged and forced a smile. 'And imagine how much more pissed he'll be when he realises what we did in his study.'

He laughed as he followed her out of the door.

When they settled into the front of Jake's pick-up, she pulled a wrapped package out of her pocket and handed it to him. He raised his eyebrow enquiringly. 'Christmas present,' she told him.

'I haven't got you one,' he said.

'That's OK – it's nothing much.'

When he opened the glossy red wrapping paper it was to reveal a copy of *How the Grinch Stole Christmas*. He looked at her, as if not quite sure what it meant.

'Christmas isn't Christmas without a Grinch,' she said.

He smiled. 'Thanks, Tabby.' He leant across to kiss her, then threw the book casually on to the floor at his feet. Tabitha could tell he didn't really understand or appreciate the present. But then that was hardly surprising: she'd originally bought it for Mark. She wondered if he would have known what she meant by it.

PART THREE

Second Semester

Chapter Twelve

Release the Pressure

Tabitha was dreading her first seminar. She hadn't returned to work with Mark after Christmas Day, the wages he'd paid her being enough to support and house her for the remainder of the vacation. And she and Jake had met at the small motel room she'd hired, never where his brother might see them. Jake had suggested a few more secret trysts at the house when his brother was out at work but Tabitha had declined, not quite sure why but very sure that she didn't want Mark to see her with his brother again.

Now, though, she couldn't put off the inevitable any longer. She packed her books into her bag then sat down on her bed, wondering if it would really matter if she chickened out.

'Not looking forward to getting your end of semester grades?' Fiona asked.

'Shit!' Tabitha slumped backwards on the bed. She'd entirely forgotten about those and, since it would be Mark who was awarding them, she couldn't imagine they were going to be good. Then she looked back up at Fiona and saw the dark circles under the other woman's eyes and the white drained look to her skin. 'Don't tell me *you're* worried about your grades.'

Fiona shook her head. 'I'm fine.'

Tabitha's suspicions instantly increased. In her experience, people only told you they were fine when they very definitely weren't. But she really was going to be late for Mark's class, which would be worse than not showing up at all, so she reluctantly got to her feet and left the questions for later.

The class was, if anything, worse than Tabitha had anticipated. Jake hadn't shown up at all, leaving her to face his brother on her own, and Fiona was off at her advanced psych class, having already passed this one last year.

She found herself thinking that Mark looked tired, the startling blue of his eyes underscored with shadows so deep they were almost purple. But his tongue had lost none of its razor edge, and he seemed to spend most of the hour using it on her.

It began as he handed out the results for the previous semester. Tabitha looked at her C minus with dismay. She'd thought she was doing better than that. Admittedly, she'd spent more evenings and weekends partying with Jake than working on her papers, but she'd handed every one of them in, and shouldn't that be enough to secure her at least a B?

Her thoughts must have been clearly visible on her face because suddenly Mark was hovering at her shoulder, looking down on her with the same cold disdain he'd shown her last semester, as if whatever closeness they'd achieved over Christmas had all been in her imagination. 'You look unhappy, Ms Stone. Do you want to contest your grade?'

Tabitha bit back a heated retort and shook her head.

'No? So you're satisfied with a C minus? You think that's a fair reflection of your abilities?'

There were a few muffled laughs round the room.

'I think it's a fair reflection of what you think of me,' she told him, glaring back into his eyes with equal disdain.

'Well, if what you imagine I think of you is that you're an idle and unmotivated student who expects to be able to cruise through the course without doing any work, you're absolutely right. In fact, most people would say that grade was overgenerous given the calibre of the work handed to me. If it doesn't markedly improve this semester, you'll be getting an F.'

He moved on to congratulate someone else on their B plus, and Tabitha was left to seethe in peace. All this because she'd dared to ask him a personal question after spilling her guts to him herself? Or was it really all about Jake? Mark had seemed to be growing to like her OK over the week they'd spent working together, but clearly no one was good enough for his baby brother. It wasn't like Jake was the perfect catch – she could tell Mark a thing or two about his baby brother that she knew would shock him. Except that she wouldn't. It wouldn't be fair to Jake.

She was so caught up in these thoughts that she didn't hear the question Mark had asked her now the lesson proper had resumed. He didn't bother to ask it again, just made a brief remark about students who hadn't bothered to do their vacation reading – as if he didn't know that she'd been otherwise occupied! – then asked someone else.

The end of the lesson couldn't come soon enough. She tried to slide out of class as soon as Mark dismissed them, hoping to avoid any further encounters with him, but he had other ideas. She felt his hand clamp around her bicep before she could reach the door.

She looked down at it, then up at him, sending a very clear signal that she wanted to be let go. To her surprise, he blushed lightly and dropped his fingers from her arm as if they'd been scalded.

'A word, Tabitha?' he said.

She folded her arms and stared him out as the other students squeezed past her. A few lingered in the doorway, clearly planning to enjoy whatever further humiliation Mark was about to mete out to her, but Mark closed the door firmly in their faces.

'I have got another class to go to,' Tabitha told him as he continued to look at her in silence.

That galvanised him out of his inertia. He folded his own arms, so that their bodies were mirrors of each other. Tabitha couldn't remember from the body-language book she'd read when she was fifteen whether that meant they were being unconsciously friendly or unconsciously hostile. Given the circumstances, probably the latter.

'You won't have any classes to go to at all if you don't start putting some real work in,' he said. 'I meant what I said earlier.'

'I passed, didn't I?' she said mulishly, knowing that she sounded like a sulky teenager.

'Only just. And if I hadn't thought you had the potential to do better, you wouldn't have passed at all. Professor O'Grady wanted to give you an F for her class. I persuaded her not to.'

'Don't do me any favours,' Tabitha snapped. She found the idea of Mark and Professor O'Grady cosying up to decide her future together unaccountably irritating. She could just see O'Grady flicking her long dark hair off her shoulder as she bent her head conspiratorially next to Mark's, sharing a little joke about some novice mistake Tabitha had made.

'Fine,' Mark said. 'If you want to flunk out of this school too, if you want to spend the rest of your life failing at everything you try, that's your choice. And you're the one who'll have to live with the consequences.' He wrenched the door open and stalked out before she had any chance to respond.

He was always, she thought, walking away rather than listening to any explanation that she might have to offer. But then what could she really say? If she failed here she *would* have to live with the consequences, and she wasn't ready for that.

Looking out of her dorm-room window later, Tabitha saw Mark walking across the courtyard, Professor O'Grady walking at his side. They paused before the entrance to the English faculty where O'Grady taught, and Tabitha saw Mark bend his head briefly to the other woman's lips. So, their decision to fix her marks really had been part of some little lovers' bargain. Tabitha wondered why O'Grady had never been to visit over Christmas, but perhaps she'd needed to spend time with her own family. The fact that Mark hadn't mentioned her was no big surprise – he hadn't shared any personal information with Tabitha about anything. Still, Tabitha felt a knot of anger in her stomach at the sight, and she realised that her right hand had curled up into a fist.

'You look ready to kill someone,' Fiona remarked. 'What's the matter, has Jake been playing the field while you've been apart?'

Tabitha shook her head and turned away from the window. 'If you think you're going to change the subject from what's the matter with you, you're very much mistaken.'

Fiona looked for a moment as if she was going to deny it. Then she sighed and sat down on her bed. 'It's nothing important. Just . . . my baby brother.'

'Baby brothers are important.' Tabitha perched cross legged on the bed across from the other woman. 'I mean, I haven't got one, but I'm sure if I did I'd think he was very important. What's the matter with him?'

'Nothing. He's a genius, aced his SATS, highest GPA his high school's ever known, got an offer of a place at Yale.'

'So what's the problem?'

'He can't afford Yale. He can barely afford to go to Adirondacks U, and I don't want him to come here. He needs to get away, make his own life.'

'Can't he, I don't know, work his way through Yale or something?' Tabitha asked awkwardly.

Fiona looked at her as if she came from another planet. 'Do you have any idea how much tuition costs at an Ivy League school?'

Tabitha shook her head, dropping her eyes in shame. She'd never had it brought home to her so forcefully quite how privileged a life she'd led. Till the moment her father had hit her with his ultimatum, she'd never once had to worry about being able to afford anything. Money considerations hadn't featured anywhere in the equation of her life. Of course, that was all going to change the moment she failed this course. She fully appreciated for the first time what that might actually mean. What it would be like to have to think about money every moment of every day.

As if she was reading her thoughts, Fiona said, 'No, you've never had to think about that kind of thing, have you? And if you pass this year, you never will.'

Tabitha sighed. 'Except that I'm probably *not* going to pass.'

Fiona chewed her bottom lip as if not sure whether to let out the words she was considering or swallow them back down again. After a moment, she said, 'You will if I help you.'

'You helped me last semester, didn't seem to do much good.'

'I don't mean just telling you which chapter of the book to read.' The other woman's voice picked up confidence, committing to what she was saying. 'I'm talking about *real* help.'

'Cheating, you mean?' Tabitha said tentatively, wanting to be sure that was really what Fiona intended intended.

Fiona shrugged. 'Whatever you want to call it. I've already done the course you're doing and I've still got all my work on computer. I can just change it a little and you can hand it in as your own – it's not like Sinclair's ever going to notice. I'll even do it in your writing style.'

'And in return?' Tabitha asked, even though she had a sick feeling in the pit of her stomach that told her this was a very bad idea.

'When you get your allowance back, you give me some money for Charlie's school fees. It would only be a loan – we'd pay you back as soon as we could.'

'No.' Tabitha held up her hand to forestall Fiona's argument. 'No, if you need help, I'll give you help. You don't have to risk your career by cheating. Your brother can have whatever money he needs.'

'Except,' Fiona said, 'you're not going to *have* any money if you fail. And you're going to fail if I don't help you.'

'She's right, that's the problem.' Tabitha was curled in Jake's lap on his armchair. She ran her hand idly through his sandy hair, pulling the strands straight and watching them spring back into loose curls. 'So I said yes. Do you think I should tell her I've changed my mind?'

'I think you should close your eyes,' Jake told her.

She frowned. 'Why, is that going to help me make up my mind?'

'I've got you a present.' He eased her off his lap then stood and crossed to his large antique wardrobe.

Tabitha's heart leapt. 'Why? I mean, thanks – but why?'

'Close your eyes,' he repeated sternly. She did as he asked, and after a moment he continued, 'Because you gave me a Christmas present and I didn't get you anything. And because I wanted to.'

There was a sincerity in his voice that Tabitha knew was usually undercut by the gently mocking cynicism of his face. But with her eyes shut all she could hear was his voice and she let herself believe it.

She could hear him fumbling around inside the wardrobe, then the pad of his bare feet across the rug towards her. He pressed something soft into her hand. 'I'm supposed to guess what it is, right?'

'That's the general idea.' She felt him settle on to the ground at her feet, as if he thought it might take a while.

She ran the cloth through her hands, her fingers snagging on some threads, noting the changes in texture and material. 'It's a dress.'

He laughed. 'A dress? Come on, Tabby, you can do

better than that. I'm looking for designer and season at the very least.'

She smiled and continued to rub her present between her fingers, learning its outline. At the same time, she remembered a conversation she'd had with Jake last semester when she'd been flicking through a fashion magazine she'd bought to torment herself with. She'd told him how she wished she could afford to get something from the latest Valentino collection, because his clothes always fit her like a glove. But that would have cost a good thousand dollars. 'It's not . . . I mean, it can't be, but is it Valentino?' she asked hesitantly.

'Open your eyes,' he said, and she couldn't tell if he was pleased or upset.

She had been right. It was the Valentino she'd admired so much, a frothy confection in blue and green that managed to be youthful and elegant at the same time. She looked into Jake's eyes, feeling suddenly tearful. 'I can't believe you got me this, Jake, it must have cost your whole semester's allowance.'

'Actually,' he told her, standing up and offering a hand to pull her to her feet, 'I used all the money Mark gave me to buy a new computer and printer. So the least you can do is try it on.'

She didn't need any encouragement, shucking her jeans and T-shirt with such haste that she caught Jake grinning at her enthusiasm. As soon as she'd stripped down to her underwear, she slid the dress down over her head, material silkily caressing her body, a perfect fit. She turned to admire herself in Jake's full-length, twisting from side to side to get a glimpse of herself from every angle.

'What do you think?' Jake asked, sounding for once as if the answer really mattered to him.

'It's perfect,' she told him.

'Really?' he said critically. 'Because I think there's something missing.'

She looked down at herself, then back at the image in

the mirror, but the dress looked flawless to her. 'Like what?'

'Oh, I don't know – like maybe a matching pair of shoes.' He pulled out the most exquisite silver stilettos from under his bed.

Tabitha let out a squeal of excitement. 'Those are Gina!'

'Yeah, that's what it said on the label,' Jake drawled. 'Sit down and I'll put them on you.'

She perched on the edge of his bed and he raised each foot in turn in his hand, allowing his fingers to trail gently along her instep. The sensation was almost unbearably ticklish but also incredibly arousing. His fingers lingered as he slipped the shoes on to each foot, tracing the outline of her toes. She laughed softly and a little breathlessly. He stepped back and she stood up.

'They're beautiful, Jake,' she said seriously. 'And they go together perfectly.' Then she grinned impishly. 'Sensitivity and amazing fashion sense. Are you sure you're not gay?'

'You haven't seen my last present yet,' he said. He reached beneath the bed and pulled out one last item. Tabitha looked at it askance, wondering why he'd bought her two small pink balls to go with the very expensive designer clothes. Then she realised what they were and a light blush crept up her neck and into her cheeks.

Jake saw the blush and grinned wolfishly. 'I think it's traditional to say "you shouldn't have".' He stalked over to her, like a predator closing in on its prey, the love balls clasped in one hand, until he was close enough for her to feel the heat radiating from his body and to smell the musky aroused odour of him. 'Do you like your presents, Tabitha?' he asked huskily.

'I like them a lot,' she told him, running her hands underneath his fawn T-shirt and over the taut muscles of his stomach.

He nodded. 'That's because, unlike Mark, I know what women want.' He caught the hem of the dress and lifted it over her head in one sweeping gesture, then laid it gently on the armchair. 'I know what *you* want.'

As soon as her arms were free, Tabitha repeated the motion with his T-shirt, tossing it aside more carelessly. Then she worked on the fly of his jeans, fumbling until he took over and unzipped them easily, drawing them down over his legs. Wearing nothing but their underwear now they embraced again, her bra wispy enough that she could feel the crisp hairs of his chest through it, as the hard rod of his erection pressed eagerly into her groin. He kissed her roughly, his tongue taking firm possession of her mouth. She twisted her fingers into his hair, holding his head to her.

They kissed for a long time. The desire that built in Tabitha's body for something more was a turn-on its own right, frustration quickening her pulse and speeding her breathing. He pushed her backwards as they kissed until her legs collided with the edge of the bed and she sat then lay down as he pushed further, inching up the bed until she was spread-eagled, Jake lying on top of her. He pinned her hands above her head in one of his and drew back from her mouth to admire her.

Tabitha smiled sleepily up at him, though every nerve ending in her body was wide awake. He lowered his mouth to her breasts and suckled them through her ivory silk bra. The tips were already tight with arousal and when he nipped them between his teeth it was almost too painful, but he didn't let up and after a while she found that she'd forgotten the difference between pain and pleasure. She could feel the moisture gathering and falling from her centre, readying the way for the hardness pressing against it.

He released her hands and slid further down her body until his mouth was hovering over her centre and she could feel the moist warmth of his breath through the satin of her panties. Where he had been almost too rough with her breasts, here he was too gentle, using soft flicks of his tongue that would have been barely felt if they'd been on bare skin and, clothed as she was, were the merest whisper of sensation.

'Tease,' she groaned, but she heard the edge of real pleading in her voice, and she knew that he could hear it too.

He looked up at her, over the tiny swell of her belly. 'Want me to put them in, Tabitha?'

She'd never used toys like that before, had never really been into toys, but her whole body was a throb of desire and she wouldn't have refused him anything. 'Yes.' She lifted her hips to allow him to draw her panties down her legs and he paused, as he always did, to look at her exposed sex. The expression on his face was half-lust and half-wonder, as if for all his confidence he couldn't quite believe that Tabitha would allow him this intimacy. Then he used his fingers to gently pry her folds apart. She whimpered, so aroused that even that gentle touch was intensely felt.

The love balls weren't small. He had to work the first one gently against her entrance, rotating it until it was slick with her arousal and he could push it past the firm resistance of her muscles. Once the thickest part was inside, her body sucked the rest in then clenched tight around the cord connecting the two weighted balls, and Jake had to start the process again. The sensation was incredible, especially with the first ball inside her, an unaccustomed intrusion pressing against the most sensitive part of her.

When the second ball was inside she felt filled almost to overflowing. She groaned again. 'Oh God, that feels good.'

Jake ran his fingers lightly up the crease of her legs then over and around her clitoris. Her sex spasmed at the sensation, clenching around the balls, and the feel of them rock hard inside her caused another spasm, a wonderful richochet that didn't seem to want to stop, and to her amazement she was coming already, her toes arching with the strength of it.

When she came down the balls were still inside her and Jake's mouth was on her. She made a soft sound of protest, because she was still tender from the orgasm and she couldn't quite bear the feel of his lips against that flesh. But then once again the boundary between pleasure and pain seemed to blur and soon it was all pleasure. She could feel every curve of the balls inside her, every stroke of Jake's tongue against her skin, the even softer touch of his breath when he moved his mouth away for a second. She tangled her fingers in his hair, enjoying the silky feeling of that too.

Her second orgasm was slower to build, like an ember that had to be coaxed into flame. But when it ignited it lit a fire deep in her belly. It was almost too much. She felt out of control with the sensations and she wasn't sure that she liked being that much in Jake's power. But his lips and tongue kept on circling and nipping and there was no question of holding on. She was letting out a continual stream of sound, somewhere beyond consciousness she could hear it, but her head was too full of a sort of noiseless buzzing to pay any attention. The balls inside her seemed to grow larger and larger as her completion neared, until they were the only thing she could think about it. And then she clenched down once, hard, around them, and everything went very bright and then very dark.

It took her longer to come back to herself after the second climax. When she finally opened her eyes, it was to see Jake leaning over her, looking down intently into her face as he tugged on the cord that held the balls inside her. She almost protested at their loss, but she could feel his erection pressing insistently against her thigh and she wanted to feel that inside her more.

Jake obviously wanted that too. As soon as the balls were free, he threw them aside and put himself inside her in one hard thrust. She was a little sore from the intensity of her orgasms and the chafing of the balls and she was certain that there was no way she'd be able to come again, but there was a deeper sort of satisfaction to be had just from containing him within her. He bent his head to kiss her sloppily as he pumped in and out. She could taste herself on his mouth. He said something but the words were muffled against her lips and she wondered if he'd meant her to understand them.

She raked her nails down his back, hard enough to leave a mark, then sank them into the large muscles of his buttocks, guiding his pace, pulling him down to her. He gasped and gave one more fierce thrust before pulling out. 'On your hands and knees,' he gasped.

Tabitha was almost too tired to move, but she pulled herself up, turned her rump to face him, like an animal begging to be mounted. His hands dug into her hips as he found her centre once again and buried himself there. At the first thrust, she collapsed forwards on to the bed, arms too weak to hold her. She rested her head against her hands and just let herself be passive, allowing him to do all the work. He seemed happy to take control, speeding up as he filled her with a series of short shallow thrusts before he lost the beat altogether and a few seconds later he collapsed against her back, shouting out his orgasm as he pushed her down into the bed. His cock pulsed inside her and suddenly and unexpectedly she came again, like the aftershock of an earthquake.

After a few seconds, he rolled off her, pulling her down with him to nestle spooned against his stomach. His mouth was buried in the curve of her neck and she felt him press a few kisses against the skin there.

Tabitha enjoyed the peace for a few minutes, the mindless contentment of it. She loved the way that sex could do that. The way, even if only for a short while, that it banished everything else from her mind. But soon enough the worries of the day crowded back in. She turned round in Jake's arms until they were nose to nose.

He knew her well enough by now to raise a questioning eyebrow, recognising that she needed to talk. 'Fiona?' he asked.

She kissed him and nodded. 'Do you think I've done the right thing?'

He pressed a return kiss against her forehead. 'Of course. It's perfect. She can do what she's good at and leave you free to do what you're good at.'

'But what *am* I good at?' Tabitha asked him.

Jake grinned and ran a hand down her arm, tangling his fingers with hers when he reached her wrists. 'You're very good at this.'

Tabitha smiled back at him and allowed him to pull her back against him as he drifted into sleep. But part of her knew that wasn't an adequate answer. Or that, if it was, it didn't say anything very flattering about her.

Chapter Thirteen

Miles from Nowhere

'I only got a B minus!' Tabitha waved her paper on facial recognition accusingly at Fiona as they walked towards the canteen after class. The paths had been cleared of snow but it lay piled steeply on either side, a growing wall of ice.

'You mean *I* only got a B minus,' Fiona said.

'Yeah, exactly. What's the point of you doing my work for me if I'm still getting crappy grades?'

'The point is you're passing, and if you started getting A plusses no one would believe it was you doing it.'

Tabitha looked at her roommate out of the corner of her eye. 'Are you inferring I'm stupid?'

'No, I'm implying that you're not Einstein, and Professor Sinclair knows it.'

She looked like she was going to say something else but Tabitha nudged her in the ribs and nodded across the square where Professor O'Grady was approaching, long brown hair tucked beneath a woollen hat and thick scarf, the sort of unfashionable ensemble Tabitha would have once laughed at if she hadn't been wearing it herself. Winter here had been *unbelievable*, and the damn thing still wasn't over.

'Professor O'Grady,' Tabitha said neutrally. Outside of class she'd been avoiding the woman pretty studiously since she'd started dating Mark. No real reason, Tabitha just didn't like the way O'Grady always hung on Mark's arm, like an adoring acolyte rather than a fellow teacher, or the way that Mark would look O'Grady in the eye but not Tabitha.

'Just the person I was looking for,' O'Grady said, looking at Tabitha.

Tabitha's heart sank. 'I definitely handed that last paper in on time!' she protested. She had nearly all the English credit required for her degree, but she needed to pass O'Grady's class.

O'Grady smiled, disconcerting Tabitha still further. O'Grady *never* smiled at her unless it was a prelude to a joke at Tabitha's expense. 'Oh no, this isn't about class. I actually wanted to give you an invitation.'

'An invitation?'

The other woman nodded. 'I've finally convinced Mark to stop behaving like a disapproving Victorian patriarch with you and Jake.'

'Well, that's . . . thanks.'

'You're welcome. So I thought it would be nice if you and Jake could come away with Mark and myself this weekend, give us all a chance to get to know each other better. We've hired a little skiing lodge up at Lake Placid.'

Tabitha studied the other woman's face, but it didn't look like she was joking. 'That's a lovely idea,' she said insincerely, 'but I think I ought to concentrate on my studies. There's still plenty of catching up for me to do.'

'That's very commendable. But your grades have been much better this semester. Mark thinks so too. And Jake's already said yes, so you won't turn us down, will you?'

'Jake said yes?' Tabitha watched her breath cloud in front of her in the freezing air and wished she could float away from the situation with it.

O'Grady smiled. 'When has he ever been known to turn down a free skiing trip? Mark's driving – we'll pick you up from Jake's at eight tomorrow morning.' She walked off without bothering to ascertain if that was OK with Tabitha, as if Jake's agreement to the plan was all that really counted.

As soon as O'Grady was out of earshot, Fiona turned to Tabitha, her eyebrows raised. 'What's she playing at?'

Tabitha shook her head. 'I guess she's just being friendly.'

Fiona's eyebrows rose still further. 'If you believe that, you really *do* need my help.'

The drive to the cabin took under an hour, with Jake holding her hand for the entire journey, something he did very rarely and never in front of anyone else. Mark was at the wheel but O'Grady didn't miss any opportunity to brush against his arm or gently nudge his leg with her own. It already felt as if there was a subtext to this trip that only Jake and O'Grady – Paula – were privy to. Tabitha wondered what exactly Paula had said to Jake when she'd suggested it.

A few times during the journey she caught Mark's eyes watching her in the mirror, but as soon as she met them they flicked back to the road ahead and she couldn't see the rest of his face to read his expression.

Still, when they finally reached the cabin she had to admit she was impressed. She'd expected something small on the outskirts of town, but the place was like a miniature wood-clad palace, sprawling in the middle of its own five acres of forest. Mark set a fire while everyone else took the suitcases and skis into their rooms, Tabitha's a pair she'd begged from another student. By the time they all emerged again, the fire was crackling merrily in the grate and the scene looked deceptively domestic.

Jake slung his arm over Tabitha's shoulders as she came to stand beside him near the fire. She shot him a quizzical look, unused to these open displays of affection, but he wasn't looking at her he was looking at his brother, and when she glanced towards Paula she saw that she was looking at Mark too. Only Mark seemed oblivious to anyone else, prodding the fire with a poker to provoke it into sparks.

'Well, I don't know about anyone else, but I want to

get out on the slopes,' Paula said after a moment's more awkward silence. 'There's a green slope about ten minutes' drive away, Tabitha, or nursery slopes if that would suit you better.'

'Strictly double black for me,' Tabitha told her, trying to keep her tone as falsely friendly as the other woman's. 'I've been skiing since I was five.'

Paula arched a ruthlessly plucked eyebrow. 'In LA?'

'Believe it or not, they do let us out occasionally. To Europe, in my case.'

'Lucky old Europe,' Paula said, the malice barely hidden under a veneer of civility.

Tabitha thought that this was shaping up to be one of the longest weekends of her life.

Tabitha really did love skiing, always had. She took the first descent with Jake, jack-knifing round the corners as sharply as she could. When he cut her up on the second curve, she realised that this was a race and was childishly pleased when she beat him to the finish line.

She grinned as he skidded to a halt beside her a few seconds later. The trees were gloomy around them, crowding in on the pure white of the ski slopes, but the day was turning out to be more cheerful than she'd expected. Jake smiled up at her, then his eyes drifted away up the slope and she saw that he was watching his brother – who, it turned out, was a truly terrible skier. If anyone should have stuck to the green slopes, it was Mark.

Jake watched a few seconds longer as Mark staggered towards the bottom, then he hooked an arm around her and pulled her in against him for a kiss, his lips ice-cold against hers but his tongue and breath warm. A few minutes later, Mark skidded to a halt beside them, barely keeping to his feet.

'You certainly haven't gotten any better at this,' Jake said to his brother, drawing his lips away from her.

'No, I don't think I have,' Mark replied. Something in

his voice suggested they were talking about something other than skiing.

Over the course of the morning, they drifted apart to find challenges which suited their individual abilities. The area was home to a fantastic selection of slopes and Tabitha set herself the aim of trying each of them at least once over the next two days. She was about to attempt her seventh when she saw someone sliding on to his ass on a slope below her and after a moment recognised the dark-blue and purple ski jacket belonging to Mark. As Tabitha watched, he dragged himself to his feet – only to fall inelegantly back down again.

Tabitha looked around, but there was no sign of Paula, who was every bit as good a skier as she thought she was and had apparently lost patience with baby-sitting her boyfriend. Jake was nowhere to be seen either, probably enjoying a beer somewhere in town. He too was a competent skier, but true to character was more of a fan of the *après* than the actual skiing.

Tabitha hesitated a moment, then pushed off with her sticks and cut across open ground to reach Mark. She glided to a stop beside him as he finally made it to his feet. 'Jake's not kidding,' she said. 'You really do suck at this.'

'Really? I thought I was doing so well.'

Curls of Mark's fair hair were poking through the hood of his top, and Tabitha felt an unexpected urge to brush them back into place with her fingers. They just looked so *untidy*.

'You could try taking lessons. Or is that idea just too radical?'

'I've tried lessons. The instructor told me I was a lost cause. No natural sense of balance.'

She could have just accepted that, skied away and left him to his own devices, but she found that she didn't want to part company from him so soon, so she said, 'Why don't you follow me, do what I do, and we'll see if that works?' Here, away from the college and away from Jake, it was easier to speak to Mark as if they really might be friends.

He shook his head. 'There's no need. I don't want to slow you down.'

'It's no problem. Think of it as a thank you for not kicking me off the course at the end of last semester.'

He looked at her suspiciously, bright-blue eyes narrowed to slits. 'You just want to see me fall on my ass again.'

She grinned. 'Yeah, that too.' Then she pushed off, careful to keep her pace slow, and eased down the gentle slope.

Mark managed about a hundred yards this time before tumbling helplessly to the ground. He looked so indignant sitting there, one foot splayed to the side, the other stuck out in front of him, skis scattered to either side, that Tabitha couldn't help laughing.

'Oh, you think that's funny, do you?' He was smiling broadly and Tabitha didn't think she'd ever seen him so relaxed.

'I think it's hilarious,' she told him. She was taken totally by surprise when a large ball of snow hit her square in the face and stood there open mouthed and blinking before she'd quite registered that Mark of all people had thrown a snowball at her. He was laughing too now, head thrown back in a carefree gesture she wouldn't have thought him capable of.

'You should see your face,' he gasped.

'A sitting target really shouldn't start a snowball fight,' she told him, bending to put together the biggest wettest snowball she could manage. She made as if to throw it at him – then skied straight up to him and deposited it down the back of his jacket. He roared and leapt to his feet – only to fall immediately back down, on to his face this time.

Tabitha was laughing so hard at that that she finally lost her footing and her skis too, tumbling down to fall on her tailbone with a hard jolt. They sat there, ten feet apart, until their laughter had finally subsided. Tabitha felt warm with it, as if something inside her had physically melted the ice between her and Mark.

When she was completely in control of herself she got carefully to her feet, put her skis back on, then went over to help Mark. He was a big man, but she felt him using the power of his legs to lever himself up and he only let her take a little of his weight on her arm. When he'd found his feet, his fingers lingered for a moment inside hers. They were both wearing gloves, but it still felt like a disturbingly intimate contact. She lifted her eyes and found his looking straight back, another contact more intimate than it should have been.

Very clearly, she found herself thinking, I'm with the wrong brother. But that was ridiculous. She barely knew Mark and what she did know she didn't like. For his part, he'd shown little evidence of thinking of her with anything other than contempt. Just because they'd had a moment of fun together didn't mean that they were suddenly bonded for life.

Still, he didn't let go of her hand and she didn't look away from his startling blue eyes.

They were standing like that when Jake and Paula found them and Tabitha knew that the way she guiltily pulled her hand back from Mark's made it look far worse than it actually was. Then they were all talking and Jake was teasing his brother for his clumsiness and challenging Tabitha to an off-piste race and Paula was offering to show Mark how to do a snow plough *again*, and maybe it had all been in Tabitha's mind. Except that she knew that it wasn't. And from the way Mark's eyes followed her as she skied away with Jake into the surrounding trees, she knew that he knew it too.

When they finished the day's skiing, Tabitha found herself alone in the cabin. Mark and Paula had gone into town to buy some food and drink for the evening, and

Jake had stayed outside to collect a little more firewood. Tabitha felt exhausted from the day's exercise and she lay down on the bed still fully clothed and allowed herself to drift off into the pleasant twilight zone between waking and sleeping.

Except that today the only thing waiting for her there was that image of Mark, looking into her eyes so intently as he held her hand. She sighed and got up. There was only one bathroom in the cabin but it held a big tiled shower stall and she thought that a long hot shower might wash away the uncomfortable thoughts as well as the grime of the day.

She turned the water up almost unbearably hot at first, enjoying the scorch of it on her chilled skin, the contrast with the cool of the tiles when she leant her back and buttocks against them. In that position the powerful spray of the shower hammered straight into her sex and, despite her exhaustion, she found that she was becoming aroused. She squirted a dollop of soap into her hand, then ran it down her arms, over her belly, round and between her breasts, enjoying the sensuality of it. Her eyes slid shut and she let her mind drift, but it returned again to that image of Mark, only now it was mixed with an earlier image of him she hadn't even realised she'd stored so precisely, the way he'd looked when she'd seen him emerging from his bathroom, nothing but a towel around his waist. The precise muscles of his stomach and the light dusting of hair over his chest and around his nipples. She imagined him stepping into the shower with her, touching her where her own hands were touching herself, and it turned her on even more.

She didn't want to have this fantasy, but now she'd thought it she couldn't seem to unthink it, and she was too turned on now just to stop. Instead she tried to turn the fantasy to something else, to change Mark for Jake. But then she just found herself imagining both Jake *and* Mark in the shower with her, and that was something she really didn't want to be getting herself off thinking about.

Her eyes opened, frustrated at her inability to control her own thoughts – and saw Jake's staring straight back at her.

She let out a small startled yelp. 'What the hell are you doing?'

'If you will leave the door unlocked.' He was as naked as she was, the perfect shape of his body, tapered waist leading into lean legs and his cock already half-ready for her. His face was wreathed in the steam from the shower, mouth quirked in a smile of pure mischief, like a water spirit. 'I'm wounded you started without me.'

He looked downwards and she realised that one of her hands was still at her sex, her fingers parting its folds. She blushed and tried to move it away but his hand covered hers, curving one of her fingers with his to gently insert it into her body. She let out a low groan, this unexpected reality coupled with her fantasy almost too much for her to deal with.

In silence now, he moved behind her, taking the soap into his own hands and repeating her early motions, running them over her arms, her belly, her breasts. He lingered on the nipples, touching them lightly with just the tips of his fingers and then squeezing them hard. All the while her own finger was still moving inside her, keeping rhythm with his motions. Her head fell back weakly against his shoulder.

'You're a very dirty girl, Tabitha, have I ever told you that?' he whispered in her ear. One of his hands kept toying with her breast, the other drifted lower, pausing to swirl inside her belly button, making her squirm and smile, and then lower still to join hers on her sex. He circled her clit, the joint stimulation of her finger and his allowing her to focus only on the sensations, not the identity of the person evoking them. Then his hand moved again, round to her buttocks. He squeezed them rhythmically, a deep hard massage that pulled at the flesh of her centre. Then he put a dollop of soap on his index finger and slowly eased it inside the small puckered hole there, a new intrusion that her mind wasn't entirely comfortable with but her body obviously wanted, because she found her hips swaying involuntarily backwards and forwards between the twin invaders, her finger and his.

Her eyes were closed to the world and water was pouring down over her head, disorienting her. She didn't feel him turn her round, only realised it had happened when she felt something larger and harder push forwards to fill her sex and realised that the foreplay was over and now he was fucking her.

He pressed her back against the tiled wall of the shower, hooked his hands underneath her buttocks and lifted her till the angle of penetration was perfect. But the wall was slippery and so was the floor and it was hard to keep the position. He started to ease her back down again, so Tabitha wrapped her legs around his waist and dug her nails into his back to urge him on.

Every stroke of his pushed her into the wall, hard enough that she was sure her skin would be marked with the square pattern of tiles. She dug her nails in deeper, determined to mark him too. It just seemed to spur him on and he pushed into her harder and harder, grunting with effort on each thrust. She was groaning too and she was just coherent enough to realise that it was very loud. Loud enough to be heard over the sound of the water raining down around them. But there was no way they were stopping, not when they were both so close.

And then it was over for him before it was over for her, and either his knees collapsed or he lost his footing because they both went sliding down to the shower floor, his legs folded beneath him and her still impaled on him. The landing drove his flesh even deeper into her and it was enough, more than enough, to send her over the edge too. Her scream of satisfaction echoed round the tiled room.

A few seconds later, she started laughing and he did too, though it soon turned to a drowned sort of spluttering in the water cascading all around them and they were forced to finally climb out of the shower. Tabitha was hoping that he would dry her off, a nice intimate finale to the more physical prelude. But he just grabbed a towel and patted his hair dry before slinging it around his waist, so she was forced to do the same.

'I don't think I feel any cleaner,' she told him, tucking her own towel just above her breasts.

He smiled, but it looked half-hearted. She wanted to ask what the matter was, then decided that the steamy bathroom just wasn't the right venue. She opened the bathroom door – and nearly walked into Mark's arms.

It hadn't occurred to her that anyone else might be home yet. She took a startled step back into the doorway, bumping into the emerging Jake, and her towel came loose and began to shimmy down her body. She grabbed it and hastily pulled it back up, clutching it tightly around her, but she was damn sure that Mark had got a good look at everything first.

'Sorry,' she said. 'I didn't realise you were there.'

'Obviously,' Mark said icily, his eyes on his brother.

'We were just –' Tabitha began, then realised there was almost nowhere she could go with that. Her eyes slid away from Mark's face but the only other place they seemed to want to go was the tense angry lines of his body, and she ended up looking intently at the wall just over his left shoulder. 'We thought we'd save on hot water, make sure there was enough for you and Paula.'

He waved his hand in a dismissive gesture, telling her not only that he didn't believe her excuses but that he wasn't interested in hearing them. 'Paula's cooking steaks,' he said flatly. 'They'll be ready in ten so make sure you are too.' He disappeared down the corridor and Tabitha ducked into the bedroom before Paula could emerge and make some pointed remark too.

Jake followed her in but stayed in the doorway, blocking

it. She realised that *his* body was tense with anger too, though she couldn't imagine what she'd done to piss him off in the two or three minutes since they'd both had a very satisfactory orgasm together.

'*We thought we'd save on hot water,*' he mimicked.

Tabitha shrugged, using the gesture to slip her blouse down over her arms. 'Sorry – I suck at making excuses.' She scrabbled through her suitcase, trying to find the Armani pants she'd packed to make sure she had something as elegant as Paula to wear for dinner.

'Why do you *need* to make an excuse?' He'd started getting dressed himself but his body was still so stiff with annoyance that she half-expected his clothes to snag and tear on the sharp angry angles of it.

'Well . . .' Tabitha realised that she didn't have a good answer, but she attempted one anyway. 'Because he's on our case all the time and I didn't want to make it any worse.'

'It's none of his damn business!' Jake said fiercely. His wide mouth was squeezed into a thin hard line.

'No, you're right, it's not.' Tabitha went to him and rested a hand on his arm, but she could still feel the muscles knotted beneath it and they didn't relax. 'I'm sorry. I'm not ashamed of what's going on between us, if that's what you're thinking.'

'Fine, whatever.' He put his hand on the door handle as if he was intending to leave the room with whatever this was still simmering between them.

She yanked his arm angrily and spun him round to face her. 'For God's sake, Jake! I just got a surprise when I saw him, that's all. I mean, you could at least have told me he was home.'

'Why? Why would that have made a difference to anything?' He pulled his arm free from hers and they stood fuming at each other two feet apart. Jake was the first to look away. 'Sorry. I'm sorry.'

She relaxed a little but she didn't want to let this drop. 'Really, Jake, what is this all about?'

He shook his head and she thought he wasn't going to answer. Then he looked up, his golden-brown eyes wide. They were usually like an open book to her, but this time she couldn't read them at all. 'I love you, Tabitha. I didn't mean to, but I do.'

'You *what*?' She realised as soon as she'd said it that it was the worst possible response. But one minute they'd been at each other's throat, and now *this*? She didn't know how to process it, let alone deal with it.

Jake's mouth curled as if he'd put something foul tasting in it. Then he walked out of the door and slammed it behind him.

Chapter Fourteen

New York State of Mind

'I just didn't know what to say to him.'

Fiona rolled her eyes. '"I love you too" is the traditional response.'

'But do I?'

'*Don't* you?'

Tabitha flopped back down on her bed, staring at the ceiling rather than at the question she couldn't answer in the other woman's eyes. 'I don't know. It's just – I've never let myself think about it, you know? Jake and me, it's never been a hearts and roses kind of relationship. He's never even called me his girlfriend – and now he's telling me that he loves me. It's like we've gone from zero to sixty without passing through two to fifty-nine along the way.'

'You're overthinking it,' Fiona told her. 'It isn't a question you analyse. You either do or you don't.'

Tabitha tried to think about what she did feel for Jake. She cared about him, she knew that. And the sex was – well, the sex was fantastic, there was no doubt about that. She enjoyed his company, he made her laugh, she made him laugh. And then she realised that she was doing exactly what Fiona had told her not to do, analysing it. So did she love him? But that just brought her back round to the beginning, thinking, I like his company, he makes me laugh . . .

Tabitha sighed then rolled off the bed and over to her wardrobe, scrabbling in the bottom to find the small wallet she'd secreted there right back at the start of her first semester. 'There's only one solution to a problem like this – shopping.'

'You haven't got any money,' Fiona reminded her.

'No. But my dad has.' Tabitha opened the wallet and held out a fan of plastic.

Fiona frowned. 'I thought you said he cut up all your credit cards?'

'He did. But being a man, he forgot all about my store cards. I've been saving them for the new season – which by my reckoning starts around now. We should be able to max them out before he notices. So, want to spend the weekend shopping?'

'Hang on,' Fiona said, peering at the cards. 'Aren't those all Manhattan stores?'

Tabitha grinned. 'Yep. It's time for a road trip.'

Tabitha stood on the sidewalk of Fifth Avenue, feeling like an explorer who'd just returned to civilisation after months lost in the jungle. The crowd surged around her and she took a moment to soak it all in. Then she grabbed Fiona's arm and led her towards Saks, as good a place to start as any.

Fiona looked bemused and a little alarmed, like an emissary from some isolated tribe being shown the wonders of the modern world. She'd confessed to Tabitha that she'd only been down to New York three times in her life, and one of those had been a school trip to the Natural History Museum.

'Are you really sure this is a good idea?' Fiona asked nervously. 'Are you certain your dad isn't going to have you arrested when he realises what you've done?'

Tabitha took a moment to consider it. 'Maybe, but that's OK, I won't tell anyone you were involved. I ain't no rat.'

Fiona smiled weakly as they pushed through the big swing doors into the store.

'First,' Tabitha told her, 'we're going to get you some new PJs, because the ones you've been wearing are frankly criminal. Then we're going to start on your shoes, and we'll work our way up your body from there.'

Fiona stopped in her tracks. 'I thought we were looking for clothes for *you.*'

Tabitha shook her head. 'Shopping for other people is so much more fun.' She headed determinedly for the lingerie and nightwear department. She thought they could pick up some new bras and panties for Fiona while they were there, ones which didn't look like the next generation of chastity belt.

Fiona trailed reluctantly after her. 'Basically, this has all been an excuse to finally give me that make-over.'

'It's the only thing I'm good at. And it's the least I can do for you.'

They ended up getting two pairs of PJs, two bras – one black and one purple – and six silk panties. Then they hit the shoe department. Fiona stared down dubiously at the Jimmy Choos Tabitha had insisted she try on, as if wondering whether they really were intended to be worn on her feet, but when she looked back up at Tabitha she asked a different question. 'Do you really think shopping is all you're good at?'

'No, I'm good at wearing the clothes I buy too,' Tabitha said airily. 'And I throw a mean party – when I've got the resources.'

Fiona shook her head impatiently. 'No, I mean it. There must be something else.'

Tabitha concentrated on picking out some Jil Sanders wedges for Fiona to try on, avoiding her friend's eyes. 'I know what I'm not good at,' she said eventually. 'Studying.'

'That's hard to argue with,' Fiona said wryly. 'What does Jake say you're good at?'

'I thought we came here so I could stop thinking about him.'

'No,' Fiona said, 'we came here so you could make your mind up about him. What does *he* think your talents are?'

Tabitha blushed lightly. 'Well . . .'

Fiona rolled her eyes. 'Apart from that.'

That was another question Tabitha realised she didn't have the answer to. She thought about it all through their short walk to Allesandro Dell'Acqua on Madison Avenue.

'What does Adam think you're good at?' she asked Fiona as the other girl slipped a white jacket over her shoulders. The pair of them were surrounded by bags of already purchased goods and they'd soon have to make a trip to Fiona's car to unburden themselves of some of it.

'He admires my mind,' Fiona said, then scowled when Tabitha laughed. 'No, really. He's – I guess he's a feeler, and I'm a thinker, which seems to work for us. And he thinks I'm a great cook, which I am. And he says I always buy good presents. He says it's because I understand people so I know what they'll want. I'm not the kind of person who just buys other people what I'd want to get myself.'

Her words made Tabitha think back to the present she'd bought for Mark and given to Jake, the one Jake hadn't appreciated at all. 'I guess Jake and I don't really know each other that well,' she admitted. 'He's not an easy person to get to know.' That was true about Mark as well, but, though Mark was more obviously closed off than Jake, she thought that Jake kept more hidden beneath his veneer of easy openness.

'What about you?'

'Oh,' Tabitha said, 'I'm an open book.' But then she thought about Jake and Mark, both at different times looking into her face as if they were trying to read something there in a language they couldn't quite grasp. 'At least, I think I am.'

'What is it that you like about Jake, if you don't understand him.'

That was an easy one. 'He's fun to be around. We have a good time together.'

'He reminds you of your life back in LA,' Fiona suggested.

'Yeah, in a way.'

'And he's easy to be with because he doesn't expect anything of you except having fun together.'

Tabitha thought about Mark, who always seemed to expect more of her than she was able or willing to give. 'What's wrong with that?'

'Nothing.' Fiona turned sideways to admire the jacket in the mirror then grimaced as she noticed the way the material pulled under her breasts. 'I'm just trying to help you decide what you think about him.'

'Do *you* like him?' Tabitha asked. It had never occurred to her to ask her friend the question before. And in the other girl's suddenly closed expression she had her answer. 'You don't, do you?'

'It's whether you like him that counts.'

'But why don't you like him?'

Fiona sighed and sat down on a nearby bench, clearly realising that she wasn't going to be able to get out of answering. 'It's not that I don't like him. I just ... I don't know if I trust him.'

Tabitha felt a sick feeling in the pit of her stomach. In the early days of her relationship with Jake she hadn't really been bothered by the thought of him sleeping with other people. Lately she'd chosen not to think about whether it was happening or not. 'Do you know something I don't?' She wasn't sure what answer she wanted.

Fiona shook her head. 'It's not that. What I mean is, I think Jake comes first in Jake's world, and he'll tell you whatever he thinks will get him what he wants.'

'Well, it's not like he had to tell me he loves me to get in my pants,' Tabitha said a little angrily, because Fiona's words rang uncomfortably true. 'He didn't have to buy the cow, he's already getting the milk.'

'Exactly. So why *did* he say it?' Then, seeing Tabitha's closed-off expression, she said, 'I'm sorry. Like I said, what I think of him doesn't matter. The question is whether you love him or not.'

Tabitha looked away. 'But you're saying that if I did love him it would be a mistake.'

Fiona laid a hand on Tabitha's arm, her expression soft. 'I don't want you to get hurt.'

Tabitha made to answer, then realised that the insistent sound she could hear was a phone ringing, and that it was coming from one of the bags on the floor. Fiona registered it too. 'Mine,' she said.

The conversation that followed was short, but Tabitha was amazed at the way Fiona's expression changed during it, like a light had been switched on somewhere inside her. It made her look almost beautiful. When she'd finished, though, she looked at Tabitha contritely. 'I'm sorry, I'm going to have to head back right away. Adam's got a couple of days' shore leave and he's coming over to see me. Do you mind?'

Tabitha shook her head, smiling. 'That's great news. You go home. I'll stay here tonight and catch the coach back tomorrow.'

'Are you sure?'

Tabitha nodded and Fiona gave her a quick hug. 'Don't worry about what I've been saying,' Fiona told her. 'I've always been a crappy judge of character. If you love Jake, then go for it, life's too short not to give things a chance.'

Tabitha nodded, but all she could think about as she helped the other woman carry their purchases to the car was the way Fiona's face had looked as she'd talked to Adam, the startling joy on it. Tabitha wondered if she'd ever looked like that when she was speaking to Jake.

Though snow-free, Manhattan was still bitterly cold, but Tabitha found that she didn't want to continue shopping now Fiona was gone, so she went for a walk in Central Park, winding through the Rambles and across the big open playing fields before walking a circuit of the reservoir. The things Fiona had said were circling round in her head, but they didn't make anything clearer. Was Fiona right that Jake couldn't be trusted? He'd never given her a reason not to trust him, but then he was hardly Mr Dependable either.

That made her think of Mark, who was precisely Mr Dependable. She couldn't imagine him ever not keeping his word. That was the trouble with him, she supposed – he held everyone to the same high standards he adhered to, but not everyone else was able to meet them. She'd always felt judged when she was with him. She thought back to what Fiona had asked, about whether Jake expected anything of her. Mark seemed to expect a whole lot of her, but she wasn't sure that was a good thing. Who wanted to be with someone who made them feel bad about themselves? And the whole line of thought was ridiculous anyway, because when had being with Mark ever been a possibility? She was wasting her time thinking about the wrong brother.

But thinking about Mark made her remember a conversation they'd had over a late dinner one night, a stupid West Coast v. East Coast thing. She'd claimed that LA had to be the best place to live in the country because it had the best weather, not to mention the Pacific. And he'd said he loved New York because of the chess players in Central Park. He liked how intellectual New York was. It was a city that thought far too much, and that wasn't something you could ever say about LA.

She doubted there'd be any players out today, especially now the sun was beginning to slink beneath the grey clouds on the horizon, but she still found herself heading towards the Pavilion where he'd told her the chess players met.

It was as deserted as she'd expected. She sat down at one of the tables anyway and looked at the board, wondering what it would be like to be a great chess player. Simpler than life, that was for sure. So many possible moves, but at least you knew exactly what they were and where they might lead.

'I thought you told me you'd never played chess in your life,' a voice said behind her. She didn't need to turn around to see who it was, but she did anyway. He was running a hand back through his barley-coloured hair, his normally unreadable face showing obvious surprise at seeing her, and maybe something else. Tabitha, on the other hand, wasn't surprised to see Mark at all. For some reason, she'd almost been expecting him.

Chapter Fifteen

Stumble and Fall

Mark, it turned out, was in town for an academic conference at NYU. He told her what it was about over an apple martini in the bar of the Mandarin Oriental but she didn't really pay any attention, just enjoyed the sweeping view out over the Manhattan skyline. She wasn't quite sure why she'd accepted his invitation to a drink, except that with Fiona gone she was all alone and it was nice to see a friendly face, or at least a familiar one.

'What are you doing here?' he asked. 'Visiting friends?'

'No,' she told him, 'something much more important than that.' At his frown, she held up her cache of store cards. 'Shopping.'

'I thought you didn't have any money.'

She put the cards away. 'It's only a temporary injection of funds. So, have you got any more psychologising to be doing, or are you all finished for the day.'

'Finished,' he told her.

'I guess now you're planning to find the biggest dullest museum in the city, then head to bed in a couple of hours with a warm cocoa and a good book. Probably about retrograde amnesia.'

He smiled slightly. 'Why, did you have any better ideas?'

Tabitha realised with a shock that they were flirting with each other, and couldn't quite figure out how or why, except that they were away from Adirondacks U and away from Jake and the normal rules didn't seem to apply. She studied Mark across the table, the strong lines of his cheekbones and the controlled line of his mouth.

Mark seemed to realise what they were doing too, and she could almost see the shutters coming down over his eyes as he pulled back from it. 'I can give you a ride back if you need one,' he told her, all professional distance again. 'Assuming you've got somewhere to stay tonight.'

She smiled. 'Don't worry, I'm not planning on sleeping out in Central Park – I've got enough cash for a cheap room somewhere. And, as far as better plans go, I was thinking about hitting the bars down in the Meatpacking District and maybe finding a club later.'

'Nothing too cultural then.' He relaxed a little. She realised that he'd always enjoyed teasing her, but he did it with such a straight face it was sometimes difficult to tell if he really meant it.

'Not if I can avoid it.'

They sat in silence for a few minutes and Tabitha was on the point of offering him some money for the drink then heading out into the city. Except that things seemed more relaxed between them than they had been since that awful Christmas Eve. And, if things were getting more serious with her and Jake, it seemed like a good idea to patch things up with his brother. Or at least, that was what she told herself.

'Tell you what,' she said and he looked up from his drink, startled, as if he'd forgotten she was there. 'I'll swallow some culture if you'll have some fun.'

He tipped his head to the side, clearly not sure what she meant.

'You can take me to a museum or a gallery or whatever,' she clarified. 'And, in return, you let me take you to a bar.'

His eyes narrowed and at first she thought that he was going to brush her off, but after a moment of internal debate – maybe the same debate she'd had with herself – he nodded. 'OK. But you have to actually look at the paintings. It's not good enough just to walk past them.'

* * *

He took her to MOMA, perhaps on the assumption that she'd be more inclined to pay attention to works of art which didn't also require a history lesson. At first, Tabitha was more struck by the building itself than the paintings. She loved the balcony that gave a vertiginous view down over the central well, and the clinical whiteness of it all.

'It kind of reminds me of LA,' she told Mark, feeling a sudden stab of homesickness.

He leant over the balcony so far she had to fight an urge to grab his arm and pull him back from the edge. 'The architect was actually Japanese.'

'Yeah, I know.'

He peered round at her, surprised, and she waved the small leaflet they'd picked up at the entrance.

'It says in the guidebook. I guess it does look kind of Japanese too. It's very . . . precise.'

His smile widened at that. They sauntered off through the exhibition, not following any particular route, just heading towards any display that looked interesting. She wasn't surprised to find that he knew a great deal about modern art. Still, 'If you like this stuff so much,' she asked him, 'why haven't you got more of it in your house?'

'I like a lot of modern art because it disturbs me. That's what one of the COBRA school of artists said, that art had to work at both poles. It couldn't just be pretty, it had to be pretty and ugly at the same time, or comforting and disturbing, if it was going to be complete. But I don't really want something that makes me feel vaguely uneasy hanging on my wall.'

Tabitha thought about her and Jake and it occurred to her that they had a relationship which was just at one pole. They had fun, they laughed, they had sex – all the easy things in life. But the harder things they never seemed to tackle. She shook her head to drive out the thought, and listened to Mark instead as he talked about a new display of African tribal masks which on closer inspection turned out to be images of Ronald McDonald.

It was fully dark by the time they strolled through the West Village. It wasn't an area Tabitha had spent much time in before and she was charmed by the quaint tree-lined look of it. She liked it because it wasn't like anything you found in LA. Again, she found her thoughts returning to Jake, and to what Fiona had said about him, that Jake was very like her. Mark wasn't at all. He had his head down, lost in his own thoughts, his profile sharp. He was as different from her as Wiltshire Boulevard was from Lexington Avenue.

She suddenly noticed a sign outside one of the bars and took Mark's arm to stop him walking on. He started slightly at the touch of her fingers and she found herself looking at them a moment where they rested against his wrist before lowering them again.

'What's wrong?' he asked.

She grinned. 'Nothing, we're just gonna make a stop here.'

'Why?'

She pointed at the sign. 'Because this may be my only chance to whupp your ass at pool.'

He raised an eyebrow. 'That's what you think is going to happen, is it?'

'You should have pretended not to know how to play and then hustled me,' she told him an hour later when he'd beaten her five times in a row. They'd had a couple of beers each by then, and Tabitha was feeling a pleasant buzz. She'd finally managed to stop thinking about Jake or about anything really except enjoying the moment.

'I'm not that dishonest,' he told her. 'And I don't need the money.'

'It's not about the money. It's about taking me down a peg.'

'Oh, I think I've done that fairly effectively,' he said,

and she slapped him playfully on the arm. He shook his head disapprovingly but didn't retaliate. He was leaning against his pool cue, top button of his blue shirt unbuttoned in the heat of the bar, beer bottle clasped in his other hand, and it was the first time she'd ever seen him looking like a regular guy.

'You know,' she told him, 'you're almost a normal person when you relax.'

His mouth quirked in a smile. 'And what am I the rest of the time?'

She shrugged, suddenly uncomfortable, because the real answer was *Jake's brother*. 'Why don't you relax more?' she asked him instead. 'Or is that one of the questions that's going to make you walk out of here and start treating me like the shit beneath your shoe again?'

He laid the pool cue carefully back in the rack. When he turned back to her, she saw a novel expression on his face: remorse. 'I'm sorry I – I overreacted back at Christmas. I don't –' He shrugged. 'There are some things I prefer not to talk about.'

'Why?' she asked, genuinely curious. 'Does that actually make them hurt less?'

He stared at her, then shook his head. 'No, it doesn't. But I'm still not going to talk about them.'

'Maybe you should make a list of all the questions I can't ask you. It might save a few awkward moments.'

He laughed and held out his hand to her. She saw that he'd picked up a couple of table tennis rackets for the small courts at the end of the big pool hall. 'I'd rather make a list of all the ways I'm going to wipe the floor with you.'

In fact, Tabitha turned out to be better at table tennis, beating him three games to one. She would have liked to change her clothes after the game, though she hadn't really raised much of a sweat, but they'd had another beer each by then and moving on to another bar ended up seeming like a better idea. The place they found was in the Meatpacking District and full of the kind of New

Yorkers who gave New York a bad name. For the first time since she'd come east, Tabitha felt herself being judged for not wearing the right clothes or choosing the right shoes.

Mark was also casting a disapproving eye over the other patrons. 'I bet these are your kind of people,' he said.

Tabitha felt vaguely insulted. 'What makes you say that?'

He shrugged. 'They look like they spend more time thinking about what clothes they're wearing than about any other single thing in their lives.'

Now Tabitha definitely did feel insulted. 'And that's how you see me, is it?'

'Well, what else do you think about?' He was leaning forward on the bar, shirtsleeves rolled up, arms crossed and muscles knotted. His third or fourth beer was in his hand. He definitely didn't seem drunk, but there was no doubt the alcohol had loosened him up. He looked, she thought, a little dangerous.

'I think about a lot of things.'

He raised an eyebrow.

She felt a knot of hurt untangle itself inside her, realising that he was just teasing her. She leant on the bar beside him, head resting on her hand, face only a few inches from his. He didn't pull back. 'I think about how my make-up's looking. And I think about my hair. And I spend a lot of time thinking about my shoes.'

'Clearly you have hidden depths.' He smiled, but his eyes darkened and his smile slipped as he studied her. He started to say something, stopped, then seemed to make up his mind to say it anyway. 'What is it that you see in my brother?'

It was as if he'd splashed cold water in Tabitha's face. She leant back away from him but he kept his gaze locked on her, not letting her get away without answering. 'He's fun,' she told him. 'He's easy-going. He makes me feel good about myself.'

Mark took a slug of his beer, allowing his eyes to slide from hers. 'The complete opposite of me, in other words.' His tone was carefully neutral.

Tabitha reached a hand out to touch his arm. He flinched slightly but she didn't move it. 'Yeah, you're very different. But you don't make me feel bad about myself, not really. Or at least, you only make me feel bad about the bits of me I *ought* to feel bad about.'

He shook his head, bringing his other hand up to touch hers, resting his fingers against hers where they rested against the bare flesh of his forearm. 'I don't think there are any parts of you you ought to feel bad about.'

'So you think I'm perfect the way I am?' Tabitha intended it as a light joke, but somehow it came out sounding like a real question.

He looked at her a long time before answering. 'I think Jake's lucky to have you.'

His hand moved from on top of hers and hers fell from his arm. Since she'd first met Mark that was what she'd been wanting to hear. She tried to feel happy that he'd actually said it. The music in the bar was some slow number by Coldplay and she felt a sudden urge to ask him to dance but it wasn't that kind of bar or that kind of song. 'Want a nightcap back at my hotel?' she said instead. 'Get away from all these people who remind you so much of all those bits of me you don't think I should feel bad about.'

He smiled, seemingly glad of the distraction. 'Where *is* your hotel?'

'Actually, I don't have one yet, so it can be anywhere that's convenient. And cheap.'

'My hotel's only a few blocks away,' he said. 'Why don't we go there?'

She could see in his eyes that he knew this was a bad idea, that they should have just said their goodbyes and maybe shared a car drive back to Crystal Lake tomorrow. She knew it was a bad idea too – but she said yes anyway.

* * *

The place he was staying was a little boutique establishment down in Tribeca. 'You've found somewhere that looks just like your home,' she said, looking around at the tasteful antique-decorated lobby and old-fashioned furnishings. 'It's like you never left Crystal Lake.'

'I know what I like,' he said quietly, very deliberately not looking at her as he said it. He nodded to her left, where a gothic arch led into an area of plush leather armchairs and discreet lighting. 'The bar's that way.'

She very deliberately didn't look at him as she said, 'But isn't there a minibar in your room?'

He turned to her at that, his expression for once not hiding anything. She couldn't quite believe they'd gotten to this point so quickly, but she ached with desire for him, a desire that was somehow as much emotional as physical. There was a lump of guilt in her chest about Jake, but wasn't this answering her question for her, about whether she loved him or not? And they'd never made any promises to each other. She'd never once asked him about other women, and she was quite sure there had been some, though the part of her that couldn't lie to itself told her that *other women* and *your brother* were two very different categories.

Then Mark put his hands on her shoulders and his mouth on hers and she didn't have to think about anything else any more. His lips were demanding against hers, and she'd probably have guessed they would be if she'd allowed herself to spend any time imagining this. His hips pressed her back uncomfortably against the wall of the lobby and she could feel the eyes of the hotel staff on them, but none of that mattered because they were in their own private universe where only the two of them existed. She couldn't believe how turned on she was, just from this. But it wasn't what he was doing, it was who was doing it. It was *Mark*. She splayed her palms against his chest as he twined his fingers in her hair and held her to him as if afraid that she might change her mind.

After a few minutes, she pulled back and gasped, 'What the hell are we doing?'

He looked at her fiercely, eyes burning over the arch of his cheekbones. 'I don't know. I can't control myself when I'm around you, Tabitha.'

She felt a hot triumph at that. A part of her had always tried to force him to let go, and she saw now that this was why. That this was what she had always wanted. 'Then let's finish what we've started,' she said and there was an agonising pause before he nodded, once, the agreement another admission she had dragged out of him.

They stopped four times on the stairs to kiss. Like horny teenagers, Tabitha thought, but she was beyond shame. This was nothing like her first time with Jake. That had been a game, meaningless fun, both of them doing it because they wanted to, not because they had to.

This thing between her and Mark felt like a compulsion. He pressed her back against the door to his room, unwilling to release her even as he fumbled his keycard into the lock behind her. She stumbled backwards when the door opened unexpectedly and he followed, holding her up, one arm like a vice around her waist, the other cupping the back of her head to keep their mouths sealed together.

But they were still fully clothed. If they changed their minds they could just pull themselves apart and she could walk away and it would be as if nothing had happened. She couldn't bear the thought of that. She eased her hands inside his shirt, enjoying the rough feeling of the hairs against her palms, then pulled them roughly apart.

She couldn't help pulling her head back to laugh as his buttons flew everywhere, and he gave her a look that was for one brief moment the old disapproving Professor Sinclair. Then she fastened her mouth around one of the tight brown nipples she'd exposed and bit down hard and his mouth slackened with desire and he just looked like Mark, a man.

His hands fisted in her hair as she suckled, then moved down to grasp the hem of her T-shirt. As soon as he'd removed it, exposing her breasts to his avid gaze, she dropped to her knees in front of him and began working at his fly.

'Tabitha,' he said, sounding suddenly uncertain as if this might be an intimacy too far. She didn't give him a chance to reconsider, just fumbled him free of his pants and briefs and put her lips around him. He was thick and solid and she loved the feel of him in her mouth and the helpless groan he made when she took him deeper. A second later and he'd fallen to his knees beside her, capturing her lips in a rough kiss. His fingers tangled in her hair as he pushed her back to lie on the carpet, pinning her beneath his weight. She felt a primal need to have him in her, mastering her with his cock as he overpowered her with his body. But instead he pulled back to look at her, brushing a strand of hair from her forehead in a tender gesture that made her stomach clench.

'You're so beautiful.'

She studied his face, the careful shape of his mouth and the strong line of his brows, his brilliant-blue eyes softened with feeling. She didn't know what to say to him. She was afraid if she said anything it would be too much.

He moved his mouth over her face, barely touching her now, brushing over her eyelids, her eyebrows, the complex shell of her ears. He bit down on her earlobe and she could feel him smile against her at her indignant yelp. Then he sucked the lobe into his mouth, teasing it delicately with his tongue, and the yelp turned into a low moan.

She used her fingers to explore his chest and stomach, learning it by touch, the surprising softness of his skin there and the hard muscles just underneath it. His arms were still covered with his shirt so she yanked that down and off so she could explore them too. Her touch seemed to enflame him and he moved from her face to lick hungrily at her breasts before suckling the nipples with a gently insistent rhythm.

She moaned when he moved away from her but he drew her into his arms and carried her across the room to the bed, almost stumbling in his haste.

He frowned when she giggled at him. 'You laugh at me too much,' he told her as his fingers unsnapped the waistband of her jeans and pulled them down her legs. She liked how rough he was about it, as if he couldn't wait to see the rest of her.

'You don't laugh at yourself enough,' she told him.

Their eyes met, teasing. She felt a sudden cold stab of doubt, because she couldn't pretend that this was just about bodies any more. It was about her making love to him, to Mark. But the doubt melted into a warm certainty which burnt to a white-hot heat when he stroked his hands down her legs, gently parting them, and bent his head to taste her there.

As soon as his mouth touched her she realised that she was only a few seconds away from orgasm. 'Mark, please,' she begged him, 'don't make me come.' He raised his head to look at her, uncertain, and she said, 'Don't make me come until you're inside me.'

For a moment his face assumed its usual expressionless mask, except this time she thought she might be able to read it and that it meant he was feeling too much rather than too little. Then he stood and hurriedly pulled his own jeans and briefs away. He had a runner's legs, strong and toned with a light dusting of fair hair on them, another pointing like an arrow down his chest to the straining tip of his erection.

'Tabitha . . .' he said. He looked like he was going to say something else, perhaps ask her if she was sure, but she shook her head because that wasn't a question she wanted to be asked. Then he was on top of her again, skin against skin this time. She could feel his blood pulsing through every contact point of their bodies. His cock was at her centre, nudging for entrance. His fingers touched her there delicately, perhaps thinking he needed to prepare her further, but she was more than ready. She brushed his hand aside with her own and guided him inside her.

He slid in like something clicking into place. There was a moment of stillness and absolute clarity as Tabitha knew that this was like nothing she had ever felt before. Then there was only urgency. They struggled with each other to set the pace but he was stronger and more sure of himself and she gladly submitted to the deep relentless rhythm of his thrusts. He'd got the angle just right and every stroke sent a jolt of pleasure from her centre to her brain and back again.

She reached up to touch his face, tracing her fingers along his lips until he sucked them inside and gently licked and bit their tips. After that it was too hard to keep her eyes open and she let her vision slide into darkness so that her body could concentrate on the sensation of Mark touching every part of her that mattered. She knew that she was going to come, very soon and very hard. A few more strong thrusts and she cried out helplessly as she felt her inner muscles clenching around him as if she never wanted to let him go. He groaned at the intensity of his pleasure. His thrusts became jagged and desperate and he buried his head in her shoulder and exhaled harshly as he gave all of himself to her.

He lay on top of her for only a moment, then rolled to the side, sliding out of her, to pull her into the curve of his body. She rested there, content, until after a few minutes she rolled over to face him. They were both glowing with exertion and she could see strands of his fair hair plastered to his forehead with sweat. She mimicked his earlier gesture, brushing the hairs clear of his forehead, letting his fingers linger on his cheek.

There was so much they needed to talk about. Tabitha didn't know where to start so instead she reached out and kissed his lips and then his chin and further down his neck and even though they'd only just finished they found that they were more than ready to start again.

When Tabitha woke up with the first light of dawn on her face and the warmth of a male body wrapped around her, she felt a moment's disorientation. She thought she must be in her room in the dorms and she wondered why the mattress was suddenly so soft and why Jake was sleeping here with her when they always stayed in his room.

Then she remembered. The arm curled around her waist was too sturdy to be Jake's. The fingernails she could see resting against her stomach were short and a little ragged unlike the careful manicure Jake always gave himself. Even the breathing she could feel stirring the hairs at the nape of her neck was unfamiliar. Her head felt a little muzzy from last night's drink but it wasn't a full-blown hangover and certainly not a good enough excuse for what she'd done.

She didn't know how she could have betrayed Jake so badly, except that last night had felt outside her power to stop it. It had felt like an inevitability. But how could she tell him that she was leaving him for his brother? She thought that it might break him.

She felt the breathing behind her hitch and then restart at a carefully controlled pace and she knew that Mark had woken and guessed that he was asking himself the same questions. Then she felt the arm around her middle stiffen and withdraw.

She turned over to face Mark, suddenly apprehensive. His mask was very firmly back in place but she could read him better now and she saw the regret underneath it. It felt like a body blow.

'Tabitha.' There was no expression in his voice when he said her name. 'I'm sorry. We should have known better – we're both with other people. That was ... a terrible mistake.'

She couldn't believe how much that hurt, but she was damned if she'd let him see it. With a huge effort of will she schooled her face into a carefully neutral expression, then shrugged. 'No big deal. It didn't mean anything.'

He sat up, the sheet falling back to expose his stomach and despite everything she felt a stirring of desire. She could see red welts across his shoulders where her nails had scratched him. She was glad she'd managed to mark him. He might want to forget this, but he wouldn't be able to, not straight away.

'This should never have happened,' he told her.

She nodded, not looking at him, just trying to find her clothes and pull them on as quickly as possible. She felt him looking at her and knew that he could see the marks he'd left on her body, too: the small bruise on her shoulder where he'd bitten her as he'd come for the second time, and the rough burn of his stubble across her thighs from when they'd woken in the middle of the night and she'd allowed him to finish what he'd started earlier.

'Then we'll just pretend it didn't happen,' she told him. She made herself turn to face him as she pulled up and buttoned her jeans. She hadn't been able to find her panties but she'd just buy herself some new ones before she caught the train back. 'The thing is,' she told him. 'Jake told me that he loved me when we were away last weekend.'

His expression froze. 'I see.'

She nodded. Keeping her tone level was one of the hardest things she'd ever done. 'Yeah, it really threw me, you know? But this has been ... Well, this has helped me make up my mind. I love him too, and I guess I needed to do something as stupid as this to realise that.'

She thought she saw a brief flash of pain in his face then. She was glad. She wanted him to hurt too.

* * *

Tabitha hadn't stopped to change and when she knocked on Jake's door she was still wearing the same outfit which Mark had stripped off her the night before. Her body was still aching from his touch.

Jake looked taken aback to see her on his doorstep. He bent to study her face and she drew him into a hug before he could read whatever was written there. 'I'm sorry, Jake,' she told him. 'I love you too.'

Interlude

Spring Break

It had been easier to slip back into her routine with Jake than Tabitha had imagined. Their mutual declarations of love didn't seem to change very much. He didn't talk about her moving into the room with him and he didn't start sending her roses or chocolates. But he seemed more relaxed around her, confident in their relationship. It was almost like love for him was more about possession than feeling. She had no right criticising anything Jake did, though, not after what *she'd* done, so she just let herself enjoy the fact that she'd miraculously managed not to kill the only functioning relationship in her life with her one night of madness.

Classes were unbearable, of course. She saw Fiona studying her as she did everything she could to avoid ever meeting Mark's eye, but she never gave her friend a chance to ask her what had happened in New York after she'd left. Mark acted like she didn't exist, which hurt like hell but was probably better than any of the alternatives.

It was a huge relief when Spring Break came. Her father hadn't invited her back to LA, in fact he hadn't spoken to her since he'd discovered her little store-card-fuelled shopping spree, but two days before she was due to finish and while she was wondering exactly how she was going to support herself this time, she'd had a letter from Jessica, her oldest friend back home. The letter had said that they'd realised Muhammad wasn't going to come to the mountain, so the mountain was coming to Muhammad. Her friends had booked a cottage on the sea down in North Carolina and they expected her to join them there for a week. She didn't need to worry about money because they'd got all that covered. A plane ticket down to Wilmington had been shoved into the envelope alongside the letter.

Tabitha had been so moved she'd had to fight back tears. She'd barely had any contact with her friends over the last few months, too out of their social loop to know what to say to them. The letter suggested she bring that boyfriend they'd been hearing so much about and a friend too, if she wanted. The cottage had plenty of rooms. Jake was more than happy to tag along and a concerted campaign of persuasion and emotional blackmail eventually convinced Fiona that she should come too, since Adam was at sea for the duration and if she was going to be studying she might as well do it somewhere sunny and sandy.

Tabitha watched Fiona as the two of them finished off packing. She was carefully folding the clothes Tabitha had picked out for her in New York into her suitcase. Tabitha considered her own increasingly out-of-date and threadbare selection and it occurred to her that her friend was looking more fashionable than she was.

They were interrupted by a sharp knock on the door. Tabitha looked at Fiona but the other woman shook her head, not expecting a visitor either. Tabitha shrugged and answered the door, still clutching the T-shirt she'd been folding against her chest.

It was Mark. Tabitha rocked back on her heels and Mark took a step backwards too, as if even though he'd come calling he hadn't actually expected her to answer.

'Hi,' Tabitha said coolly, hyper-aware of Fiona's interested gaze behind her.

He nodded, though his eyes wouldn't meet hers. 'I came over to see if you're going back to LA for the break.'

'I'm not. Why?'

'If you need work for the duration, I'm short a research assistant again.'

She felt a leap of hope. She started to smile, but then registered his expression. Lips pressed together, stance tight. It was a sense of duty which was motivating him, not anything else.

'That's big of you,' she told him. 'But I'm going away for the week. With Jake.'

One of his hands was resting against the frame of the door, and Tabitha had a sudden intense sense memory of how it had felt as it smoothed over her body. 'Fine,' he said and walked away without another word.

Fiona was staring at Tabitha when she closed the door. When it became obvious that Tabitha wasn't going to volunteer anything, she asked, 'What was all that about?'

Tabitha shrugged. 'Just what it looked like. Sinclair offering me some work.'

Fiona gave her a long hard look.

'What?' Tabitha knew that she sounded as guilty as hell.

'Nothing,' Fiona said, looking back down at her packing. But it was clear she thought it was anything but.

The house Tabitha's friends had booked turned out to be a strange dark wooden structure standing on stilts in the sand of the long promontory that paralleled North Carolina's coast. It looked, she thought, like somewhere the Addams Family would go for their vacation. The land here was less than a mile wide, edged with sea at either side, and she could hear the restless shuffle of the waves. She wondered if it would start to drive you crazy after a while, the way that it never let up.

There was no one in the house when she, Jake and Fiona knocked then cautiously stepped inside. It was big, though, big and a little too empty in the way that only a rental could be. 'Hello?' she called. No answer. 'Must be on the beach.'

A short walk through the white-painted main room led out to a sea-view balcony, and there they all were. Brad was the first to see her. He nudged Jessica beside him and they both rose, smiling, and sauntered towards her. Tabitha remembered that they never did anything in a hurry, even greet a friend they hadn't seen for six months. Showing any kind of enthusiasm would have seemed too uncool.

She found herself rooted to the spot, unable to run to them either. It suddenly seemed a long time and a lot of water under the bridge since they'd last been together. Then Jessica was air-kissing her on both cheeks and the others had all realised she was there too and she was surrounded by what felt like everyone she'd ever known back in LA.

Jessica pulled back to look at Tabitha, then she looked at Jake and her eyes widened appreciatively. 'Well, well,' she whispered in Tabitha's ear. 'Haven't you done well?' Her eyes flicked at and then over Fiona, dismissing her as unworthy of interest. Tabitha had forgotten Jessica's habit of doing that. As she watched Brad casually asking Jake what he drove and Corey checking out the design of his shoes, she realised that there were a lot of things she'd forgotten about her friends.

They spent the day lazing on the beach, Fiona crouched under a parasol to protect her pale skin, and Tabitha slathered in lotion and stretched out on the sand, wearing the white Melissa Odabash bikini which was the one new item of clothing she'd splashed out on. She'd almost forgotten what it felt like to be really warm. Jake's eyes warmed her still further, tracing out the shape of her body like he wanted to memorise it. He looked pretty good as well in a pair of surfer's green swimming trunks that hung low on his hips, framing the firm muscles of his stomach.

She noticed that Brad was checking her out too. They'd had a thing a couple of years back, nothing major, but she hadn't thought he'd been carrying any kind of torch for her. Still, he was definitely noticing her and she knew that Jake was noticing him noticing. Jake seemed mildly amused by Brad's interest. It was a contrast to his behaviour around Mark, Tabitha realised, where he had always been very territorial, as if unconsciously aware that there was something more than student and professor to their relationship.

When the sun began to chill, they retreated inside and Jessica and Corey – who'd had some professional training as a chef – set about preparing supper while the others made a start on the cellar's worth of beer and wine they'd brought. Conversation ebbed and flowed, about people and places Tabitha hadn't even thought about for months. She did her best to explain the background to Fiona and Jake but found that half the time she didn't know what was going on either. LA life was a fast-flowing river and she began to feel like an observer on the shore, waving as it all passed by.

When they were eating the mango crème brulee which finished off the meal, Jessica turned her laser eyes on Jake. 'So, where *did* Tabitha find you?'

'I'm hard to miss,' he told her.

'I can believe it,' Corey said, looking Jake up and down appreciatively even though his boyfriend Michael was sitting right next to him.

'Seriously, though, don't tell me you're a student at Backwater U too?'

''Fraid so.'

Jessica pursed her mouth jokingly at Tabitha. 'You cradle-snatcher.'

'I think it was Jake who did most of the snatching,' Fiona said, one of her only contributions to the conversation that evening.

'An assertive man – I like that even more,' Corey said, and Michael slapped him, but it was clear he didn't mean it.

Jake smiled, seemingly flattered rather than bothered by the attention. 'What can I say, Tabitha's hard to resist.'

Jessica clapped ironically. 'Good answer. But you still haven't told me what a boy like you is doing in a place like that.'

There was a small but discernible silence as both Tabitha and Jake hesitated to answer the question. It was left to Fiona to say, 'His brother's a professor there.'

'Really?' Jessica licked her lips. 'Now a sexy young professor definitely has possibilities. The question is, is he available and is he anything like as gorgeous as you?'

'Oh, I'm one of a kind,' Jake said lightly.

'Anyway, he's with someone,' Tabitha added, then wished she hadn't when Jake shot her a sharp look.

'Actually,' he said, 'I think they split up a few weeks ago.'

Jessica smiled like a lion stalking its prey. 'So he *is* free. You really must introduce us.'

Tabitha gathered herself enough to make a joke about Jessica's man-eating ways but her heart was racing and she didn't want to examine why.

Later that night, Jake made love to her with a more urgent passion than he usually showed, pushing in hard enough that she cried out with a mixture of pleasure and discomfort. It took her longer than usual to come, and she kept her eyes open throughout, fixing them on Jake's face so that a different one wouldn't be able to slip into her consciousness.

The second day followed the same routine as the first, but after her initial enjoyment of her friends' company Tabitha began to feel more and more isolated from them. All they wanted to talk about was a life she was no longer leading, and they weren't interested in hearing very much about the one she *had* led.

Jake didn't seem to have any problem, joining in with his own stories about the wild time he'd had at Columbia, stories he'd never bothered to tell her. She'd never noticed before how very like all her LA friends Jake was.

She guessed that was why she'd been attracted to him right back when she first came to Adirondacks U.

Fiona didn't seem to be enjoying the company too much, and Tabitha felt bad about that. A few times she caught Michael and Corey making bitchy comments about her, nothing serious, the kind of thing you could write off as a joke, but Tabitha didn't like it. She especially didn't like it because she could imagine herself saying the same kind of thing not that long ago.

The third day Jessica decided she wanted to go clothes shopping and dragged Tabitha on the three-hour drive to find a store that wasn't the Gap.

'You know I can only window shop, right?' Tabitha told her.

'Oh don't worry.' Jessica held up her platinum card. 'I'm buying.'

Tabitha shook her head. 'No way. I'm not taking any more of your money. It's bad enough I'm not paying my way for this trip.'

Jessica took her eyes off the road to give Tabitha a disbelieving stare. 'Since when have you had a problem spending other people's money? Anyway, my dad always covers this card. Spending my dad's money or spending your dad's – where's the difference?'

Tabitha gave up, unable to think of one. But also knowing that that made both things equally wrong, not equally right.

In the end she surrendered and let Jessica buy her one Anna Molinari dress, which she had to admit looked fabulous against her newly tanned skin. Brad whistled appreciatively when he saw it and Jake insisted she keep it on when they made love that night, kneeling to go down on her beneath its loose skirt.

'Brad can't take his eyes off you,' he said to her when they were curled together in bed afterwards, enjoying the afterglow.

'Oh, Brad's just Brad,' she said uncomfortably. 'He'll get over it, just ignore him.'

But over the following days Brad didn't seem to get over it, and Jake wasn't willing to ignore him. Two days before they were due to leave, Tabitha padded into the house from the beach, searching for some more factor-10 lotion for Fiona, who had managed to go beet red despite avoiding the sun more assiduously than a vampire.

She was fumbling in her bag when she heard someone else enter the room, but she just assumed it was Jake, looking for the Frisbee they'd been talking about tossing. It was only when she turned to leave and walked into an entirely different male body that she realised it was Brad who had been watching her these last few minutes.

She made herself laugh. 'Brad, quit stalking me.'

He smiled but didn't release his light hold on her arms. 'Ah, come on, Tabby, you've been checking me out too – admit it.'

She shook her head because she really hadn't. Brad was well put together, there was no denying it – tall and tanned with a surf bum's blond hair and an agent's calculating eyes – but there was just nothing about him that attracted her any more. 'In case you hadn't noticed,' she told him, 'I'm with someone else.'

'Yeah, I know,' Brad said. 'That's why I asked him if this would be OK.'

He bent down and pressed his lips against hers, forcing his tongue briefly inside her mouth before pulling away.

She pushed her hands against his chest and even though it had about as much effect as pushing against a wall, he let her go. Brad might be a shark but he didn't swim where he wasn't invited. 'You asked Jake *what*?' she said disbelievingly.

'Whether he'd mind me and you having some fun for old time's sake.'

'And I said that was fine,' Jake said, 'as long as I got to watch.' He was framed in the doorway, one arm leaning against it, wide mouth quirked in a sly smile.

Tabitha was so frozen with surprise that she didn't react as Brad stepped behind her and put his arms around her waist, splaying his hands across her stomach. She knew that the two men's eyes were meeting over her head, but she had attention for no one but Jake. 'Don't you think you should maybe have mentioned it to me first?' she asked, trying to keep her voice calm because she didn't want to seem like she'd turned into some kind of prude.

The light from the window fell across half Jake's face, leaving one eye entirely in shadow. 'I'm mentioning it now,' he said, equally calmly. As he spoke, Brad's hands began to move, one tracing lazy circles on her stomach, the other moving up to cup her breast through her bikini.

Tabitha saw Jake's other eye darken till it seemed the same colour as the one that was in shadow. She could see that this excited him and there was definitely a part of her that was turned on too, the part that enjoyed breaking taboos and trying new things. But there was something in Jake's expression she didn't like. He got off on this, she realised, because it was another form of possession. He showed that she was his by showing that he had the right to give her away to another man, if he chose.

But he didn't have that right. She stepped forward, out of Brad's arms, then turned to face him. 'Sorry, Brad. This just isn't happening.'

Brad looked at Jake for confirmation, then seemed to realise that it really wasn't the other man's call and held up his hands in a gesture of surrender. 'Sure, Tabby, no biggie. But, once you and Jake have sorted this out, if you change your mind ...' He left the room before she could tell him that wasn't going to happen.

Jake shut the door behind Brad, then turned to face Tabitha. The darkness had lifted from his eyes and he looked a little ashamed. 'I'm sorry. You're right – I should have talked to you about that first. I just knew you'd been with him before and I thought you might think it was fun.'

'You were wrong,' Tabitha told him. 'I don't want

anyone else.' But as she said the words the full untruth of them struck her and she had to turn away from Jake because she didn't want him to see what must be written so plainly on her face. Only, after a moment, she did turn back, because she realised that Jake had every right to see what she was thinking, and that it was something she should have been honest with him about some time ago. But of course she hadn't been able to be honest with *herself* till now.

Jake must have read something in her expression because his suddenly fell and he took a step towards her.

She held out a hand, wanting him to keep his distance. This would be hard enough as it was. 'I'm the one who's sorry,' she told him. Sorry that she had stayed with one brother when really she wanted to be with another. The fact that the brother she wanted didn't want her back really wasn't the point.

He knew what she meant immediately. 'You're ending it?' he said incredulously. 'Because of that?'

Tabitha steeled herself. 'No. I mean yes, I am ending it, but not because of that.'

'Then why?' She could see the hurt in his face, and simmering beneath it a scorching anger. 'I thought you said you loved me.'

'I did. I did say it, but –'

'But what?' Jake said bitterly. 'You didn't mean it?'

'I was lying to myself,' she told him. 'Not you.'

'And that's supposed to make me feel better? You bitch!' He turned and ran his hand along the shelf behind him, smashing books and ornaments to the floor.

Tabitha jumped and took a step back, but there was one more truth she owed him. 'There's something I – there's something I did, and I know it was wrong, and I'm so, so sorry, but there's something else I have to tell you.'

His eyes burnt into hers. 'There's nothing you could say that would make this worse.'

'I slept with Mark,' she blurted. 'In New York. We were drunk, but that's no excuse and I felt terrible. I wanted to tell you, I just didn't know how. It was a one-night thing and I told myself it didn't mean anything. But I was lying to myself about that, too.'

His whole face froze, brittle with fury, and she saw both his hands curl up into fists. For the first and only time in their relationship she was afraid that he might hit her. But he just said, 'Get out.'

She and Fiona drove to the airport together. She'd told her friend only the bare bones, that she and Jake had split up and she wanted to head home right now. Fiona didn't seem upset to be leaving the LA gang a day early and neither, truth be told, was Tabitha. She couldn't imagine spending much time with them again, and wasn't really sure how she ever had. Mostly, though, she was thinking about Jake and trying not to think about Mark. She watched the scenery slide by outside the car, sand dunes giving way to woodland, hills rising in the distance to mountains.

She felt a strange mixture of sadness and relief and guilt and fear. Fiona seemed to sense her mood and reached out a hand from the wheel to clasp Tabitha's. 'You've made the right decision,' she told her.

Tabitha gave a shaky laugh. 'Yeah, but you never liked him.'

Fiona shook her head. 'I didn't dislike him. I never thought he was right for you.'

'But we're so alike,' Tabitha protested, wondering why she was trying to talk herself back into a relationship she'd just irrevocably ended.

'That's why. The last thing you need is someone just like you. You need someone who balances you.'

Tabitha instantly thought of Mark. She guessed they did balance each other, in a way, like people sitting on the opposite ends of a seesaw. But when you were that far apart, how did you meet in the middle?

'Something happened between you and Mark, didn't it?' Fiona said.

Tabitha snapped her head round to look at her, shocked.

Fiona laughed, not unkindly. 'Unlike you, I'm very good at psychology. No one goes to that much trouble to avoid someone without a very good reason.'

Tabitha looked back out of the window again, at the scruffy nowheresville town they were leaving almost as soon as they'd entered it. 'We slept together, in New York. I didn't mean for it to happen. I didn't think that I even liked him.'

'And now what do you think?'

Tabitha swallowed. 'I don't know, just that I think about him too much to be seeing his brother.'

'Are you in love with him?'

'He thinks I'm a moron,' Tabitha said, 'and I guess now he also thinks I'm a slut.'

Fiona stared at Tabitha in silence but didn't ask any more questions. Both of them knew that she hadn't really answered the first one.

Chapter Sixteen

Every Day is Like Sunday

The flight back to Lake Placid felt like one of the longest of Tabitha's life. She stared out of the window of the plane like she'd stared out of the window of the car and tried not to think about anything but the scenery. Both she and Fiona had parked their cars at the airport, so they drove back separately.

Tabitha knew she'd be the first back; Fiona had told her she was going to pick up some shopping before she went home. She found that she couldn't face the prospect of going back to the empty room and stayed in her car, staring vacantly at the brick cube of the faculty building. She couldn't quite believe that she'd broken up with Jake. And for what? A man who almost certainly didn't want her.

As if her thoughts had summoned him, she saw Mark heading across the parking lot towards her. She sank down in her seat, hoping he'd pass by without seeing her. She didn't feel up to talking to him at the moment and anyway had absolutely no idea what she was going to say to him about breaking up with Jake. It was no use – he'd already spotted her. Her stomach churned but she squared her shoulders and got out of the car, knowing she'd have to face him sooner or later.

Up close, she could see that his face was a study in icy rage. 'I knew you were bad news the moment I saw you,' he spat, as if each word was a mouthful of something poisonous.

She realised that she was shaking, but she managed to keep her voice steady when she said, 'I'm sorry I told

Jake about us, but I thought I owed it to him to be honest.'

He looked at her contemptuously. 'Don't pretend this has anything to do with me. Jake told me what you did – what he caught you doing.'

'I didn't do anything!' Tabitha protested, suddenly unsure what he was talking about. 'Or at least,' she added bitterly, 'I didn't do anything that you weren't there doing right along with me.'

'Yes, and I let myself believe that that actually meant something. I guess my brother and I have more in common than I realised – we're both fools when it comes to you.'

Tabitha shook her head, baffled. She'd been expecting a confrontation, but not this one. 'What the hell are you talking about?'

'I'm talking about Jake catching you whoring around with your old boyfriend.'

'*What*?' Tabitha felt almost speechless with fury. 'That's just – it was *Jake* who wanted me to sleep with Brad.'

'That's your excuse for doing it, is it?' he said disgustedly.

The anger in his voice, the contempt in his expression, burnt her like acid. How could Jake have said this about her? But, far worse, how could Mark believe it?

'I *didn't* do it,' she told him, ashamed to realise that her voice was thick with incipient tears. 'Nothing happened, I told him no.'

Mark looked utterly unmoved. 'So you're telling me my brother's lying to me.'

'Yes!'

'And just why would he do that?'

She looked at Mark, his face harsh with condemnation, and she knew the answer, though she'd never really faced it before. Jake had lied because he didn't want Tabitha with Mark, and the reason he didn't want it – maybe the reason he'd been with Tabitha all along – was that he hated his brother. She didn't know why, but when she thought of everything Jake had ever said about Mark, the way his face looked when she spoke about him, she knew that it was true. But that was the one thing she couldn't say to Mark.

She looked away instead, at a small group of students who had stopped at a distance to watch the interesting confrontation between Professor Sinclair and his student. 'I don't know. But it is a lie.'

'Really?' He folded his arms and glared at the students until they walked away. 'And is it also a lie that you've been cheating all semester, handing in another student's work as your own?'

Tabitha felt like the bottom had dropped out of her world. It hadn't crossed her mind that Jake would betray her so comprehensively. She gathered herself and opened her mouth to deny it, but she knew that her face had already betrayed her. 'All right,' she said, 'that is true.' It occurred to her that this could get Fiona into terrible trouble as well and there was no need to ruin both of their lives. 'Fiona shouldn't have left her password lying around,' she added. 'It made it too easy.'

He nodded sharply, seeming to accept that explanation. 'Well, at least when I get you kicked out no one's going to think I'm being vindictive.'

As the initial shock wore off, Tabitha found that a burning anger was growing inside her. How dare he act like he'd had no part in any of this? And now he was planning to ruin her entire life just because he was too dumb to see through his brother's lies.

His eyes swept over her one last time before he turned to go, as if he'd already dismissed her from his thoughts.

She grabbed his arm and pulled him back round to face her. 'There's no way I'm letting you do that.'

He looked at her hand as if it was diseased. 'Just how are you planning on stopping me?'

'I don't know,' she said, her voice shaking now with anger rather than hurt. 'Probably by threatening to tell the faculty what happened between us in New York. Maybe I'm wrong, but last time I checked there was a rule against professors sleeping with their students.'

His eyes widened, shocked. She was shocked at herself too, but she was damned if she'd take it back. He and his brother weren't the only ones who could fight dirty.

She read Mark's acceptance of his defeat in the slight droop of his shoulders. But she couldn't feel any triumph because the contempt in his eyes when he looked at her had deepened still further. 'Yes, I should have expected that of you. Fine. But you'll redo every single piece of work that you cheated on. You'll do all the new papers on your own. And you'll still fail the exams, without any help from me, because you just haven't got what it takes to stay the course at anything.'

This time when he turned and walked away she didn't stop him. She drew in a few deep breaths to steady herself, refusing to give in to tears until she was in the privacy of her room.

Tabitha had finally managed to cry herself out two hours later when Fiona returned. Her eyes felt gritty and they must have looked red because Fiona immediately realised that something was wrong. She sat down on the bed next to Tabitha and put her arm around her, resting her chin against Tabitha's hair. The sympathy was too much to bear and Tabitha realised that she wasn't done crying as she buried her face in the other woman's neck.

'It'll all be OK,' Fiona murmured, stroking her hair. 'You're better off without him.'

Tabitha let out a sound that was halfway between a sob and a laugh. 'Yeah. He told Mark he caught me screwing Brad. He said that's why he finished with me.'

Fiona's arms stiffened around her. 'That lying bastard! Did Mark believe him?' She read the answer in Tabitha's expression. 'They're both bastards. You're too good for either of them.'

Tabitha smiled bitterly. 'He told Mark about me cheating on my papers, too.'

Fiona's faced paled. 'He did what?'

Tabitha pulled away and swiped at her eyes with her sleeve. 'Don't worry. I told Mark it had nothing to do with you.'

'That's not the point,' Fiona said, though the relief in her voice said that it partly was. 'You should have told him it was my idea. You don't need to take the blame for that too.

Tabitha suddenly felt filled with a restless energy. She walked to the window, leaning her head against the glass. Her face was flushed from crying and the glass felt almost icy cold. Like the look in Mark's eyes when he told her she wasn't worth anything. 'Why not? It's not like I said no, is it? Anyway, there's no point fucking up both our lives and you deserve to graduate. I don't.'

'You do!' Fiona said fiercely. 'Tabitha, you're not stupid. You might not be the world's greatest psychologist but you're perfectly capable of passing this on your own. You just have to do some work.'

Outside the window, Tabitha could see students drifting into the courtyard, gathering and parting like clouds. One figure walked on its own and she realised after a second that it was Jake. She thought that he might have looked up at her window but he was too far away for her to be certain. 'Sure,' she said. 'It's not like there's anything else to distract me.'

Tabitha tried to persuade herself that if she actually got her head down and studied some psychology she might discover a hidden talent for it, or at least a sudden fascination. She soon discovered otherwise: it was something she'd chosen to do because she couldn't think of anything better and she had no great aptitude or interest.

But she did the work. Like she'd said to Fiona, there was nothing else to occupy her time. After two days, she was able to leave her first rewritten assignment in Mark's pigeon hole, an essay on the development of language which Fiona had written for her early in the semester. He returned it to her without comment in his next class with a circled C at the bottom and red scribbles all over it. Still, it was a pass.

She thought about confronting Jake over his lies but decided in the end that there was no point. Besides, she'd slept with his brother while she was still with him – he probably had a right to hit back at her. She thought about trying to explain herself to Mark too, but one look at the freezing expression on his face whenever he saw her convinced her it would be pointless.

Jake started seeing someone else a couple of weeks after she came back. He seemed to bring her with him wherever he went, and his hand was always somewhere on her body, as if he wanted to be absolutely sure that Tabitha got the message. She did feel a stab of something painful, but she didn't think it was really jealousy. Maybe it was regret, that she'd had this guy who'd made her feel pretty good and she'd lost him because she couldn't stop thinking about a guy who'd only ever made her feel bad.

She phoned her father for the first time in weeks, tired of everyone in her life being angry at her. He was cautious on the phone, clearly distrusting her motives for calling, but she didn't ask him for anything and she thought he was probably pleased to have spoken to her. He told her he'd booked a ticket for her graduation and that he hoped he wasn't going to have to refund it. She told him she was working hard, which was about the only thing she could safely say.

Finally, almost unbelievably, the end-of-semester exams were approaching, and then they were the next day. Tabitha had done every bit of work Mark had asked of her by then, and passed all of them, even if it was by the skin of her teeth. But doing that hadn't left her much time for revision. She thought that it would be a nasty sort of irony if she passed the coursework and failed the exam. She didn't imagine Mark was going to be marking it leniently.

The evening before the exam, when both she and Fiona were hunched at their desks, heads bent over their textbooks, Jake came to see her.

Fiona took one look at him then stood up, saying, 'I'll get out of your way.'

'Don't be silly,' Tabitha told her, 'you need to work.'

'I'll do it in the library.' Fiona shot Jake an unloving look, then walked out of the door and shut it behind her.

'I don't think she likes me,' Jake said lightly.

'She never did.' Tabitha retreated to sit back at her desk, leaving ten clear feet of floor space between them. 'But she definitely likes you even less now.'

He looked down at his hands, his fingers fidgeting with the hem of his jacket. 'Can we talk without arguing?'

She glared at him. 'That depends. Can you talk without lying?'

'Hold on a minute,' he said, a hard edge in his voice. 'You don't get to play the victim here. You were the one who slept with my brother. I only told him those things because I was angry with you.'

But he didn't look angry now. She couldn't read his expression at all, as if Mark had recently taught him the trick of keeping all his emotions locked away behind closed doors.

Tabitha knew that his answer made sense and, yes, he did have every right to be angry. But deep inside her she knew that it wasn't the truth, or at least not all of it. 'Is this really about me? Has it ever been about me, Jake, or is it just about you and him?'

He took a step nearer then halted, as if not sure of his welcome. 'I don't know what you mean.'

She studied him, the familiar lines of his face, the generous curve of his mouth, and she wondered if she really knew him at all. She thought about Mark's face too, how it was like a foreign language, only unintelligible until you learnt to translate it. 'Did you ever really love me?'

'Of course I did!' He closed the distance between them further, only a couple of feet separating them now. 'I still do. That's why I want you back.'

Tabitha expected to feel something at that, relief or even joy. She couldn't have Mark so why shouldn't she have Jake, who for everything that had happened in the last few weeks had made her time here bearable? But she looked in his golden-brown eyes and she knew that if she went back to him Mark would still be there between them. 'I'm sorry, Jake.'

'*Why*?' He reached his hand towards her but it halted in midair, as if bumping up against an invisible barrier.

'Because you only want to have me so your brother can't.'

The hand clenched and she saw his knuckles whiten. 'That's ridiculous – you know it isn't true. You and me got together long before anything happened with you and Mark.'

Tabitha remembered Mark's face in her first lecture, the expression she'd found so unreadable and cold then. The same look when he'd picked her up in the cells, the way he'd looked when she told him that she wanted him inside her. 'But you saw the way he looked at me,' she told Jake. 'And you knew he wanted me.'

'You think he's got feelings for you?' Jake said derisively. 'Christ, do you think he loves you? You know what you are? You're just some student he didn't have enough self-control not to bone.' He saw that he had wounded Tabitha and carried on relentlessly. 'Have you thought that maybe he only wanted you because he knew you were mine?'

Tabitha shook her head, trying not to let Jake's words cut her. 'No, that isn't true. You might hate him, Jake, but the one person he does love is you.'

He began pacing the floor like a caged animal.

'Bullshit. What, you think he's some kind of fucking saint? You don't know anything about him. But you'd still rather be with him than with me.' He turned to face her, suddenly pleading. 'Just tell me something. Was there one moment together when you weren't happy? When we weren't having a good time?'

'No, there wasn't,' she told him gently. She knew that he might not love her, but she still had the power to hurt him, and she didn't want to do that. Whatever lies he'd told about her, and whatever horrible things he was saying now, he didn't deserve that. 'I had a great time. But that's all there was, and in the end that wasn't enough.'

'What, you wanted more sex? I didn't fuck you good enough?'

She bit down an angry retort. 'The sex was great. But you know how it was, Jake. We never thought about anything *except* sex and partying when were together.'

'What's wrong with that? Jesus, you're starting to sound like him, like you think having a good time is some kind of crime. We're both rich, Tabitha, we don't ever have to do anything except keep on having fun.'

She stood up and gazed out of the window to watch the sun setting behind the college buildings. 'Yeah, that's what I thought too. Then I realised in the last few weeks that I've been living my life like it's a mirror image of my mom's. I thought I was making sure I'd never have any regrets, but I was wrong. If I carry on the same way, I *will* have regrets, they'll just be different ones.'

'You'll regret you had too much fun?'

'I'll regret the fact that my life's been completely empty.'

'Maybe having fun is all you're good for,' he said nastily. 'Have you thought of that?'

Tabitha watched the last golden rays of the sun darken to red. 'Yeah.'

She turned back to Jake, saw his chest rise and fall with the force of his breath as he tried to control himself.

When his voice came out it was hard with fury. 'He won't have you back, you know. You're kidding yourself if you think he will.'

'This isn't about what I feel for him!' Tabitha shouted, her control finally snapping. 'Don't you get it? It's about what I don't feel for you.'

All pleasant emotion was gone from his face. She knew she was seeing the raw angry feeling that had always lived inside him but that he'd kept hidden from everyone, probably even himself. 'That fucking selfish bastard! He's taken everything I ever cared about.'

'It's not –'

'Don't say that again!' he roared. 'If you think this isn't all about him then you're even more of an idiot than I thought.' He stalked to the door and wrenched it open. 'Enjoy the rest of your *meaningful* life, Tabitha. And, when you realise what a mistake you've made, don't come crawling back to me.' The door shook when he slammed it behind him.

Tabitha realised that she was shaking too. Jake's fury had felt like a physical assault but she found that she wasn't really angry with him. She felt angry with Mark instead, who'd made her see things about herself she didn't want to see and then left her on her own to deal with them. And she was angry with him about Jake too, who Mark seemed to have brought up so badly. Because there had to be a reason Jake hated his brother so much, didn't there?

Chapter Seventeen

Blistered Heart

Tabitha woke at six on the morning of her first exam. The sun was peering round the edges of the blind but Fiona was still asleep so she stayed in bed, mentally running over everything she'd been trying to cram into her head in the last few days. It didn't feel like enough.

At seven o'clock Fiona finally woke and Tabitha rose, brushed her teeth, showered, her entire morning routine cruising by on auto-pilot. When she was dressed and ready she sat down at her desk and cracked open a book, but the text blurred and merged in front of her eyes.

'If you don't know it by now,' Fiona said ten minutes later when she returned from the shower, 'then it's too late.'

'That's what I'm afraid of.'

Fiona was right, though. Tabitha decided to take a walk instead, feet unconsciously seeking the road that led down to the lake. She'd sat on its shores plenty of times since, but as she watched the waves licking the beach she was inevitably reminded of her first time there, when she'd played her first game with Jake. Everything had seemed so simple then. She didn't quite know how it had managed to get so complicated. She mentally shrugged, letting it go, letting her mind drift out over the surface of the water, refusing to think of anything in particular, just trying to soak in some of the calm. Half an hour later all she'd managed to soak in was the sun and she headed back to the campus more tanned but no more ready for what lay ahead of her.

* * *

The moment Tabitha turned the examination paper over she knew that she was in trouble. The questions just didn't seem to make sense, asking her about subjects she hadn't even known she was supposed to know about. Was this some kind of joke? Had Mark specifically written the paper to make sure she failed it?

Despairing, she sat back in her chair. Her eyes unfocused and she let her gaze roam aimlessly round the room, wondering how soon it would be before she could walk out. Two seats ahead of her and three rows to her left she could see Jake. He had his head bent over his own paper, exposing the nape of his neck to her. She had a sudden intensely tactile memory of touching him there, feeling the velvety texture of the closely shaved hair over his skin. She felt a momentary sharp regret that it was something she'd never feel again. He was right, they had been good together. Against her will, her eyes drifted further, to the front of the class where Mark sat at his table, watching over the proceedings with a cool eye. His hand was playing with a pencil, twirling it round and round between his fingers.

That brought another memory, the picture of that hand touching her, the delicate way it had traced over her skin, more tender than she ever would have expected of him. And that image seemed to unlock a flood of others: the dark burn in his eyes when he'd found her and Jake in the cells together; the wry tilt of his mouth as he'd watched her working, knowing she was bored and keeping her amused with stories of his travels in Europe; the way his face looked when he talked about art, more open and unguarded than when he talked about himself and his feelings.

Annoyed with herself, she closed her eyes and tried to banish the images. When she opened them again he was staring straight at her. Probably wondering why I'm not writing, she thought. Or no, knowing that I'm not writing because I can't do it. She felt a flash of anger and allowed it to grow. He'd told her she was going to fail the first time she'd met him and the last. Well, she was damned if she was going to live down to his or anyone else's expectations of her.

She looked down at the questions again, just for the hell of it, and read them more carefully this time. Slowly, she realised that they might be written in a different way, but they were still subjects she'd studied. Maybe she could do this. If nothing else, she could try.

Two hours later she walked out with her fingers cramped from hurried writing and her brain feeling like it had tied itself in knots, but possibly productive ones. Students were pouring out of the exam hall around her, already conducting a post-mortem on the paper, but she didn't want to hear how many things she'd gotten wrong and she hurried away from them as quickly as she could.

She didn't realise that Mark was hurrying after her until she felt his hand on her shoulder. He was wearing a midnight-blue dress shirt which made his eyes seem deeper and darker than usual and his hair as fair as corn. She thought she'd learnt to read his face but it was once again inscrutable to her. Like an arms race, she thought, his ability to hide his feelings always just keeping ahead of her ability to read them.

'Come to gloat?' she asked.

He dropped his hand. 'I came to ask how it went.'

She shrugged. 'I guess you'll be telling me soon enough.' She kept her expression equally closed, knowing all too well that he could pierce her through any chinks she left in her emotional armour.

'So,' he said. 'Jake tells me he wanted to mend fences with you.'

'Yeah. I guess he told you I threw that back in his face.'

'He said you weren't receptive to the idea.' He studied her, but he couldn't seem to figure out her feelings either.

There was a long awkward silence. She expected him

to lay into her, maybe ask why she had to keep on hurting her brother, but he seemed atypically inarticulate.

'Well, thanks for the great chat,' she told him eventually. 'Really appreciate you taking the time to straighten everything out.' She nodded at him once, then walked away.

'Tabitha –' He took a step towards her.

She spun round, still walking backwards, away from him. 'I think we've said everything we ever need to say to each other. Don't you?'

He looked like he was going to argue for a moment, then shrugged and turned away. Tabitha realised that Fiona was standing only a few paces away, watching them. Her eyes followed Mark for a moment, then switched to Tabitha. 'I came to wish you luck, but you'd already gone in.'

Tabitha managed to smile. 'Wish me luck in a "you're going to need it" kind of way?'

Her friend smiled back. 'In a "you deserve to pass" kind of way.'

Tabitha felt a sudden lump in her throat. 'Thanks. You know, despite everything, I'm glad I came here. I'm definitely glad I met you.'

Fiona shuffled awkwardly, never comfortable with displays of sentiment, but Tabitha could see that she was touched. 'I'm glad you came here too. I thought you were a total airhead when I first met you, which just goes to show that everyone deserves a second chance.' Her eyes shifted and Tabitha knew that she was looking at Mark's back retreating across the court.

Tabitha grimaced. 'There's second chances. And then there's believing that someone cheated on your brother and threatening to get her kicked out of college.' She held up her hand, forestalling any further comment from Fiona. 'Forget it – it's over.'

Fiona nodded reluctantly. 'Have it your way. So what

are you going to do now? Not straight back to the books, I hope.'

'Actually,' Tabitha told her, 'I thought I might go for a walk, a good long one. I need to clear my head.'

'Good idea. You should try Cascade Mountain. It's only twenty minutes' drive from here and you won't get a better view in all of the Adirondacks.'

'But doesn't climbing a mountain involve, you know, climbing?'

Fiona frowned in mock disapproval. 'Has no one ever told you that exercise is good for the soul.'

Tabitha laughed. 'Yeah. And my soul needs all the help it can get.'

Fiona was right, the view from the mountain was astonishing. Some other walkers she'd met on the way up had told her she was lucky: the scraped-bare granite peak of Cascade was usually buffeted by merciless winds, but today an almost unearthly calm had descended and she could stand on the summit bathing in the sunlight and marvelling at the world.

Up there on the peak, she could see a full 360 degrees around her. There were other people up there, little clumps of them staking out their own rocky perches but Tabitha still felt like she was all alone. The sky was a clear and brilliant blue, just a few wisps of cloud trailing across it. The Adirondacks stretched off to every horizon around her, only the occasional sign of human habitation scarring the primordial vegetation. Native Americans could have come up here a thousand years ago, she thought, and seen pretty much the same thing.

She took a few more minutes to enjoy the vertiginous feeling of height, the privilege of having everything laid out so carefully for her, clear and precise and far enough away that the trees looked like a vast green carpet, individual leaves and branches and twigs and all the messy, unmanageably complex reality of it disguised by distance. Then she found a convenient slab of granite, far enough from the small metal plaque marking the highest point that she wasn't going to be disturbed by the steady trickle of new arrivals putting their foot there to prove they'd made it to the top. She lay down on her back, stretched out her legs and lifted her face to the sun, eyes closed.

She had almost drifted off to sleep when she felt a shadow drift over her and stay put. She opened her eyes, wondering how the sky had clouded over so quickly, but it was still an unrelenting blue. When she shifted her eyes to the side it was to find another blueness gazing down at her, eyes far less open than the sky. The sun was shining through his fair hair, haloing him in light.

'Well.' She sat up, drawing her legs under her arms. 'Bumping into you in New York I could put down to coincidence, but this . . .'

Mark ran a finger over the rock, idly tracing a vein of quartz. 'Fiona told me where to find you.'

'Why the hell did she do that?' She should have realised that her roommate had given up the argument too easily. Fiona never backed down when she thought she was right.

He shrugged, dismissing the question. 'She told me it was her idea for you to cheat on your papers. She said you tried to talk her out of it. Is that true?'

Tabitha wondered whether she should deny it, but there didn't seem much point now. She nodded.

'She also said that you never slept with anyone but Jake while you were on Spring Break. Is that true as well.'

Tabitha felt her anger at him washing back into her. 'What do you think?'

'I think it is true,' he told her. 'I think I should never have been so ready to believe what Jake told me about you.'

'Thanks,' she said bitterly, because it still felt like too

little too late. 'What brought about this great change of heart?'

He stopped moving his finger over the rock and rested it carefully on his knee. 'The fact that Jake moved right on to his next conquest after the break-up and I haven't seen you with a single man. And the fact that the thing Jake told me, it's just not something you'd do.'

'You didn't seem to think that a few weeks ago. You thought it was *exactly* the sort of thing I'd do.'

His mouth twisted into a small bitter smile. 'I was angry with you for going back to him after you'd been with me.'

'Angry? But you practically shoved me back into his arms,' Tabitha said incredulously.

He shook his head. 'What people say isn't always what they mean. And I didn't want to believe that Jake would lie to me about something so important.'

She studied him in silence for a moment. She didn't think he'd ever been so emotionally open with her. She could feel a hard painful hope building inside her, but she ruthlessly suppressed it. He wasn't making her any offers, just an apology. 'OK,' she told him. 'I suppose I get that.'

They sat in silence for a few minutes, both looking out over the mountains, northwards towards another country. She could have left it at that, just walked away and been satisfied that they could part as – well, at least not as enemies. But, however much he wouldn't want to answer it, there was one question she had to put to him, something that had been hanging over the three of them from the moment they met. So she turned to him and asked, 'Why *does* Jake hate you so much?'

He drew in a deep shaky breath. 'Because I killed our parents,' he told her. 'And he's never forgiven me.'

She shook her head. 'But ... I don't understand. How could you have done that?'

His gaze tracked a solitary bird as it skimmed the peak

of the mountain. 'I was eighteen and I was ... out of control, much worse than Jake's ever been. I was drinking, smoking, partying all night. My parents begged me to stop but it was pointless, I didn't want to hear it and there was nothing they could do except worry.'

Tabitha saw the way he held himself entirely rigid, as if the slightest movement might shatter him. She reached out a hand, tentatively, not sure of its welcome, and rested it against his forearm. He didn't acknowledge it but he didn't push it away either.

'Then it came to New Year my senior year and I went out with some of my friends and managed to get myself caught, driving drunk and with a week's supply of grass in the glove compartment. The sheriff was an old friend of my parents, so he did them a favour. Rather than booking me like he should have he put me in a holding cell and called them to come fetch me. They'd had a drink or two themselves but what were they going to do, leave me in jail for the night?'

Tabitha felt herself go cold, feeling as if she was there, on that night, knowing where all this was heading and powerless to do anything to stop it.

His eyes glittered when he turned them back to her. 'They never even saw the truck coming. The driver was drunk too, and high – just like me. The doctors told me they died instantly, but I've never known if they said that just to make me feel better. Jake was eight years old and suddenly the only person he had left in the world was the person who'd made him an orphan.'

Tabitha realised that she was crying. She wiped the tears away with her fingers. 'You were *eighteen*, Mark. And you couldn't have known what was going to happen. It's – it's misplaced guilt.'

'I'm the psychologist, do you think I don't know that?'

She let her hand slide down his arm until it met his hand, twining her fingers with his. 'You've given up your life to take care of Jake. It's not fair of him to keep on blaming you.'

He looked down at their hands for a long time, the elegant strength of his fingers enfolding the slender whiteness of hers. Then he raised them to his lips and pressed a kiss against her palm. She felt the contact with a warm shock that was both physical and emotional. 'But he does,' he said softly. He gently disengaged his fingers from hers and laid her hand back in her lap. 'That's why I can't be with you. I can't let you be one more thing I've taken away from him.'

'What century are we living in?' Tabitha protested hotly. 'I'm not some bit of property you get to decide which of you owns. Doesn't what I want count for anything?'

He stood up, silhouetting himself against the falling sun. She stood up too, unwilling to let it all end like this. 'You wanted Jake before – can't you give him another chance? I know he can be difficult but now you know why can't you forgive him for what he said?' His voice was strained, as if he was getting the words out at a high cost.

Tabitha stepped towards him. He tensed but didn't step away. 'No. It's over with us. You were right in what you said about us all along. We aren't good for each other.'

'I'm not good for you either,' Mark said. He looked like he was going to say something else, but instead he just reached for her, cradled her face between his hands and kissed her. It was instantly intensely arousing. And it was completely right, whatever he said. But she could feel in the desperate way his mouth moved over hers that it was meant as a goodbye. After a minute he pulled back, eyes burning into her face. 'I'm sorry, Tabitha.' Then he turned and walked away.

Chapter Eighteen

I Want

Tabitha's uniform was too tight, she was sure that the sleazebag at table nine was only asking for regular coffee refills because it gave him a chance to look down her cleavage and she'd collected a grand total of $20 in tips all morning – but Tabitha was trying not to mind because in exactly half an hour she was leaving Fat Sam's Diner and she hoped that she'd never be coming back. The university had promised to post up the final exam grades on the psychology noticeboard at three-thirty and Tabitha planned to be there waiting for them at three-twenty-nine.

Of course, if she failed she'd be coming back to Fat Sam's and asking if her part-time job could become permanent. She didn't think she'd ever felt so nervous in her life. The second hand on the big clock above the door ticked round with agonising slowness. She refilled the sleazebag's coffee twice more, looking into the middle distance with a grimace as he looked at her breasts.

With one minute to go, the bell above the door chimed and her heart sank, expecting to be held up seating and serving a customer when all she wanted was to be getting the hell out of there. Then she saw who the entrant was and grinned. 'Fiona!' She hadn't seen her roommate since she'd headed home two weeks earlier to spend some time with her fiancé.

Fiona swept her into a brief hard hug, then held Tabitha at arm's length and smiled.

Tabitha frowned. 'What?'

Fiona laughed. 'Just enjoying the sight of you wearing something that wasn't designed by Versace.'

'You won't be enjoying it for long,' Tabitha told her. 'Give me two minutes to get changed, then we can walk back together.'

It was a blazing-hot day, humidity so high that Tabitha thought there might be storms later. Fiona seemed totally relaxed. She clearly wasn't too worried about the results, Tabitha thought, but she didn't resent the other woman her confidence. Fiona deserved all the success she got.

'I can't believe the wedding's in a month,' Fiona said. 'I feel like I've been planning it half my life.' Her face was glowing with happiness.

'I feel like you've been planning it half *my* life too,' Tabitha teased.

Fiona grinned, the smile gradually slipping into something more thoughtful. 'I've brought your invitation with me.'

'Good, because I hear it's bad form to crash a wedding.'

'I've made it a plus one.'

'You,' Tabitha said, 'couldn't be less subtle if you tried.'

'I think I probably could.' Fiona's expression was entirely serious. 'Have you spoken to Mark?'

Tabitha looked away. 'No. There's no point.'

'Or Jake?'

'Even less point. Look, I appreciate what you tried to do with me and Mark, really. Especially since it could have gotten you into a lot of trouble. But some things just aren't meant to be.'

'I know,' Fiona told her. 'But are you sure this is one of them?'

Tabitha didn't bother to answer because suddenly they were at the gates of the school and only a few minutes away from learning exactly what her future had in store for her.

Fiona seemed to sense her change of mood and grasped her arm reassuringly. 'You'll be fine.'

'Is that a promise?' Tabitha tried to make it a joke, but her voice came out shaky.

Fiona didn't answer, just squeezed her arm tighter. The results were due to be posted on the noticeboard outside the canteen, and Tabitha could already see a group of students bunching around it, their nervous chatter drifting over the still air towards her. It seemed a peculiarly barbaric institution to make them all find out their fates in front of each other, but Tabitha knew that public humiliation would be the least of her worries if she'd failed.

Naturally, the results hadn't yet been posted when they arrived at the board. Tabitha was aware of the tension humming through her body till she felt like she was vibrating on a low sustained note. She closed her eyes, trying to calm herself and persuade herself that she'd cope whatever happened. To her surprise, she realised that this was true. She *would* get by without money if she had to.

Which was not to say that she'd rather not.

Her reverie was interrupted by Fiona's soft: 'They're here.' There was something in her voice, some warning note, that made Tabitha open her eyes apprehensively.

It was Mark, of course. She should have realised he'd be the one to do this. He was head of department, after all. He didn't look at her once as he pinned the results to the board, though he must have known she was there. But when he'd finished he turned to face her. 'You deserve this, Tabitha,' he said.

She didn't quite dare to hope. 'You mean –?'

'You've passed!' Fiona shouted, pushing her way out of the crush around the board. 'You did it!'

Tabitha whooped and gathered Fiona in a huge bear hug, lifting her off her feet and spinning her around. When she put her down again, it was to find that Mark was already gone. Tabitha ruthlessly suppressed the hurt.

'I think this calls for a drink,' Fiona said.

'Several,' Tabitha agreed. 'Right after I've called my dad.'

He picked up on the second ring, as if he'd been waiting for the call. Maybe he had. She wouldn't put it past him to have phoned the school and found out exactly when the results were due.

'You won't need a refund on that ticket,' she said before he could get a word in.

There was a slight pause. 'Really?' he asked cautiously.

'Really,' she told him. 'You're now talking to Tabitha Stone, graduate. OK, I got a sucky grade, but that wasn't part of the deal, was it?'

'No it wasn't.' She could hear the pleasure in his voice now. 'I'm proud of you, Tabby.'

'Thanks, Daddy.' She took a moment to swallow past the lump in her throat, then added, 'Now since I've held up my side of the bargain, it's time for you to hold up yours. I need, well I guess ten thousand dollars ought to be enough to start off with.'

Her father sighed. 'Fine. I'll have a cheque for you at graduation.'

'Great – but it isn't for me. Seeing as how you're so keen on people getting college educations I thought you could pay for someone else's.' Fiona looked at her sharply, her mouth open in a surprised 'oh'. 'Fiona's brother has a place at Yale,' Tabitha told her father as she smiled at Fiona, 'but he can't afford to go without a scholarship. Fiona's the only reason I got through this year, so I think it's the least you can do.'

Throughout her childhood, Tabitha's father had never been on time for a single event in her life – delayed at work, he'd even arrived three hours late for her tenth birthday party. But he walked into the hall two hours before the graduation ceremony was due to start. She felt her heart leap and contract at the sight of him, the shock of greying hair on top of the pockmarked granite of his face. She hadn't realised how much she'd missed him.

He grunted when she flung her arms around him, but he squeezed her right back and when she drew away to look at him she thought she could see the glimmer of tears in his eyes. Then he pulled back, holding her at arm's length to inspect her.

'Don't tell me,' she said, 'the whole gown thing really isn't working for me.'

'I've never seen you looking better,' he said seriously. 'I'm glad you stayed the course.'

'I learnt a lot this year,' she told him. 'Though most of it wasn't on the exam.'

Fiona was a few feet away, standing with what appeared to be her entire family. Tabitha pulled her father over to introduce him.

He shook hands gravely, then pulled out a cheque and handed it to Fiona. 'I believe this is for you.' Tabitha could see a lot of zeros on the paper.

Fiona, for almost the first time since Tabitha had met her, was stunned into speechlessness. After a second, she tried to hand the cheque back. 'Thank you, Mr Stone, but I can't possibly take this.'

Tabitha's father gently closed her fist around the money. 'Of course you can. If you've been looking after my Tabby then I owe you much more than that. And everyone should have a Yale education. Went there myself, more years ago than I care to remember.'

Fiona smiled, blushing with pleasure as Tabitha's father waved off her family's thanks, scanning the hall with his eyes as if looking for someone else. His gaze returned to Tabitha. 'And where's that young man of yours?'

'Oh,' Tabitha said awkwardly, 'Jake and I broke up a couple months back. I thought I told you.'

'That senior you were dating? I don't mean him, I mean that lecturer of yours you kept telling me was so horrible.' He laughed at Tabitha's dumbfounded expression. 'I'm your father, Tabby. I learnt to read between your lines a very long time ago.'

Tabitha smiled sadly. 'That's over too. Not that it ever really started.'

Her father studied her, seeming to read more into her expression than she wanted to reveal. But then he just nodded.

The ceremony went on forever, but none of them minded because this was their graduation and who'd ever thought the day would come? When Tabitha was called to the stage she remembered her high-school graduation and how all she'd wanted was to get out of there and get on with the partying. But now, when she clutched the scroll in her hand, she felt a sense of pride which was hokey but real.

She saw her father smiling at her across the audience as she descended from the stage. But just before she reached him a hand touched her arm and she found herself face to face with Jake. She nodded stiffly at him.

Her father stopped a couple of feet away, sizing up the scene. 'The flight back to LA leaves in three hours,' he told her, looking between her and the young man facing her.

'So no time for small talk,' she told Jake with forced cheerfulness.

He looked at her father, as if hoping he'd go away, but the older man just folded his arms and glared at him, sensing his daughter's discomfort.

'Fine, I'll keep it brief,' Jake told her. 'It's about Mark.'

Tabitha backed away, towards her father. 'I don't want to talk about this, Jake. I'm leaving now and neither of you will ever have to see me again.'

'Which is why I need to say this now.'

'Please, Jake,' she said desperately.

'Mark's in love with you,' he told her.

She shook her head, trying to figure out why he was telling her this, what he hoped to achieve by it.

'I mean, I thought he just had a hard-on for you – excuse my language –' he looked briefly at Tabitha's father '– but, no, it's the full hearts and flowers deal.'

'Your brother can't help what he feels,' Tabitha told him, feeling a mixture of hope and pain. And how could it be true, when Mark had been so ready to walk away from her?

'I know. And then he goes and gives you up for my sake, and suddenly I'm feeling guilty – which is not how it's supposed to be at all. *I'm* the one supposed to be making *him* feel guilty. That's how our relationship works.'

Tabitha stared at him, speechless, still not sure she knew what he was trying to say.

'For fuck's sake, Tabitha,' Jake said impatiently, 'just go and tell him you love him too, will you? That way I can carry on hating him without having to feel like maybe he's not such a monster after all.' He turned away, then turned back to her for one last parting shot. 'I'm staying with Tessa tonight, so you'll have the house to yourselves.' He smiled, the mischievous carefree smile which had attracted her to him in the first place. And then he was lost inside the crowd.

Tabitha felt like too much blood was pumping through her body, energising and heating her almost past her ability to bear it. Her father was looking at her with an expression as inscrutable as any Mark had ever worn. Then he grinned, looking suddenly, startlingly boyish. 'Phone me when you need a ticket home,' he told her. 'And maybe you'll think about bringing your young man with you.'

Tabitha hesitated for a very long time outside Mark's door before knocking. But, when he pulled it open, blinking in the bright sunshine, she breezed straight past him, trying to ignore the way her stomach rearranged itself at the sight of him.

'You see,' she said, walking purposefully into the living room. 'I don't really think you mean it when you say you don't want me.'

He was wearing jeans and a worn green T-shirt and she didn't think she'd ever seen him looking better. His feet were bare, looking oddly vulnerable against the stained brown of the floorboards. His face looked vulnerable too, more open than she was used to seeing it. 'I never said I didn't want you.'

'No, that's right, you didn't. You just had some bullshit explanation about how you had to stay away from me because it would break your brother's heart if you didn't, even though Jake never showed much evidence of having a heart in the first place.' He looked like he was going to argue, so she held up her hand to stop him. 'Newsflash is, Jake says he's fine with the two of us being together. So what's your excuse going to be now?'

She was delighted to see that for the first, and probably last, time she'd managed to render him completely speechless. But beneath his shock she thought she could detect a mounting happiness.

'I know you're messed up, Mark. I'm messed up, we're all messed up. But that's the point of life, sorting ourselves out not just wallowing in it. I mean, you're the psychologist – aren't you supposed to believe in self-actualisation?'

He was definitely smiling now, with half of his mouth but all of his face. 'I'm not really a subscriber to Rogerian humanist theories.'

She moved closer, close enough to feel the heat of his body. 'Another newsflash – this isn't the time for a lecture.'

He bent his head towards her, his breath brushing against her lips. 'What is this the time for?' He didn't give her time to reply, just caught her lips with his own. She didn't understand how she could have been missing this so much, when she'd barely known it at all. But, as his hands moved up to frame her face and their bodies pressed together, she knew that she didn't want to have to do without it again.

She rested her hands against his chest, pushing gently until he moved his lips from hers and looked in her eyes. 'I don't know why,' she told him, 'because you're as annoying as hell, but somewhere along the line I fell in love with you.'

He laughed, a breathy incredulous sound. 'You did?'

She nodded, moving her mouth in to kiss his cheek, his chin, the proud arch of his brow. 'I guess I am pretty dumb after all.'

He pulled her head against his chest and held her tightly for a moment.

'You know,' she said, 'it's customary for you to say something at this point.'

When he still didn't answer, she felt a second's insecurity and pulled back to look at him. His face was that still mask that she'd learnt to recognise as a sign that he was fighting against emotions too strong for him to handle. He lifted his hand to brush his fingers gently over her lips, closing his eyes for a moment when she pulled one inside her mouth and sucked. When he opened them again, they were the darkest she'd ever seen them. 'I love you too, Tabitha.'

His other hand moved to the back of her dress and he pulled the zipper down in one smooth move. All that extra blood she'd been feeling earlier suddenly felt like it was moving and settling in her belly, her breasts and her groin. She was aching for him to touch her.

He didn't keep her waiting. As soon as he'd slipped the dress from her shoulders he traced his hands down her back, round the arch of her shoulder, moving them down to cup her breasts, his thumbs flicking gently over her nipples. She groaned, so turned on she thought she might come just from that. 'You're the most beautiful woman I've ever met,' he told her. 'I thought that the first time I saw you, wandering around outside wearing less than this.'

'You *saw* that?'

He nodded, moving his fingers lower, over her belly, then running them teasingly over the top of her lace panties. She worked her hands up under his T-shirt, raking her nails over the hard muscles of his chest. 'I thought you were the most uptight person I'd ever met the first time I saw you. I didn't notice you were a man until that day you came in from your run and I got my first look at this.' She pulled his T-shirt up and over his head, exposing the sculpted shape of his body, like an exhibit in his own museum.

'I didn't notice you noticing,' he said.

'I can be subtle when I want to,' she told him, then silenced his derisive snort by fastening her mouth around his nipple, washing it with her tongue and nipping gently with her teeth.

He groaned low and animal. When he pulled back, the humour was gone from his face, only raw desire left in it. His mouth returned to hers, hard and possessive as she snapped the button of his jeans and let him kick them away from his legs. His erection pushed insistently against her through his grey briefs, demanding her attention. She cupped her hand around it, holding it then stroking it in time to his gasping breaths, then dragged his briefs down and away so that she could repeat her caresses against his velvety smooth bare flesh. She felt his knees buckle and she loved that she had the power to weaken him.

Then he took control again, pushing her backwards as his own lips fastened around her nipples. Her legs struck the back of the couch and she let him force her to sit. He knelt in front of her, tore her panties from her legs and put his mouth where she most wanted it. His tongue pressed into her, then two satisfyingly thick fingers as his mouth moved to her centre, lapping and lapping until she felt like her whole body was pulsing in time to its movements. She came abruptly, arching her back away from the seat. 'I love you, Mark,' she said again and he groaned as if the words had physically touched him.

He let her rest only a moment, then pulled her up and sat behind her, turning her around until she was kneeling above him. She moaned as she settled on top of him, sinking slowly over his length. His head fell back against the cushions, breath hissing out of him at the feeling. On top she could set the pace, and she set it hard and fast, feeling like she wanted to brand him into her, make up for all these weeks she'd been without him.

His hands moved to her buttocks, massaging them in time to the movements of his cock inside her. Then his mouth latched on to her breast, suckling fiercely and it was almost too much, too many sensations to concentrate on at once. But still she wanted more and she clenched her inner muscles around the rock-hard length of him. His hands went slack on her for a moment, then he thrust up into her with a wild abandon, nothing gentle about their love-making at all. But she didn't want this to be gentle. She needed to know that he was as starving for her as she was for him.

As his strokes grew ragged with his nearing climax, he took his mouth from her breast and his hands from her ass and moved them to stroke down her face as he stared straight into her eyes. 'Mine,' he told her fiercely.

She nodded and said his name as they both came.

When she started thinking clearly again, they were spooned up together on the couch, his already hardening cock pressing against her back. She could smell the fresh male scent of him, subtly altered by the molecules of herself she'd left on his body. She turned round to face him, enjoying the relaxed look of his face, more peaceful than she'd ever seen him.

He lifted a hand and gently stroked her hair, letting one curl play between his fingers. Then he smiled teasingly. 'So what *do* you want to do with your life, Tabitha?'

She bent to press a kiss against his chest. 'I want to go

to Fiona's wedding with you. I want us both to spend some time with my dad, and with Jake too. I want us to teach him that there's more to life than having fun.' She looked back up at Mark. 'And I want to teach you that there's nothing *wrong* with having fun. I want to go to Europe with you and have you explain all the stuff in those churches and museums that bored me so much the first time. And I think maybe I want to learn about art – I think I might have an eye for it. But right now . . .' She kissed him hard on the mouth and she knew from his response that she didn't have to say any more.